The Faith and the Rangers

The Faith and the Rangers

A Collection of
Texas Ranger & Western Stories

James J. Griffin

iUniverse, Inc.
New York Bloomington

Texas Ranger Novels
by
James J. Griffin

Trouble Rides the Texas Pacific
Border Raiders
Trail of The Renegade
Ranger Justice
Panhandle Raiders
Big Bend Death Trap
Ranger's Revenge

Forthcoming Novels:

Death Stalks the Rangers
Dancing Fox Publishing, Winter 2009

Ride for Redemption
A Texas Ranger Cody Havlicek Story
Condor Publishing, Inc. Spring 2010

Bullet for a Ranger
A Texas Ranger Jim Blawcyzk Story
Six Guns Westerns, Spring 2010

The Faith and The Rangers

A Collection of Texas Ranger & Western Stories

iUniverse books may be ordered through booksellers or by contacting:
iUniverse
1663 Liberty Drive
Bloomington, IN 47403
www.iuniverse.com
1-800-Authors (1-800-288-4677)

Author Photo: Patricia Johnson

As always, thanks to Texas Ranger Sergeant Jim Huggins of Company A, and Karl Rehn and Penny Riggs of KR Training, Manheim, Texas, for their invaluable assistance.

Thanks to Paul Dellinger for the title Left Handed Law.

ISBN: 978-1-4401-9320-0 (pbk)
ISBN: 978-1-4401-9321-7 (ebk)

Printed in the United States of America
iUniverse rev. date: 12/02/09

For my readers, with thanks and gratitude.

Table of Contents

On The Border

1

Texas Rangers Bill Pierson and Ben Judwin rode slumped with weariness as they pushed their tired horses down the single dusty street of Cotulla. They had been riding hard, southward from San Antonio, for the past several days. The pair still had at least three more long days ahead of them before meeting Company D, which was camped somewhere along the Rio Grande between Laredo and Eagle Pass. Both men were looking forward to a good meal and a night in a comfortable hotel bed, rather than their usual trail supper of bacon and beans, then sleeping on the hard ground.

"There's the livery stable just ahead," Pierson noted. "We'll put up our horses, then find a room for ourselves."

"Some decent grub and a few drinks will taste good too," Judwin answered.

After placing their horses in the stable and arranging feeding and rubdowns for the mounts, the two men tossed their saddlebags over their shoulders. They headed for the Ransom House Hotel, where they obtained a room overlooking the street.

While Pierson stretched out on his bed, Judwin peeled off his sweat-stained shirt. He stepped over to the washstand.

"You gonna clean up a mite too, Bill?" he asked. He poured water into a cracked basin from a chipped pitcher, then ducked his head into the tepid liquid.

"Perhaps a bit later. I'm not out to impress the gals like you are," Pierson grinned.

While he rolled and lit a quirly, Pierson studied the young man riding with him. Ben Judwin was only nineteen, and had joined the Rangers just a few weeks previously. He was tall and thin to the point of lankiness, with sandy hair and light brown eyes. From the little Pierson had learned so far about the new recruit, Judwin had no family. His parents had died of the influenza several years back. The boy then fended on his own as a cowpuncher, until deciding to join the Rangers.

"Maybe someday I'll be an old married man like you, Bill, but until then I'm gonna have some fun with the ladies," Judwin retorted. He ran a rough washcloth over his chest. "Might play some poker, too."

"I ain't exactly old, kid," Pierson snapped back.

Despite his protest, the veteran Pierson knew he was indeed getting old for a Ranger. He was pushing forty. Years of exposure to the Texas sun and wind had weathered his face so he looked several years older. The deep wrinkles around his clear gray eyes and the blonde hair bleached even lighter testified to that. In addition, he was starting to detect the beginning of a slight paunch around his middle. Neither Pierson nor Judwin wore their badges in plain sight, although they both carried one, Pierson a battered silver star on silver circle, Judwin a half-finished badge he was still carving from a Mexican ten peso coin.

"Ben, are you gonna leave some skin on your bones, or are you gonna scrub it all off?" Pierson grumbled. "I'm ready for some grub."

"Be right with you," Judwin answered.

The young Ranger dug in his saddlebags for his spare shirt. He shrugged into it, retied his bandanna around his neck, and shoved his dark Stetson back on his head.

"You about ready, Bill?"

"'Bout time you finished dudin' yourself up, kid," Pierson shot back. "Let's go."

∧∧∧∧∧∧∧∧∧∧∧∧

After a quick supper, Pierson and Judwin settled in at the High Lonesome Saloon for a few drinks. Pierson was nursing his last beer for the night, while Judwin was drinking whiskey and making plans with one of the saloon women, Betty Jean, a bosomy blonde in a low cut scarlet gown.

"How about your partner? Does he want some company too?" Betty Jean asked Judwin.

"Bill? Not hardly," Judwin chuckled. "He's got a wife and three kids at home, so he's not interested in another woman. And he quit gambling a long time ago."

"Really?" Betty Jean gazed thoughtfully at Pierson.

"You could still have some fun, Mister," she suggested.

Pierson ran an appreciative glance over the woman before he replied.

"Thanks, but no thanks, honey. You and you friends are sure easy on the eyes, all right, and it's fine to look. But that's all I've done since I got married, look."

"Suit yourself," Betty Jean shrugged. "Ben, if you're ready to play cards, I'll introduce you to Joe Pickett, our chief houseman."

"I sure am. Then you and I'll have some more fun afterwards."

Ben grinned in anticipation.

"Ben, I'm heading back to the hotel. Don't stay out too late," Pierson warned. "We're ridin' out at sunup."

"I won't," Judwin promised. "C'mon, Sugar, let's go."

Pierson watched his young partner and the saloon woman head for the gambling tables. He lingered over his beer for a few minutes, then drained the mug. He tossed a coin on the table in payment for the drinks, and stepped out of the saloon for the short walk to the hotel.

Pierson paused halfway across the street to roll and light a quirly. As he touched a match to the smoke, two men emerged from the general store. One of them shouted in recognition and grabbed for the gun on his hip.

"Pierson!"

"Clete Hardisty!" Pierson dropped the match. He clawed for his own sixgun.

Pierson was too late in reacting as the gunman leveled his Colt and fired. Hardisty's bullet tore into the Ranger's stomach.

Pierson grunted and buckled at the bullet's impact. He tried to bring his gun in line with Hardisty's chest. Before Pierson could thumb back the hammer, Hardisty fired twice more. Both slugs ripped into the Ranger's belly. Pierson clawed at his bullet-torn gut, then jackknifed to the dirt.

Clete Hardisty gazed disdainfully at the lawman he'd just downed.

"C'mon, let's get outta here," he ordered Pete Stone, his partner. The two men lifted their horses' reins from the hitchrail, climbed into their saddles, and loped away.

∧∧∧∧∧∧∧∧∧∧∧∧

Ben Judwin leapt from his chair at the sound of gunfire, scattering his cards.

"I've gotta go," he told Betty Jean. He pulled his gun from its holster, shoving men aside to force his way out of the crowded saloon. He jumped from the porch of the High Lonesome to join the crowd gathering around a man lying in the dusty street.

"What happened?" he demanded.

"Some hombre got plugged," a bystander replied.

"I'm a Texas Ranger. Let me through!" Judwin ordered. He pulled his half-finished badge from his pocket.

The crowd parted to let him pass. Judwin hauled up short when he saw Bill Pierson lying there, blood spreading over his shirt.

"Bill! What happened? Someone get the doc," Judwin shouted. He leaned over his partner, who was still breathing raggedly.

"Doc Slade's already on his way," someone answered.

After what seemed an eternity to Judwin, an elderly man carrying a black satchel arrived.

"I'm Doctor Slade. Stand aside," he ordered.

Slade knelt beside Pierson, made a cursory examination of the wounded Ranger, then tsked softly.

"There's nothing I can do for him here. Some of you bring him to my office."

Judwin and two other men lifted Pierson and carried him to the physician's small home, where the wounded man was placed on a table in a tidy examining room.

"Doc, is there anythin' you can do for my pardner?" Judwin pleaded.

The doctor opened Pierson's shirt.

"I'm afraid not," he replied. Slade washed the blood off Pierson's belly, then placed a clean white cloth over it. More blood immediately soaked through the fabric.

"He's been gut-shot. Your partner took three bullets right through his abdomen. Frankly, I'm amazed he's still alive. He doesn't have much longer. I wish I could do more for him, son."

"Bill," Judwin murmured. He placed a hand on Pierson's shoulder.

Pierson's eyes flickered open.

"Ben..."

"I'm here, Bill. Who did this?"

"Hombre name of... Clete Hardisty," Pierson gasped. "He's head of the gang Company D's been after. Must've... gotten around them, if he's this far... north. He usually stays closer to... the border, since his outfit holes up in Mexico when they're not... causin' trouble in Texas. He surprised me and... plugged me."

"I'm goin' after him," Judwin gritted.

"No, you're not, son," Pierson ordered. "Pete Stone, Hardisty's segundo, was with him. That means his whole gang's not far off. You can't take on that bunch of killers single-handed. Just keep ridin' until you locate the company. Tell Captain Moore what happened, and he'll get the boys on Hardisty's trail right quick."

"But Bill," Judwin began to protest.

"No buts. That's an order... Ranger," Pierson snapped.

"All right," Judwin reluctantly agreed. "Anythin'... anythin' I can do for you, Bill?"

"Just make sure word... gets back to... my wife and kids that... I love them. Sell my... horse. I won't be needin' him. Send the money... to my... wife."

The dying Ranger's voice was barely a whisper.

"I'll do that," Judwin promised.

"Good. I guess this...this is...Adios, kid."

Pierson's voice trailed off, and blood welled in his mouth. His body shuddered, then went limp.

"He's gone, son. I'm sorry," Doctor Slade intoned.

Judwin dug in his pocket and came up with a gold double eagle, which he handed to the physician.

"Take care of the arrangements for me, will you, Doc?"

"I'll do that if you wish," Slade promised. "But won't you be here for your friend's funeral?"

"I've got another funeral to attend. The funeral of the hombre who killed my pardner. And I'm the man who's gonna send him to Hell."

2

Despite his vow to track down Clete Hardisty, Ben Judwin had few clues to go on when he rode out of Cotulla before dawn the next morning. He'd sold Bill's horse to the livery stable owner, who assured Judwin he would send the money to Pierson's widow. Armed with information from two eyewitnesses to Pierson's murder that the killer had ridden south out of town, and their sketchy description of the gunman, the young Ranger headed in the same direction. He took the main road heading toward Mexico. Along with his own Colt, he was now wearing Bill Pierson's Peacemaker.

"I don't know where those hombres are headed, Charcoal," Judwin admitted to his steeldust gelding. "I sure can't pick out their tracks from any of these others. I've just got a gut feelin' they headed this way. If the worst happens, and we can't find them, we'll just hook up with the company like Bill ordered."

Judwin fell into a pensive silence. He pushed his horse at a mile-eating pace, stopping only to allow the steeldust a brief breather or short drink. It was almost dusk when he spotted a dim trail turning off the main road, a trail marked with the hoofprints of twenty or more horses.

"That's got to be Hardisty's bunch!" Judwin exclaimed. "C'mon, Charcoal, get movin'!"

The young Ranger urged his weary mount into a full gallop. Less than half an hour later he hauled the horse down in a sliding stop, when they topped a rise overlooking a ranch in a small valley.

Sure looks abandoned, Judwin thought. Through the gathering gloom, he studied the buildings, spending several minutes looking over the spread.

"Guess we'll head down there careful-like, Charcoal," he murmured to his gelding. "Although I've got a sick feelin' in my belly Hardisty's already paid that place a visit and moved on."

Judwin didn't hear a sound when he walked his horse into the ranch yard and dismounted. He tied Charcoal to the porch rail, then lifted his Colt from its holster before climbing the stairs and pushing open the door. The minute he entered the house, the barrel of a rifle was rammed into his spine.

"Hold it right there, Mister, or I'll drop you in your tracks. Lose that gun and get your hands up," a harsh voice snarled.

Judwin let his gun fall to the floor and raised his hands shoulder-high.

"Now turn around, real slow."

When the Ranger turned to face his captor, the rifle barrel was jabbed deep into his belly, driving air from his lungs. Judwin grunted. He found himself looking into the face of a cowpuncher little older than himself.

"Just who are you, Mister?" the cowboy demanded. "Tell me why I shouldn't blast your guts out right now."

"The name's Ben Judwin. I'm a Texas Ranger."

"You got any proof of that?"

"My badge is in my shirt pocket, and my commission's in my billfold."

"Take them out and let me see them. Easy. Once false move and I'll splatter your insides all over this room."

Judwin reached carefully into his pockets to remove the badge and commission papers. He handed them to the cowboy. As his vision grew accustomed to the dim light, he realized the house had been thoroughly ransacked.

The cowboy studied Judwin's commission for a moment, then handed it and the half-finished badge back to him. He lowered the rifle.

"I reckon you're who you claim to be, Ranger. I'm Jake Sheehan. You can put your hands down and pick up your gun."

Sheehan suddenly broke into great gasping sobs.

"I'm sorry, Ranger," Sheehan apologized. "I just buried my wife. I came home and found her dying."

"Let me guess. She was murdered," Judwin said. He slid his Colt back in its holster.

"You're right," Sheehan confirmed. "Murdered… and worse. I wish those hombres had just killed her rather'n… you know what I mean. Better still, I wish I'd been home when they showed up. I would've done in every last one of 'em before they ever got to Becky."

Judwin tried to offer some small comfort to the distraught cowboy.

"If it's the same bunch I'm trailin' all that would've happened is you would have gotten yourself killed while your wife watched. That would've been even worse for her. Then, once you were dead they still would've had their way with her. The head of that outfit gunned down my pardner, and Bill was one of the smartest and toughest Rangers you'd ever meet."

"You say you're trailin' 'em?" Sheehan asked.

"That's right."

"Then I'm goin' with you. I was just getting ready to saddle my horse and take after those men when I spotted you up on that rise. I thought you might be one of them comin' back, which is why I was waitin' on you. If you had been one of that bunch, you'd have a couple of slugs in your guts right about now."

"I don't think I can let you ride with me," Judwin answered. "This is the Hardisty outfit I'm after. They're one of the most vicious gangs to ever hit Texas. We'll be outnumbered ten to one."

"I've got nothing left," Sheehan replied. "My wife's dead, and she meant everything to me. Anything of value on the spread's been taken, and the stock all driven off. There's nothing holding me here. Besides, you can't stop me from following you. When you do catch up with Hardisty and his men, my gun'll sure come in handy."

Judwin rubbed his jaw thoughtfully before answering.

"I reckon you're right, Jake. I'll water my horse while you saddle up. The longer we stand here jawin' the more distance those renegades can put between us."

3

It was around ten o'clock the next night when the Ranger and cowboy reined their horses to a halt on the edge of the Rio Grande. The tracks of the outlaws' horses led straight to the riverbank.

"Well, it looks like they beat us into Mexico," Sheehan sighed. "I don't know about you, Ben, but I'm still goin' after 'em."

"The border ain't gonna stop me," Judwin answered.

"But your Ranger badge ain't worth a dime in Mexico," Sheehan protested.

"That doesn't matter," Judwin explained. "Those renegades have got to pay for what they did to Bill. Besides, someone has to stop them before they do any more killin'. Appears it's up to us, so I'll either bring them back to Texas or die trying. And no matter what else happens, Clete Hardisty is gonna die with my slugs in his belly, or hang. Let's go."

Judwin put his steeldust into the shallow water. Sheehan and his sorrel gelding were close behind. The river, low this time of year, barely came to the horses' bellies as they reached midstream, then climbed the bank onto Mexican soil. Once the horses had shaken themselves off, their riders pushed them into a dead run yet again.

The two men, one determined to see justice done, the other seeking revenge for the death of his wife, rode hard for half an hour, then slowed their mounts to a walk. They moved cautiously now, since they could not chance riding up on their quarry unexpectedly. It was an hour later when Judwin caught the faintest whiff of wood smoke, and reined Charcoal to a halt. The dim entrance to an arroyo was just ahead.

"Hold it, Jake," he ordered. "I'll bet my hat that's Hardisty's bunch up there in that canyon. We'd best walk from here. We'll take the horses along, in case we need them in a hurry. Make sure your sorrel stays quiet."

Sheehan clamped his hand over the gelding's nose.

"He won't make a sound."

"Good. Let's check our guns before we head in there."

Quickly, and as silently as possible, the two men checked the actions of their Colts and Winchesters.

"What if there's a guard?" Sheehan questioned.

"I doubt there'll be one," Judwin explained. "Those hombres probably figure no one'll follow 'em into

Mexico. We're goin' to show them how wrong they are. Let's move."

Judwin paused for a moment.

"Jake, if we don't come out of this, I want to thank you for siding me."

"Por nada," Sheehan shrugged. "I'm just grateful you let me ride along, so I'll have a chance to get even for what they did to Becky."

Leading their horses, the Ranger and cowboy headed slowly up-canyon. They rounded a bend, and could now see the flickering of a campfire behind a cluster of boulders. The voices of the outlaws drifted through the still air.

"Those sons of Satan," Sheehan hissed. "They're bragging about what they did to my Becky."

Indeed, the outlaws were raucously celebrating the success of their latest foray into Texas, boasting about how much they had stolen, the women they had violated and the men they'd killed.

"They won't be braggin' for long," Judwin promised. "Let's circle 'em."

"Just give me time to get in place," Sheehan answered.

While Sheehan disappeared into the dark, Judwin pinned his badge to his shirt and leveled the Winchester he carried. He waited two minutes, then stepped around the boulders to emerge into the renegades' campsite. At the same moment, Sheehan appeared from the opposite side of the rocks.

Judwin's voice cut through the dark like the crack of a whip.

"Texas Ranger, boys! You're all under arrest. Don't try for your guns unless you're lookin' for a bellyful of lead."

The stunned outlaws fell silent, frozen for a moment in disbelief that their hiding place had been discovered. Then, with a curse one of them went for his gun. Judwin dropped him with a bullet through the stomach.

The rest of the renegades pulled their guns and began firing. Their vision still dimmed from gazing at the fire and their targets shrouded in darkness, the outlaws could only fire blindly in the direction of Judwin's voice and the flashes from Sheehan's rifle. Seven of them went down with Judwin's or Sheehan's bullets in them.

Judwin heard a grunt of pain. He glanced sideways to see Sheehan staggering from the bullet which had slammed into his side. Sheehan jacked another shell into the chamber of his Winchester and fired. The bullet ripped through a cursing outlaw's throat. Sheehan fired again, and another desperado went down. Then an outlaw's slug tore through Sheehan's thigh, dropping him to one knee.

Judwin put a bullet through another renegade's belly, the man screeching in agony as he jackknifed. The Ranger was slammed back against the rocks by a bullet which struck him high in the chest. His return shot plowed into the chest of the man who'd shot him.

Jake Sheehan had tossed aside his now-empty rifle. He held a Colt in each hand, blazing away at the outlaws. However, the remaining men had recovered from their initial surprise, and were aiming more precisely. Bullets were thudding into the cowboy's chest and stomach. His desire for revenge keeping him upright long after he should have been stretched out in the dirt, Sheehan gunned down several more of the killers, until Pete Stone put two finishing bullets into him. Both slugs buried themselves deep in the cowboy's gut. Stone cursed in triumph when Sheehan began to sag. With one final effort, Sheehan fired twice more, his bullets ripping into Stone's chest. Stone was slammed onto his back, dead. As Stone fell, Jake Sheehan crumpled to the ground.

Ben Judwin had also taken several more of the outlaws' bullets. He was braced against a Boulder, his vision was beginning to blur, and he could barely keep level the Colts he now held while he shot at the few surviving members of the Hardisty gang. He was vaguely aware of the screams of a badly injured horse, then another, and realized outlaws' slugs had found his and Jake's mounts.

Tex Lloyd, Hardisty's next in command after Pete Stone, had crawled undetected to within a few feet of

Judwin. He lifted his .44 Remington, fired, and put a bullet low into the Ranger's belly. Judwin dropped one of his pistols. He clamped a hand to his gut, buckling, but still managed to aim his other revolver at Lloyd's head and put a slug between his eyes.

As Judwin began to double over, another bullet ripped into his chest, slamming him back against the rocks. Through his fading vision, Judwin saw Clete Hardisty closing in. A wicked grin twisted the outlaw's powder-streaked face.

"I've got you, Ranger," he sneered.

Before the outlaw leader could thumb back the hammer of his sixgun, Judwin fired twice, both slugs taking Hardisty in the stomach. Hardisty began to slump. Judwin put his last two bullets through the killer's belly.

"That was for Bill Pierson," Judwin muttered, as Hardisty hit the ground.

Judwin gazed at the Colt he still held, the Colt Peacemaker that had belonged to his partner, Ranger Bill Pierson.

"I reckon it's over," he half-whispered, then slowly collapsed to his face.

With the last of his rapidly ebbing strength, Judwin dragged himself to where Jake Sheehan lay, face-down in a puddle of blood. He rolled the cowboy onto his back.

Sheehan's eyes flickered open.

"Ben… did we get them… all?" he weakly gasped.

"We got them all," Judwin answered.

The cowboy let out a last long sigh. The Ranger's eyes slowly closed as he took his final breath.

4

Several weeks later, the Rangers of Company D were speculating about what had happened to the new Ranger who had been riding with Bill Pierson to join them. Captain Daniel Moore had received a telegram informing him of Pierson's death; however, no further word had been received about Ben Judwin. It was a chilly night where they were camped along the Rio Grande. A full moon brightly illuminated their campsite and the muddy river.

"I guess the kid lost his nerve after seeing Bill dying with those bullets in him," Sergeant Jim Huggins theorized.

"I don't know," Bob Murphey mused. "I met Judwin up in Austin, when he was first thinking of joinin' up. He didn't seem like the type who'd turn yellow to me."

"Rider comin' in, Captain," Lefty Hall, the sentry, announced.

Fifteen minutes later, a middle-aged Mexican, riding a wiry pinto, rode into the camp and dismounted.

"You are the capitan, Senor, si?" he questioned, looking straight at Moore.

"I'm the captain of this Ranger company, yes," Moore confirmed. "What do you want, hombre?"

"Capitan, I am Don Jose de la Vega. I own a large rancho just outside of Guerrero, close to the Rio Bravo. Quite some time back, I heard the sounds of a horrific gun battle, not far from my hacienda. When the next morning came, I went to investigate. I found many men who had died from bullet wounds, twenty-two to be precise."

"Yes, yes. And did you recognize any of those dead hombres?" Moore impatiently asked.

"Si, Capitan," de la Vega replied. "Most of them were muy malo hombres, best avoided. They were the men who rode with Clete Hardisty."

"You mean the Hardisty gang is wiped out?" Moore asked in disbelief.

"Si, Capitan," the Mexican confirmed. "However, two of the dead men were off from the rest. One of them wore this."

De la Vega handed Moore a half-finished star on circle badge.

"A Ranger badge?" Moore exclaimed. "What'd the man wearing this look like?"

"Blonde, very slim, light brown eyes," de la Vega described. "He and his compadre must have been muy valeroso hombres, to take on the Hardisty gang with such odds against them."

"Ben Judwin," Moore half-whispered. "He didn't run after all."

"Senor, what did you do with the bodies?" he asked de la Vega.

"The bodies of Hardisty and his men I left for the coyotes and buzzards, for that is all they deserved. But I buried the man wearing this badge, and his compadre, in a small grove of cottonwoods. Such bravery must be respected."

"Indeed,", Moore assented. "Gracias, Senor de la Vega. Would you care to spend the rest of the night here with us, so you can rest? We still have hot coffee and warm beans on the fire."

"Gracias, Capitan. I would appreciate that very much indeed," de la Vega gratefully accepted.

Later, with most of the Rangers still awake, two horses' whinnies, loud and insistent, drifted across the camp. Several of the Rangers' mounts answered. The men looked toward the ridge from where the sound had come.

"I don't believe what I'm seein'!" Captain Moore exclaimed.

"We haven't been drinkin', so it ain't the red-eye," Lefty Hall declared.

Up on the ridge the ghostly images of two men, one wearing a Ranger badge and riding a steeldust, the other riding a sorrel, were clearly visible under the light of the full moon.

"That's Ben Judwin!" Bob Murphey shouted.

While the Rangers watched, the two men reared their horses, whirled them around, and galloped off.

"Those are the men I buried," de la Vega stated, in awe. He dropped to his knees and made the Sign of the Cross.

The Rangers of Company D stood in stunned silence, until Captain Moore finally whispered, "Adios, Ranger Judwin and your pardner. Vaya con Dios!"

The Faith and The Rangers

Prologue

Bandera, Texas February 2, 1855

Two young men, in Roman clerical collars and black coats, descended from the stagecoach. Three others awaiting their arrival hurried up to them.

"Father Nowicki? Father Jankowski? I'm Thomas Mazurek. Allow me to introduce Franz Jureczki and Kaspar Kalka. Welcome to Bandera. We're very pleased to have you here, since we've been anxious to start our parish. How was your trip?"

Mazurek was a sturdily built man who worked in the cypress shingle mill. He spoke in his native Polish.

"Thank you. We're happy to have received this assignment," Father Robert Nowicki answered, also in Polish. "Our journey was rather long and tiring. We would like to freshen up a bit."

"Of course," Mazurek replied. "We'll get your luggage and take you to Maria Bish's boarding house. You'll be staying there until the rectory is completed."

The priests climbed into Kalka's waiting buckboard. Their belongings were retrieved from the stage and loaded into the wagon. Once that was completed, the parishioners joined them. Kalka picked up the reins and slapped them on the horses' rumps, putting the team into a brisk walk.

"Have you chosen a name for the church, Thomas?" Father Stefan Jankowski queried.

"Yes, Father. It will be Ul. Stanislawa Kosciol. The bishop has already given his approval."

"Saint Stanislaus Church," Father Jankowski translated. "Excellent choice."

1

Bandera, Spring 1878

"Father Nowicki? That rancher, Jack Taylor, is here again. Shall I tell him you're busy?"

"No, Regina," the pastor told his gray-haired housekeeper. "You may send him in. I must say, he is persistent."

"He's a pain in the dupa," Regina Grosecki mumbled under her breath. Aloud she answered, "Very well, Father."

She bustled out of the pastor's office.

"Mister Taylor, Father will see you. Although why he allows you to keep pestering him is beyond my understanding. Perhaps he hopes to save your immortal soul. I'll say a rosary for you myself. You need all the prayers you can get."

Father Nowicki frowned, but couldn't suppress a chuckle at the feisty, widowed housekeeper's scolding of the most influential rancher in the county. He rose from his chair when Jack Taylor entered the office.

"Hello, Father. I hope you don't mind my stopping by so early."

"Not at all, Mister Taylor. Please, have a seat."

"Thank you."

Taylor settled into a straight-backed chair, which seemed barely able to hold his weight. He was a big man, close to six feet tall and almost two hundred pounds, broad-shouldered and lean-waisted, tanned from years of exposure to sun and wind. Dark brown eyes peered from under his broad-brimmed hat. He removed the Stetson to uncover a shock of brown hair.

Father Nowicki settled behind his desk once the rancher was seated.

"May I have Regina bring you some coffee?" he asked.

"No thank you, Father," Taylor replied. "My time is limited. I just came by to ask if you have reconsidered my offer."

"There is nothing to reconsider. I thought I made that clear the last time we met."

"You did, but I want to be absolutely certain you're aware how much your land means to me."

"Not my land. The parish's," Nowicki clarified.

"Of course. The parish's," Taylor repeated. "Father, your parish controls a considerable amount of water rights, along with some good grazing land. So do several of your parishioners. I need that water and land for my ranch. Certainly you can understand that. My herds are growing, and Bandera has become a central point for organizing trail drives from Texas to Kansas and Montana. I am willing to raise my offer for your buildings and land. But I do want them."

"And as we have discussed numerous times, Saint Stanislaus Parish is willing to negotiate an agreement to share those water rights, which will be mutually beneficial to both the parish and yourself. There is more than enough water for all of us. In addition, some of the land might be available for lease."

"Father, that isn't good enough," Taylor insisted. "I must have complete control of that land and water. Just having access to some of the water won't do. You can build another church nearly anyplace, but I can't find water everywhere. If you talk sense to your parishioners they'll go along. Once you give up the church's property they'll be willing to sell theirs."

The normally even-tempered pastor struggled to maintain his composure. His clipped words came out softly, but edged.

"Mister Taylor, our community has been here since 1855. We came to a strange land and fought both man and nature to survive. The men worked long hours in the shingle mill to support their families. We celebrated

Mass in parishioners' homes for the first three years, until we were able to erect a log structure for a temporary place of worship. We made many sacrifices, and struggled to raise funds to build a proper church. Our sanctuary was completed only two years ago. The Sisters of the Immaculate Conception arrived a few years back to staff our school. Their convent was built two years before the church. Many of our deceased members are buried in the old cemetery on church grounds. My parishioners' lands are their homes, homes they could never have hoped to own in their native land. You cannot expect them to start over."

"A church built by a bunch of foreigners," Taylor snapped.

Nowicki's blue eyes grew frosty.

"Mister Taylor, most of our parishioners, or their parents, emigrated here from Poland over twenty years ago. They became citizens and worked hard to rebuild their lives. Many of them fought, and some died, for the Confederacy. They are every bit as much Texans as you are. Now, we have nothing further to discuss. Good day, sir."

"You're making a mistake, priest," Taylor answered. "I want that land and water, and I'll do whatever's required to get them. Is that clear?"

Taylor rose from his chair, his hand on the butt of his pistol.

"Is that a threat?" Nowicki asked.

"Just a statement of fact." Taylor's tone was flat and deadly. He lifted the gun half out of its holster, then slid it back.

"Then perhaps you had better leave. Regina will see you out."

"Fine."

Taylor stalked out of the office. He slammed the door so hard the windows rattled.

A moment later Father Jankowski entered. He had just finished offering the morning Mass.

"What did Jack Taylor want?" he asked. "As if I didn't know?"

"That's right," Nowicki answered. "The same thing he's been after for months. He refused to even discuss anything less than taking everything the parish owns."

"Well, you sure put a burr under his saddle, Robert," Jankowski grinned. The younger priest had picked up many of the cowboys' expressions during his tenure in Bandera.

"I'm afraid I did, Stefan," Nowicki sighed. "He made a not-so-veiled threat about what might happen if we didn't give in to him. In fact, for a moment I thought he was going to shoot me."

Jankowski sobered.

"That explains why he nearly knocked me over rushing out of here. What should we do about him?"

"Nothing. I'm certain he won't do anything rash. He had his chance just now."

"I'm not so sure," Jankowski disagreed. "Taylor is ambitious. I'd bet my hat he's ruthless enough to trample anyone who gets in his way. We should notify the sheriff."

"That would be pointless," Nowicki answered. "Taylor would merely deny our accusations."

"Then all we can do is wait and hope," Jankowski answered.

"And pray," Nowicki added.

2

Father Nowicki looked up from his breviary at the sound of the church bell urgently pealing. The rectory door slammed open, and Stanley Mazurek burst into his office

"Father, there's a brush fire along the river!" Mazurek shouted. "The wind's pushing it this way. If we can't stop those flames before they jump the Medina, the church will be set ablaze!"

The pastor tossed aside his prayer book and started for the door. Father Jankowski had also heard the bell, and hurried downstairs.

"What's the commotion?" he asked.

"Fire!" Mazurek replied.

"Let's go!" Jankowski urged.

Regina emerged from the kitchen.

"I heard Stanley. I'll make coffee and sandwiches."

"They'll be appreciated," Mazurek said.

He and the priests rushed outside.

The acrid odor of burning brush assailed their nostrils. Thin tendrils of smoke, pushed up the riverbank by a gusty wind, swirled around the church and rectory. Answering the summons of the bell, men and women hurried toward Saint Stanislaus. Several nuns had already assembled in the church yard.

"Some of you get on the church roof with water buckets in case any embers land up there. The rest grab all the buckets and burlap sacks you can find and head for the river," Mazurek ordered. He jumped onto his plow horse and sent the animal lumbering toward the river, less than two city blocks distant.

Father Jankowski and several men gathered the fire buckets from the church. They passed several to the others, then ran for the riverbank.

The fire was spreading rapidly, flames leaping fifty feet into the air. Sheriff Ben Musgrave led about thirty townspeople who were battling to contain the blaze to the south bank of the Medina.

"Don't bother to cross the river!" Musgrave ordered. "We can't save anything on that side. You men in the river start filling buckets. The rest of you keep any embers that blow across from catching. If we lose here the whole town will burn to the ground."

The firefighters filled pails and soaked burlap sacks. When an ember landed in the dray grass and brush, it was doused with water or smothered under wet burlap.

"There's a wagon tryin' to get across!" Mazurek yelled. The firefighters saw a hard-driven team pulling a buckboard holding a husband, wife, and six children galloping along the riverbank.

"That's the Markewicz's!" Anton Bach shouted.

Jerzy Markewicz found a gap in the flames and urged the terrified horses through. Barely slowing, they plunged into the Medina. The buckboard tipped on two wheels, hung for a moment, then settled back and lurched up the opposite bank. Markewicz sawed the reins to pull the panicky horses to a halt.

Several firefighters and nuns surrounded the wagon.

"Is everyone all right?" Father Jankowski asked.

"Yeah. But we lost everything," Markewicz answered. His wife was trying to comfort their sobbing children.

"We'll take the children," Sister Anastasia ordered. The youngsters were handed to the nuns. Once certain they were cared for, Markewicz and his wife Anna joined the firefighting efforts.

Stan Mazurek attached a log to his horse's harness, then tied sacks to that. The horse balked in fear of the flames and smoke when the farmer attempted to drive him into the Medina. With firm hand and soothing voice, Mazurek calmed the animal and urged the bay into the water. Once the sacks were drenched, he led the horse from the river and jumped on its back. Mazurek pushed the horse into a trot along the riverbank, the wet log and sacks dragging behind flattening brush and grass, clearing a rough firebreak.

Nonetheless, the blaze threatened to overwhelm their efforts. The shifting wind sent burning debris in all directions. The heat and humidity added to the firefighters' misery.

"Don't give up! We've almost got it licked!" Mazurek urged. He sent his horse plunging back into the river to soak the burlaps once again.

For hours the crew fought the conflagration, rushing to douse any new flames which flared up. Regina and several of the sisters kept everyone provided with sandwiches, coffee, and cold water. Other nuns helped battle the blaze.

Mother Mary Claire worked until the sack she was wielding disintegrated. Undaunted, she pulled the veil from her head, revealing her flowing blonde hair. She dipped the veil in the river and used it to beat back the flames.

Sister Luke, one of the novices, stared in shock at her superior. For just a few seconds so did Mazurek, before shaking his head in admiration and turning his horse again.

"Mother, I was taught we were always to wear our full habit in public," Sister Luke exclaimed.

"This is no time to stand on propriety, child," the Mother Superior scolded. A burning ember landed three feet from her. She slapped out the flames with her wet veil.

By sunset, the wind slowed to a gentle zephyr. The fire, having consumed most of the fuel on the south side of the Medina, burned itself out. With the threat to the church and town over, the firefighters settled to extinguishing some remaining hot spots and smoldering brush.

An hour later, the worn-out group stumbled back to the church. Despite the sparks and embers which had landed on its roof, the sturdily built structure of native stone stood unharmed.

Joe Urban and the men who'd defended the church descended, gratefully accepting coffee and the remaining sandwiches.

"Is that fire completely out?" he questioned.

"It appears to be," Mazurek answered. He was still taking an occasional glance at the good-looking blonde Mother Mary Claire.

"Joe, Stash, Karol, you did a fine job on the roof," Father Nowicki praised.

"It was touch and go for awhile," Urban explained. "A big ember landed on the steeple. We were fortunate to get to it before it could do more than scorch a few shingles."

"I'd like to thank everyone," Nowicki announced, "Including those who aren't parishioners of Saint Stanislaus. Tomorrow evening at seven o'clock we will celebrate a Novena of Thanksgiving to our Lord for sparing our church, our community, and ourselves from that fire. However, the Markewicz'z have lost everything. They'll be staying at Maria Bish's temporarily. Saturday we'll have a house raising for them. But for tonight, we'll say a prayer of gratitude, then get a good night's rest.

The exhausted firefighters bowed their heads while Fathers Nowicki and Jankowski led them in the Our Father, Hail Mary, and Glory Be. Nowicki concluded by blessing the assemblage with the Sign of the Cross, then dismissed them.

"Father, wait a minute," Stan Mazurek requested. He called to the sheriff and Markewicz.

"Ben, I'd like to speak with you. You too, Jerzy."

They joined the priests as they headed for the rectory.

"What's on your mind, Stan?" Musgrave asked.

"It's bothering me how that fire started," Mazurek responded. "There've been no lightning strikes, and no other way I can imagine for a fire to start down by the river. The wheat isn't ready for harvest, so no one's been working in the fields. Jerzy, did you see anything?"

"No. Anna spotted smoke, then the flames came over the ridge behind our place so quickly we barely had time to harness the team and flee for our lives. Our house was afire before we could save anything."

"Perhaps a passing cowboy tossed away a cigarette he hadn't extinguished," Nowicki speculated.

"Possibly. But that fire spread awful fast, even with the wind," Mazurek demurred. "I can't help but think of Jack Taylor."

"I don't think he'd stoop that low," Nowicki protested. "That fire could have destroyed the entire town. Would Taylor chance that?"

"I might be wrong. Lord knows I hope I am. But Taylor is hungry for control of the entire county," Mazurek answered.

"And don't forget some of the other incidents recently," Jankowski added. "Cattle rustling, never a problem before. Vandalism at the cypress mill. The crops which have been trampled. Sheriff, what's your opinion?"

"I'd hate to think someone would deliberately endanger so many lives," Musgrave replied. "It's hard to believe anyone could be that callous. However, there does seem to be a pattern. Unfortunately, what we need is proof, and we have none."

"We're all too tired to think straight tonight," Nowicki said. "Let's get some sleep. We can talk about this tomorrow."

"The best advice I've heard today," Musgrave agreed. "I'll stop by about ten. Good night, Fathers. 'Night, Stan, Jerzy."

"Dobranoc, everyone," Nowicki answered.

3

The next day's meeting provided no tangible results, except Musgrave's promise to keep investigating. Two days after the fire, Regina entered Father Nowicki's office, a disgusted expression on her face.

"Father, Jack Taylor is here again," she announced.

"Tell him to come in," the pastor replied.

"Certainly. But I'd rather tell him to go to Pieklo!"

"I heard that," Nowicki called after her. "Confession on Saturday, Regina."

"It's no sin to speak the truth," the housekeeper retorted.

A moment later, Taylor was standing in front of the pastor's desk.

"Please have a seat, Mister Taylor," Nowicki invited. "Would you care for some refreshment?"

"No thank you," Taylor answered. "I just spoke with Jerzy Markewicz. I made him an offer for his land. A fair offer, considering the fire destroyed his property.

However, he refused it. He tells me your parishioners will be rebuilding his home on Saturday."

"That is correct, along with some of the townspeople," Nowicki confirmed. "Are you offering your assistance?"

"Hardly," Taylor snorted. "I came to stop that fool idea. Markewicz's property is worthless. It will be next spring before he can replant crops. He can't survive that long. Either he accepts my offer or I'll have his land for the taxes after the county takes it."

"Jerzy's friends will provide the assistance he needs to survive the winter," Nowicki replied. "Perhaps you have forgotten about the virtue of charity, Mister Taylor."

"Charity my ..." Taylor caught himself. "Father, I'll have Markewicz's land, and all the properties I'm after. Mark my words."

Nowicki fixed the rancher with a firm gaze. He responded, "Even if it means destroying property, setting fires, and endangering lives?"

"You can't prove that!" Taylor snapped.

"You are correct, of course," the pastor agreed. "And I hope I am wrong. But even a priest can only be pushed so far. Unless you have something further to discuss, I must bid you good day."

"Just consider what I said," Taylor insisted. "I've warned you once what would happen if I didn't get what I wanted. I don't intend to warn you again."

"I already have. And I'm tired of your threats. Please don't slam the door on your way out."

Taylor opened his mouth to speak, then snapped it shut. He stalked out of the rectory, climbed into his saddle, and dug his spurs deep into his horse's flanks, sending the animal into a dead run.

4

"Regina, you certainly have a green thumb," Father Nowicki praised, looking over the rectory's flower garden. "The roses are lovely."

"Dziekuje, Father," Regina replied. She carried a basket filled with cut flowers.

Both looked up at the sound of hoofbeats of a galloping horse approaching. Deputy Jed Morrison slid his gelding to a halt in the churchyard.

"Father, rustlers hit the Z Cross last night," he said. "They shot young Tadeusz Zielinski and Jose Montoya. They're at Doc Franklin's. You need to come now."

"Of course. Regina, please get my sick room kit while I saddle Rosie."

"Certainly, Father."

The pastor hurried to the stable, accompanied by the deputy.

"Is anyone searching for those rustlers, Jed?" he asked while saddling his mare.

"Sheriff Musgrave's got a posse lookin' for 'em."

"Let's hope they find them."

Nowicki led his horse outside and climbed into the saddle. Regina met him in front of the rectory. She handed him the small leather case holding the sacred oils, candle, and stole.

"I'll return as soon as possible," he said. "Tell Father Jankowski what's happened."

"Of course, Father."

The pastor and deputy put their horses into a lope. Ten minutes later they reined up in front of Doctor Willard Franklin's office.

"I'll take care of your horse, Father," Jed offered.

"Thanks, Jed." Nowicki dismounted, handed Rosie's reins to the deputy, then rushed into the office.

"Father. I'm glad you're here," Doctor Franklin greeted him. "Tad and Jose are in back."

"How are they?"

"Badly wounded. They were both shot in the back. I was able to remove the bullets, but their survival is doubtful at best."

Franklin led the pastor into the back room. The two cowboys were unconscious, covered with blankets. Hank and Betty Zielinski, owners of the Z Cross, sat by their son's side. They looked up when Father Nowicki entered.

"Hello, Father," Betty said.

"I came as soon as I heard."

"We know, and appreciate you being here," Hank assured him. "I'm not sure what you can do, though."

"I can pray for Tad and Jose. So can you."

"Father is right, Hank," Betty agreed. "If it's the Lord's will, they'll be fine. We can't lose faith."

"I'm going to administer Extreme Unction," Nowicki said. He opened his case containing the sacramentals, removed the stole, kissed it, and draped it over his shoulders.

"In nomine Patris, et Filii, et Spirtus Sancti," he began. The pastor murmured the ancient words of the sacrament for the gravely ill over the wounded men, anointing them with holy oil and water. Once he had finished the sacrament, he knelt in silent prayer for a few moments.

Afterward, Nowicki remained with the Zielinskis, consoling and reassuring them. He was preparing to leave when Father Jankowski and Stanley Mazurek arrived.

"How are the boys?" Jankowski questioned.

"In God's hands," Nowicki replied.

"And Doc Franklin's," Mazurek added. "If anyone can pull those boys through, he can."

Mazurek paused before continuing.

"Father Nowicki, as you requested, we've all been patient. But now, things have gone too far. It's sheer luck Tad and Jose weren't killed. My father worked too hard for the land we own. My mother's buried on it. I'm not about to give it up to anyone. We have to call in the Texas Rangers. Frank Czajkowski is stationed with Company D in Laredo. He could be here in a few days."

"You're right, Stanley," the pastor conceded. "It's apparent Jack Taylor will do anything to get what he wants, and Sheriff Musgrave is powerless to stop him. But I want to make sure the rest of the parishioners agree with us. Could you ask as many as possible to meet at the church tonight, say eight o'clock?"

"I'll round up everyone I can, Father," Mazurek promised.

"I'll give you a hand," Zielinski offered. "I can't do much sitting here. Unless you don't want me to leave, Betty."

"No," his wife answered. "You go on. I'll stay with the boys."

"We'll be back as soon as possible," Mazurek stated. "Fathers, we'll see you tonight."

5

Jack Taylor was on the porch of his ranch house, enjoying one last beer before turning in, when Monte Harding, his foreman, and several of the ranch hands rode up.

"You boys are back early," Taylor noted. "I figured you'd stay in town overnight."

"We'd planned on that, but I've got some news you won't like," Harding answered.

"What's that?"

"The bartender at the Black Horse says that priest has sent for the Rangers."

"He wouldn't have dared to!" Taylor exploded, with an oath.

"Not according to Harry," Harding answered. "He claims the Rangers are already on the way."

"Where'd he hear that?" Taylor demanded.

"Couple of the cowboys from Casimir Voytek's spread let it slip. Looks like instead of givin' in, like you thought would happen, those thick Polacks called in the Rangers."

Harding spat in the dust.

"I told you they'd never leave, unless you drove 'em off."

"You were right," Taylor conceded. "But it's still not too late. If we take care of Nowicki before the Rangers get here, the rest will give up. We can handle any who don't."

"Kill a priest?" Harding looked doubtful. "Well, if we do, we'll have to get rid of the other one too. And we'd better move fast. Harry tells me Nowicki sent his request for help to Austin several days ago. That means those Rangers'll be here anytime now."

"Yeah, but Nowicki's the one I want to make sure I gun down," Taylor snarled, eyes blazing in a way that made even his foreman cringe. "Get some shut-eye. We'll head out at sunup."

6

Father Nowicki whispered his morning prayers while he vested for the Tuesday Mass. Weekday Masses were sparsely attended. The nuns, along with the regular group of elderly women saying their rosaries, occupied the front pews, while old Thomas Mazurek was in his usual place in the rear left pew. Regina Grosecki was, as always, seated next to him. A few others were scattered throughout the sanctuary.

"It's time, Peter," he said to his altar server. They went to the altar, genuflected, and started the Mass.

"Introibo ad altare Dei," the pastor began.

Nowicki recited the ancient Latin words. He led the congregation through the Confiteor, Kyrie (which is Greek, not Latin), and Gloria. He read the day's Epistle and Gospel. Then the Creed was recited, followed by the Offertory and Sanctus.

The most sacred part of the Mass was reached, the Consecration, where bread and wine would be transfigured into the Body and Blood of Christ. Nowicki bowed over the sacred Host.

"Qui pridie quam pateretur, accepit panem in sanctas ac venerabilis manus suas, et elevates oculis in coelum ad te Deum Patrem suum omnipotentem tibi gratias agens…"

Jack Taylor and three of his men burst through the church doors, pistols drawn. While his men covered the parishioners, Taylor aimed his sixgun at the center of the cross embroidered on the back of the pastor's robes.

"That's right. Say your prayers, priest!" Taylor shouted. "'Cause I'm gonna send you straight to Hell!"

Nowicki didn't turn his head. He continued the prayer.

"…benedixit, fregit, diditque discipilus suis, dicens: Accipite, et manducate ex hoc omnes:

"HOC EST ENIM CORPUS MEUM."

He lifted the Host in veneration. Taylor thumbed back the hammer of his Colt.

Nowicki lowered the Host and genuflected. Taylor fired. The bullet went over the pastor's head and into the wall, directly under the crucifix.

Not even flinching at the shot, Father Nowicki spoke the words of Consecration over the chalice.

"Simili, modo postquam coenatum est, accipiens et huc praeclarum Calicem in…"

"Turn around and look at me, Nowicki!" Taylor screamed. He again thumbed back the hammer of his gun.

"...sanctas ac venerabilis manus suas, item tibi..."

A flurry of gunfire sounded outside. The church doors were again flung open. Two men, one wearing a silver star on silver circle badge, rushed inside, guns at the ready. Taylor's men turned to confront them, but thought better of shooting, facing those leveled Colts.

"Drop your gun, Mister!" the badge-wearing Ranger ordered.

"I'm gonna kill this priest!" Taylor screeched.

"...gratias agens, benedixit, deditque disciples suis,..."

Nowicki continued the prayer.

"...dicens: Accepite, et bibite ex eo omnes:"

The Ranger thumbed back his Colt's hammer, unwilling to fire lest his bullet hit the pastor or altar boy rather than Taylor. Nowicki continued the act of consecrating the wine into the Blood of Christ.

"HIC EST ENIM CALIX SANGUINIS MEI, NOVI ET AETERNI TESTAMENTI: MYSTERIUM FIDEI: QUI PRO VOBIS ET PRO MULTIS EFFUNDETUR IN REMISSIONEM PECCATORUM."

"Haec quotiescumque feceritis, in mei memoriam facietis."

Taylor squeezed the trigger just as Nowicki lifted the chalice. A ray of sunshine burst through the stained glass window above the altar, reflecting off the upraised chalice directly into the rancher's eyes. Blinded, Taylor dropped the pistol to shield his eyes. His bullet plowed into the floor.

The badge-wearing Ranger rushed up to Taylor and jabbed his gun into the rancher's back.

"You're under arrest, Mister. Outside!" he ordered. He and his partner hustled Taylor and his men out of the church.

"Undi et momores, Domini..."

Nowicki continued the Mass.

∧∧∧∧∧∧∧∧∧∧∧

Once the Mass was concluded, Father Nowicki and the congregants headed outside, where a small crowd had gathered. Ranger Frank Czajkowski hurried up to the pastor. The badge-wearing Ranger was at Czajkowski's side. Three other Rangers guarded several prisoners, two of whom were wounded. Monte Harding lay at the bottom of the rectory steps, killed by a Ranger bullet in his chest. Father Jankowski was praying over the dead man.

"Father, are you all right?" Czajkowski asked.

"I'm fine, Frank," Nowicki replied.

"I'd like you to meet my sergeant, Jim Huggins," Czajkowski introduced.

"I'm very pleased to meet you, Sergeant. And I'm very grateful. Thank you."

The priest and the Ranger shook hands.

"Father, you're either the bravest man I've ever met, or the most foolhardy," Huggins stated. "Standing there at that altar calm as could be rather'n ducking for cover."

"I put my faith in the Lord," Nowicki answered.

"I have faith in the Lord too, Father," Czajkowski retorted, "but when you're up against a man like Jack Taylor, you'd also better put some faith in the Texas Rangers."

"What did I tell you, Father?" Regina broke in. "You need the Rangers to handle a swinia like Taylor."

"I don't even want to know what swinia means," Huggins chuckled.

"I can tell you, but it's not polite," Nowicki responded, also laughing.

"Anyway, Father, Frank's tellin' it to you straight. So's the lady," Huggins agreed. "We were lucky to get here in time. If you ever need us again, please don't wait so long to ask for our help."

"You're right. That's good advice," the pastor conceded. "However, I don't believe we'll require the Rangers' assistance henceforth."

Father Nowicki looked toward the body of Harding.

"What happened out here?"

"Taylor's men tried to stop us from reaching the church," Huggins explained. "We had to shoot it out. The one we killed was about to plug your associate. I realize you men of the cloth don't like killing, but sometimes it can't be avoided."

"I know." Nowicki sighed. "It's terrible what greed will do to a person. If Jack Taylor had accepted our offer to share water rights none of this would have happened."

"You can't reason with some hombres," Huggins observed. "Well, you won't have to worry about Taylor any longer. He's facing a long jail term."

"And now things should settle down," Czajkowski added. "Is there anything we can do for you right now, Father?"

"Once you get the prisoners to Sheriff Musgrave and they're locked up, perhaps you'll return here?" the pastor suggested. "We'll celebrate a special Mass at noon, thanking God for protecting us. We'll also pray for his blessing and protection for you Rangers."

"We'll do that," Huggins promised.

Once the Rangers, taking Harding's body and their prisoners, departed, Fathers Nowicki, Jankowski, and many of their parishioners filed back into the church. They would spend the rest of the morning in silent prayer.

Left Handed Law

1

"We're home, Sam," Texas Ranger Lieutenant Jim Blawcyzk said to his big paint gelding, as they reached Jim's small home on the outskirts of Bandera. It was just about sundown. There was no sign of his wife or three year old son in the yard, and a dim light shown through the kitchen window.

"I guess Julia and Charlie are inside eatin' supper, or Julia's gettin' him ready for bed," Jim continued. "I can sure use some rest myself. So can you, horse. C'mon pard. Let's get you settled."

Sam nickered a response, then broke into a trot. A moment later he was nuzzling the gate of his corral. Ted, Charlie's pet paint gelding, whinnied a welcome from the run-in shed.

Jim dismounted, stripped the gear from his horse and hung it on the fence, then turned Sam into the corral.

He gave the horse the last of the peppermints he always carried for him.

"I'll be back to care for you in a bit," he promised. Sam trotted off, then dropped to the sand to roll, while Jim headed for the house. The front door opened before he was halfway across the yard.

"Dad!" Charlie called from the doorway.

"Yeah, pardner. I'm home!" Jim took the stairs two at a time, picked up his son, hugged him, and perched the boy on his shoulders. He had to duck to enter the kitchen, where Julia stood waiting. Jim crossed the room in three strides, took Julia in his arms, and kissed her.

"Surprised to see me?" Jim asked, after they broke their embrace. "I'm home a few days sooner than planned."

"Only a little," Julia answered, her brown eyes sparkling with pleasure. "Charlie said you'd be home today. Somehow he seems to know when you're returning. Did you get the men you were after?"

"Yeah, Dad. I knew you'd come home today," Charlie confirmed.

"And you were right," Jim grinned. He lifted the boy from his shoulders, sat him in the corner rocker, and tousled Charlie's hair.

"Yes, I did get those hombres," he continued. "Frank Taunton and Beau Mallory are locked up. I've also got some more news. I'm gonna be home for a spell this time."

"Are you serious, Jim?" Julia asked. Usually the Rangers only allowed her husband a few days off between assignments.

"I sure am," Jim replied, "Not by my choice, though. The legislature's been stallin' about money for the Rangers again. You know politicians, always scheming to line their own pockets before worryin' about the folks they're supposed to serve. We've all been furloughed for a month. The only good news is they finally appropriated funds for the force, but they won't be reinstated until the first of next month. That means I'll be home until then."

"Which is the second piece of good news," Julia noted.

"Yeah, I reckon," Jim answered. "And there may be a bit more. The Adjutant General's asked for authorization to add twenty more Rangers to the rolls. If that's approved, we won't be spread so thin. Mebbe I'll be able to spend less time on the trail."

"That wouldn't necessarily make you happier," Julia observed. She had known from the start Jim was incapable of staying in one place for long. After a few days, his need to be on the move was almost irresistible.

"You're right again," Jim conceded. "There's no denyin' that."

"But right now you're here. That's all that matters. I'll heat up some leftover chicken for you. It will only take a few minutes."

"Good lookin' and a good cook. You're the best wife in Texas, honey," Jim answered.

"Flattery won't get you anywhere," Julia laughed, the promise in her eyes and smile denying her words. Her eagerness to be with Jim again was clearly evident. "While I'm heating your supper, why don't you put Charlie to bed?"

"Aw, Mom, do I have to?" Charlie pleaded.

"It's already past your bedtime," Julia answered.

"I'll tell you what, Charlie," Jim said. "You can help me rub down and feed Sam. After that, I'll wash up a mite, then you go to bed."

"Can we ride?" Charlie asked.

"Not tonight," Jim laughed, "I've spent enough time in the saddle the past few weeks. We'll see what tomorrow brings."

"All right, Dad."

"Remember, once we're finished, you go straight to bed and right to sleep," Jim ordered.

"Okay, dad. I promise," Charlie agreed.

"Good. We won't be long, Julia."

"You'd better not be."

∧∧∧∧∧∧∧∧∧∧∧∧∧

Charlie ended up not going straight to bed, but was allowed to remain up as his dad ate a late supper. While Jim ate, Julia caught him up on all the latest news from town.

"There's two new sisters at the convent, Sisters Angelica and Marguerite," she noted. "They seem very nice. Father Jaksina says they'll be serving as both teachers and nurses. Jason's putting an addition on the store. Three new families moved in."

"The town's growin' fast," Jim said. "And the ranchers seem to be doin' better and better. Good news for the folks around here."

"It certainly is. Oh, and remember the Havliceks were expecting their nephew? His parents both died. Since he has no other kin, he was coming from up north to live with them?"

"I do recollect that."

"He arrived three weeks ago. His name's Cody. He's going to learn the cabinetmaking trade from Stanley. I've already spoken to him about some shelves for the kitchen."

"I can do that," Jim objected. "Besides, we won't be here more'n a year or so. By then I'll have enough money saved for that place up around San Leanna we've talked about."

"You barely have time to keep the house up now," Julia pointed out. "And you can do rough carpentry, but I want nicely sanded and varnished shelves. Cody's willing to do them inexpensively, for the practice. You don't mind, do you?"

"I can never say no to you, Julia. You know that," Jim sighed.

"I know. But I have to let you think you can," she teased. "Besides, I think you'll like Cody. He's about your age, and believe it or not, you and he are distant cousins."

"We are? How's that?"

"Anna can explain it better than I. You'll have to ask her," Julia answered.

"I'll do that," Jim said. He pushed himself back from the table.

"It was sure good to have a home-cooked meal again, rather'n the burnt bacon and beans I make. I'm stuffed. Charlie, now it really is time for you to get to bed. You're half-asleep already. C'mon. I'll tuck you in, then help your mom with the dishes. Kiss her goodnight."

"All right, Dad," Charlie yawned.

Charlie kissed his mother and told her good night. Jim picked up his sleepy son and carried him to bed. By the time he pulled the blankets over Charlie and kissed his cheek, the boy was already asleep.

Julia and Jim finished cleaning up the kitchen, then headed for their own bedroom. Jim knelt alongside the bed to say his evening prayers, then pulled off his boots and socks and peeled off his shirt. He yawned hugely, then stretched.

"Guess I'm more tired than I realized," he said.

Julia ran her hand over his chest.

"Jim, exactly how tired are you?"

"Not that tired," Jim laughed. He wrapped her in his arms and kissed her. They sank slowly to the mattress.

∧∧∧∧∧∧∧∧∧∧∧∧

After feeding the horses and eating breakfast, Jim spent the rest of the next morning catching up on some of the neglected chores and repairs. Charlie, once he'd gathered eggs from the henhouse, tagged along after Jim, as always. The boy was the spitting image of his father, with the same blonde hair and blue eyes. He was holding nails for Jim, who was repairing some loose boards on the porch. Julia was sitting on the steps, shelling peas for supper.

"Dad, when can I have a puppy?" Charlie asked. "You promised I could, last time you were home."

"I know I did," Jim answered. "Tell you what. I'll check with Mister Hines and see when his collie will be having her next litter. You can pick out a nice pup then."

"Gee, thanks Dad!" Charlie exclaimed.

"Are you sure it's not too soon for that, Jim?" Julia questioned.

"Not at all," Jim replied. "A boy needs a dog. Besides, a dog will be protection for both of you when I'm not around."

"Yeah, Mom. My dog and I'll keep the bad guys away."

Charlie pulled the toy wooden six-gun he always had stuck in the waistband of his jeans and started banging away at imaginary outlaws.

"I think you got 'em all, Charlie," Jim laughed.

"That's 'cause I'm a Texas Ranger just like you, Dad," Charlie answered.

Jim's eyes narrowed when he spotted a smudge of dust on the horizon.

"Rider comin'," he said. "Are we expecting company, Julia?"

"That could be Cody Havlicek. He said he'd try and come by today to measure for those shelves," Julia answered. "If so, you'll get to meet him."

The dust cloud grew larger, and soon materialized into two riders.

"That's Stan Havlicek," Jim said. "I reckon the hombre with him must be Cody."

"It is," Julia confirmed.

Shortly, the riders reached the Blawcyzk yard and dismounted.

"Howdy, Jim, Julia. Hello, Charlie. I didn't realize you'd be home, Jim," Stan greeted. "This is my nephew, Cody. Cody, Ranger Jim Blawcyzk."

"Ranger."

"Call me Jim, Cody. And welcome to Bandera."

They shook hands. Jim looked over Bandera's newest arrival. While the resemblance between the two men wasn't striking, they were similar enough in appearance to obviously be related. Like Jim, Cody was tall and lean, a bit over six feet tall, with the same blonde hair, and blue eyes slightly lighter than Jim's. Jim would put Cody's age as two or three years younger than himself.

"I figured I'd better ride over here with Cody. It wouldn't look right for him to be here alone with Julia while you were on the trail, Jim," Stan explained.

"Stan, I told you there was no need for that," Julia said.

"I'm sure you're right," Stan replied. "But you know how some folks like to spread gossip. You wouldn't want to give some of those old bats from town an excuse to start waggin' their tongues and spreadin' scandalous rumors."

"Uncle Stan's right, Julia," Cody agreed.

"Pish-tosh," Julia retorted. "I'm not worried about those meddling old biddies."

"But why stir 'em up?" Stan pointed out. "I hate to rush, but we've got plenty to do, and Anna's got chores lined up for me for the rest of the week. Let's get the measurements taken, then Cody and I will be on our way."

"Can't I at least get you some lemonade, or a glass of cold water?" Julia asked.

"I could go for some lemonade," Cody admitted.

"That's fine. Come inside and I'll pour some while you and Stan take those measurements," Julia answered.

It took only a short while for Stan and Cody to get the figures they needed. After a brief respite to drink their lemonades, they headed back to their horses and remounted.

"Those shelves'll be ready for you in a few days," Cody promised.

"There's no need to rush," Julia assured him.

"Except for Uncle Stan. He won't rest until the job's done," Cody answered. "Thank you again for the lemonade, Julia."

"Yes, thank you," Stan added. "Will we see you at the church dance on Saturday?"

"I'd almost forgotten about that!" Julia exclaimed. "Of course we'll be there. It's not very often Jim is home to attend a social event with me. It will be fun."

"Good. We'll see you then. Cody, let's go. Jim, Charlie, good-bye."

"It was a pleasure getting to meet you, Jim," Cody added.

"Same here," Jim answered. "We'll have to get together again, when you have more time."

"That's a deal," Cody agreed. "See you Saturday."

∧∧∧∧∧∧∧∧∧∧∧∧

Jim spent the rest of the day working around the yard and corral, Charlie helping as best a three year old could.

"Jim, before we have supper, would you mind giving Charlie a bath?" Julia requested. "I've already heated plenty of water."

"Not at all," Jim agreed. "But you know what usually happens."

"You two reprobates had better not splash water all over my kitchen," Julia warned.

"You hear that, Charlie?" Jim grinned.

"Aw, Mom. You're no fun," Charlie moaned.

"Just take your bath," Julia ordered. "Jim, once Charlie's finished, you'd better take one too. You're filthy."

"I'm not that dirty," Jim chuckled.

"Don't even try and tell me that," Julia retorted. "I'll get your clean clothes while you get the tub."

Jim had worked up a sweat during his day-long toils. Both he and Charlie were grimy and dirt-streaked.

Jim got the big zinc washtub from behind the house and dragged it into the kitchen. While he filled it from the kettles Julia had heated, she got washcloths, towels, and soap from the cabinet.

Charlie pulled off his clothes.

"Into the tub, Charlie," Jim instructed. He knelt alongside the tub to lift Charlie into the water.

"I don't wanna take a bath," Charlie protested.

"You'll take a bath, or I'll shoot you right in your belly," Jim answered. He poked Charlie in the bellybutton. Charlie giggled.

"I'm not takin' a bath," he insisted, still giggling. "I'm gonna shoot you, Dad!"

He pointed his finger at Jim and shouted, "Bang!"

"Ow! Ya got me, Charlie!" Jim yelped. "Right in my guts!" He clutched his middle and fell backwards.

"No bath for me!" Charlie gloated.

"Jim, quit fooling around. Get your son into that tub," Julia ordered.

"I can't," Jim answered. "He plugged me. I'm dead."

"You'll really be dead if you don't get him into that water!" Julia warned, with a smile.

"All right." Jim rolled to his knees and grabbed Charlie before he could run off.

"Have I got to throw you into the tub, boy?" he growled.

"I guess not, Dad."

Charlie climbed into the tub, then immediately splashed Jim in the face.

"Got'cha, Dad!"

"Charlie!" Julia cried.

"Sorry, Mom." Charlie looked chagrined.

"You're not gonna try that again, are you, Charlie?" Jim chuckled.

"No, Dad."

"Good. Because if you did, I'd have to do this."

Jim skimmed his hands across the water's surface, scooped up a handful, and dumped it over Charlie's head. Charlie instantly returned the favor. Within a minute he and his father were embroiled in a full-blown water fight. They laughed uncontrollably as they doused each other.

"Charlie! Jim! Stop it, right now!" Julia ordered.

"We're sorry, honey," Jim answered, still chortling. He was soaked from head to foot. "We just can't help ourselves."

"I know. You're incorrigible," Julia sighed. Despite herself, she couldn't help but smile at the sight of her husband and son roughhousing together. "You're just as much a little boy as Charlie. That's part of what I love about you. Well, since you're already drenched, you might as well get in with Charlie. Perhaps that will keep a bit of water in the tub and save my kitchen floor."

"Yeah, Dad. C'mon," Charlie urged.

"All right." Jim stripped out of his wet clothes and climbed into the tub. Despite Julia's hopes, he and

Charlie were soon again dashing water at each other and splattering it all over the floor. Somehow, in the midst of their horseplay, they did manage to scrub themselves off.

Once they had finished their baths, Jim toweled himself and Charlie off. He pulled on his jeans, then got his razor and soap from the sideboard. He lathered up, and stood in front of the wall mirror to scrap two weeks' worth of blonde stubble from his jaw.

"Can I shave too, Dad?" Charlie pleaded.

"Sure. Why not?" Jim laughed. "Soon as I'm done."

He quickly finished shaving and wiped the remaining lather from his face. He then took the remaining soap from his shaving mug and spread that over Charlie's cheeks and neck. He removed the blade from his razor, gave Charlie the handle, and let him run that over his face, removing the lather.

"See Dad, I'm shavin' just like you," Charlie exclaimed.

"You sure are," Jim laughed. "Julia, you've got two of the handsomest men in Texas."

"And a couple of the worst behaved," Julia shot back. "If you two are finished fooling around, it's time to set the table."

"You heard your Mom, Charlie," Jim said. "Suppertime."

He and Charlie finished dressing, then Jim emptied the tub and dragged it outside. By the time he'd finished mopping the floor, Julia had supper on the table. They sat down, said Grace, and started their meal, content in the moment. With Jim's job as a Texas Ranger, times such as these were far too few.

∧∧∧∧∧∧∧∧∧∧∧∧

Later that night, Jim and Julia were lying in bed. Julia rested her head on Jim's chest while he stroked her long, brunette hair.

"Jim," Julia asked. "What did you think of Cody?"

"He seems like a decent hombre," Jim answered. "Doesn't appear to be the carpenter type, though."

"What do you mean?"

"I dunno for certain. He just struck me as a man who wouldn't want to be tied down."

"Not everyone's as fiddle-footed as you, Jim Blawcyzk," Julia chided.

"I know that. And I'm probably wrong about Cody. Why do you ask?"

"I'm thinking about introducing him to Sarah Wysocki. They'd make a charming couple, don't you think?"

"You're not gonna play matchmaker again, are you? Trap another unwary man into marriage?" Jim laughed.

"Why not?" Julia was indignant. "There's nothing wrong with bringing two people together. Since you're accusing me of matchmaking, don't tell me the thought of asking Cody to join the Rangers hadn't crossed your mind."

"The idea never occurred to me. But now that you mention it..."

"Don't you try and deny it, Jim," Julia retorted. "Besides, just look at you. You married me, didn't you?"

"That's because I'd been beaten up and shot when we met," Jim answered, chuckling. "I didn't know what I was doin'."

"Jim, you..."

Before Julia could utter another word of protest, Jim crushed his lips to hers. He held her for a long, lingering kiss.

"Jim, I'll...," Julia began, when he finally released her.

Jim pressed his lips to hers again.

"You'll do what, Julia?" he asked.

"This!"

Julia ran her fingertips along his sides. Jim trembled, then broke into uncontrollable laughter when Julia continued to tickle his ribs. She had discovered this weak spot of the big, rugged Ranger when they first met. Jim was extremely ticklish along his ribs.

"Please, don't," Jim pleaded. "Anything but that."

"Not until you say you're sorry, cowboy."

She continued to work on his ribs. In a few minutes, Jim was completely helpless.

"Well?" she asked.

"All right. I'm sorry. I'm sorry!" Jim gasped.

"You'd better be," Julia answered. "Or you'll be sleeping in the barn tonight."

Jim started to frame a retort, thought better of it, and snapped his mouth shut. Instead, he rolled onto his side and took Julia in his arms.

∧∧∧∧∧∧∧∧∧∧∧∧

Early the next Tuesday afternoon, Jim was taking a break from his chores. He and Julia were seated on the front porch, while Charlie was busy looking for grasshoppers. Jim spotted an approaching team and wagon.

"Here comes Cody. Reckon he's bringin' your shelves," he said.

"I can hardly wait to see how they look," Julia answered.

A few minutes later, Cody pulled the team to a halt and jumped from the buckboard.

"Howdy, Cody," Jim said.

"Hello. Julia, I've got those shelves. They turned out beautifully," Cody said. His gruff New England accent contrasted greatly with Jim's soft Texas drawl. "I'll bring them right in and put them in place."

"Thank you for getting them done so quickly," Julia answered.

"I'll give you a hand," Jim said.

"Me too, Dad." Charlie had come from the garden when he saw Cody arrive.

"All right."

Cody reached into the wagon bed and handed Charlie a package.

"You take these, Charlie. They're the screws for holding up the shelves."

Cody and Jim slid the shelves from the wagon and carried them inside, where they were placed on the floor. Cody picked up the top one.

"It'll make things go faster if you can hold these level for me, Jim," Cody requested.

"Sure. You did a much better job with these than I ever could."

The shelves were made of oak, sanded smooth and varnished to a high gloss finish.

"Truthfully, Uncle Stan did most of the work. I'm still not all that handy," Cody explained.

"Don't be so modest, Cody," Julia said. "These are lovely."

Cody and Jim made short work of hanging the shelves.

"How's that?" Cody asked Julia, once the last shelf was in place.

"They're perfect," Julia answered. "I'll make good use of them. Now, you boys go out on the porch and relax. I've got some lemonade and oatmeal cookies. I'll bring those out in a jiffy."

"Thanks. That sure sounds good, Julia," Cody replied.

"I can guarantee those cookies are the best you'll ever eat," Jim promised. They headed for the porch. Soon, Julia joined them. She carried a tray which held a plate of cookies, glasses, and a pitcher of lemonade.

"Help yourselves," she ordered. "You first, Cody."

"Don't mind if I do."

Cody poured himself a glass of lemonade and took several cookies. He waited until the others also had theirs before taking his first bite.

"Julia, Jim's right. These are the best cookies I've ever had, at least since my mother passed away."

"You know, Cody, Sarah Wysocki's a fine cook," Julia hinted. "I noticed you had three helpings of her apple crumble at the Saint Stanislaus social. You and she certainly made a handsome couple when you danced. She had her eyes on you all night. Quite a few of the girls did. You'd be a fine catch."

Cody blushed.

"I'm not so certain about that, Julia."

"Well, I am. You're good-looking, kind, and considerate. Once you finish learning your trade, you'll be a good provider. With all the folks moving into Texas, there'll always be work for a skilled carpenter. A woman could do far worse than marrying you."

"Perhaps," Cody replied, noncommittally.

"Cody, I haven't had a chance to show you around the rest of the place," Jim deftly changed the subject. "Lemme give you the grand tour."

"Sure," Cody agreed. "I'm free for the rest of the day."

"Bueno." Jim rose from his chair. "Julia, we won't be long."

"We sure won't," Cody agreed. "I want some more of those cookies, if I'm not being impolite."

"Not at all," Julia replied. "A woman likes a man with a good appetite."

Jim, Cody, and Charlie headed for the barn.

"You'd better watch out for Julia. She'll have you hog-tied before you know it," Cody," Jim laughed, once they were out of Julia's earshot.

"I don't notice you complainin'," Cody rejoined.

"That's right. Marryin' Julia's the smartest thing I ever did… well, that and joining the Rangers."

They stopped at the corral gate. Sam, Jim's palomino and white splotched war horse, and Ted, Charlie's two year old buckskin paint gelding, ambled up to the gate. While Sam nuzzled Jim's cheek, Charlie climbed the fence and scrambled onto Ted's back. Cody eyed the boy dubiously when he sent the young horse trotting around the corral.

"Isn't Charlie a bit young to be riding a horse?" he asked.

"No," Jim answered. "I had him in a saddle by the time he was six months old. Rode him all around while he sat in my lap. Julia was horrified, of course. But most kids in Texas start ridin' as soon as they can walk, sometimes sooner.

Sam nuzzled Jim again, more insistently.

"Of course I've got your peppermint," Jim told the horse. "One for Ted, also. Don't you try'n steal his."

He dug into his hip pocket and came up with a candy, which he gave to the horse. Sam took his treat, then pinned his ears and lunged at Cody.

"This is Sam. You'd better steer clear of him," Jim warned. "He's pretty much a one man animal."

"I can see that, and I sure understand," Cody answered. "I've got one with much the same attitude. His name's Yankee. He's also a paint. Chestnut gelding. I rescued him from a bad situation. I'm the only one who can handle him."

"Same way I got Sam," Jim answered. "Only the hombre I took him off tried to kill me. Luckily, I shot faster. Had to kill both that man and his brother."

"You didn't get arrested for murder?"

"No. It was self-defense. A Texas Ranger witnessed the entire thing. He not only didn't arrest me, he recruited me into the Rangers. I've been one ever since."

"You don't have any regrets about that?"

"Not a one," Jim answered. "Sure, I get lonesome when I'm away from Julia and Charlie, but I wouldn't trade my life for any other. In another year or so, I hope to have enough saved up to buy a little spread nearer to Austin. I'll turn that into a horse ranch. Julia's already said she'll run the place while I'm out Rangerin'. She's every bit as capable of doin' that as any man."

Jim eyed Cody thoughtfully.

"Cody, if I'm pryin' just say so, but do you really want to be a cabinetmaker and carpenter?"

"No," Cody answered, without hesitation. "Uncle Stan and Aunt Anna were real kind to ask me down here after my folks died, and I appreciate what they've done for me. But my uncle's already figured out I'm not cut out for woodworking. He hasn't come out and said so, but he wouldn't be upset if I found another line of work."

"Would you consider joinin' the Rangers?" Jim asked. "We're waitin' for funding right now, so I can't say for certain we'll be lookin' for more recruits, but if you think you'd be interested, I can let you talk with Captain Trumbull. If he feels you might make a lawman, you'd be in line once we were ready to sign up new men."

"Jim, you read my mind," Cody responded. "I was trying to think of a way to ask you about becoming a Ranger. I'd like to try my hand at a lawman's job."

"It's not an easy life," Jim warned. "You'll be on the trail for weeks or months at a time, facin' white outlaws, Mexican raiders, and renegade Indians, all of who'll be just itchin' to put a bullet in your back. The pay ain't much, thirty a month and found, when the state gets around to payin' you at all."

"Found?"

"Grub. Food."

"Oh."

"You've got to provide your own guns, supplies, saddle, and a horse worth at least a hundred dollars. Sounds like the horse won't be a problem for you. The state'll reimburse you if your horse gets killed or crippled in the line of duty. Texas will also supply your ammunition, but that's it. Otherwise, you'll be on your own. If you think you're loco enough to want to try your hand at bein' a Ranger, we can ride up to Austin and meet with the captain."

"I've got one question," Cody replied.

"What's that?"

"How soon can we leave?"

"Day after tomorrow. But boy, is Julia gonna be sore at me," Jim laughed. "She plans on doin' her darndest to get you and Sarah Wysocki hitched."

"I'm not ready for that yet," Cody answered. "But when the time comes, I sure would be interested in a woman like Sarah."

"You could do far worse," Jim agreed. "Well, let's get back to the house. C'mon, Charlie. You can play with Ted later. Here's his candy."

"Sure, Dad." Charlie slid from Ted's back and ducked under the fence. He gave Ted the peppermint, then patted his nose. Ted nuzzled the boy's chest and nickered.

"Cody, you won't want to let on to Julia quite yet that you're considerin' joining the Rangers," Jim chuckled. "You might not get the rest of those cookies if you do."

2

"Well, here we are. Ready to meet Captain Trumbull?" Jim asked.

"Sure am," Cody answered.

After a three day ride from Bandera, they had arrived in Austin, and were tying their horses to the rail in front of Ranger Headquarters. Jim had spent the trip observing how Cody handled a long horseback journey. The New Englander had held up well, taking the long days in the saddle without complaining. Cody was also a good judge of horseflesh. If pressed, Jim would have to admit Cody's horse was every bit as good as his own Sam.

"Then let's go."

The two men headed inside. With funding for the Rangers having run out, there was no one at Headquarters, save a lone clerk and Captain Hank Trumbull. Jim led Cody straight to Trumbull's office. The captain looked up in surprise when Jim entered.

"Jim! What're you doin' here? We haven't had any word from the Capitol yet on releasing our funds before the beginning of the month."

"I figured as much," Jim replied, shaking Trumbull's hand. "Those politicians always dawdle when it comes to money for the Rangers. Nope, I'm here for another reason. I'd like you to meet Cody Havlicek. Cody, this is Captain Hank Trumbull. He's the meanest hombre and toughest man you'd ever ride with. And every one of us Rangers'd follow him to the devil and back."

Cody took Trumbull's hand with a firm grip.

"Pleased to meet you, Captain."

"Same here, Cody."

"Cap'n, Cody would like to join the Rangers, if you get the authority to take on some new men," Jim explained.

"You would, son?"

"Yessir, Captain Trumbull."

"Fine. Let's talk about that for a bit. You want some coffee?"

"I wouldn't mind some," Cody admitted.

"Good." Trumbull poured three cups of coffee from the battered pot he always kept hot on the corner stove. He handed one each to Jim and Cody, then settled behind his scarred desk.

"You want a smoke?" he asked Cody, knowing that Jim never used tobacco nor drank liquor.

"No thank you, Captain. Never got in the habit," Cody answered.

"All right." Trumbull's frosty blue eyes studied Cody while he rolled a quirly, then lit up.

"Where are you from, Cody?" was his first question.

"Keene."

"Keene? You mean that town up by Fort Worth?"

"Not exactly. Keene, New Hampshire. Close by Vermont and Massachusetts."

"Ah. That explains the accent," Trumbull grunted. "How'd you land in Texas? And what makes you think you want to be a Texas Ranger?"

"The only kin I have left are my aunt and uncle, in Bandera," Cody answered. "I came down here to learn carpentry from my uncle, but it's not for me. Jim here suggested I might try my hand at Rangerin'. The thought had already crossed my mind, so when Jim said he'd see what he could do, I jumped at the chance."

"I see." Trumbull blew a ring of smoke toward the ceiling.

"Can you shoot?"

"I've done some huntin'."

"Fight? With fists and knife?"

"A bit with my hands. Never tried with a knife," Cody admitted.

"Ride?"

"Yes, pretty well."

"Cody, don't be so modest," Jim interrupted. "Cap'n, he can ride darn near as well as me. 'Course, we had to get him a good stock saddle before we left Bandera. And he's got a real good horse."

"A good horse. Figures you'd see that as qualifyin' a man for the Rangers, Lieutenant," Trumbull snorted.

"But havin' a decent horse is one of the requirements, Cap'n," Jim protested. "And Cody's is a fine animal. He even has the same temperament as Sam."

"Just what the Rangers need. Two cayuses like yours," Trumbull retorted. He turned his attention back to Cody.

"What other qualifications do you have?"

"Just that I'm willin' to try real hard to learn everything I need to know to be a good lawman," Cody answered.

"Cody's also my distant cousin," Jim answered. "So we share the same blood."

"Your cousin?" Trumbull echoed.

"Yep. Distant cousin. One of those fourth cousin three times removed deals. Somethin' like that," Jim answered. "Cody's aunt can explain it better'n me."

"Jim Blawcyzk's cousin. With a horse like his. Lord help me… and the Texas Rangers," Trumbull groaned.

"Cap'n, we've got at least two weeks before the money for the Rangers will be reinstated," Jim continued. "I can use that time to teach Cody almost everythin' he'll need to know about Rangerin'. Once you get the go-ahead to recruit more men, he'll be ready."

"You can teach him all you want, Jim, but if Cody doesn't have the instincts of a lawman he won't last a month before he gets a knife in his guts or a bullet in his back," Trumbull objected.

"I'll know about that by the time I'm finished workin' with him," Jim replied. "If Cody doesn't have the makin's of a Ranger, I'll be the first to say so. I'm sure not gonna chance any of my pards' lives on a man who can't cut it. Bet a hat on that."

"I'm certain of that," Trumbull responded. "But let's leave that up to your cousin."

"How about you?" he continued to Cody. "Did Jim explain exactly how tough a Ranger's life is?"

"He did," Cody answered.

"And you think you can handle it?"

89

"I'm sure of that."

"Cap'n, you can never be certain a man will make a Ranger until you give him a try," Jim broke in.

"I know that," Trumbull answered.

"Captain Trumbull, if you'll give me the opportunity to prove myself, I promise I won't let you down," Cody stated.

Trumbull studied Cody for a moment, liking what he saw. The young man's eyes never blinked, his expression never flinched under the Captain's icy gaze.

"All right," he decided. "I'm not makin' any promises, but if the state grants me the funds I need, and Jim says you'll make a Ranger, then we'll give you a try. Is that fair enough?"

"That's all I ask, Captain," Cody replied, a grin spreading from ear to ear.

"Cody'll be a man to ride the river with. You'll see, Cap'n," Jim said.

"I believe you're right, Jim," Trumbull answered. "Now, how about we head over to the Silver Star for some drinks? On me."

"As long as it's sarsaparilla," Cody answered.

"You too?" Trumbull questioned. "Jim won't touch alcohol, either. Next thing you'll be tellin' me you also don't cuss."

"That's right," Cody answered.

"Let me guess. You go to church every Sunday."

"Never miss Mass if I can help it."

Trumbull shook his head.

"Two of you. Both left-handed. And even your looks are similar. Dunno if Texas is ready for that."

"Reckon we'll find out, Cap'n," Jim grinned.

"I reckon we will. But I know one thing for certain."

"What's that, Captain?" Cody asked.

"Now I really need that drink. Let's get to the saloon."

∧∧∧∧∧∧∧∧∧∧∧∧

"All right, Cody. Time to find out how well you can shoot."

Jim and Cody were at the far end of the pasture behind Jim's horse corral, where Jim had set up a series of targets.

"Try for the center of that board nailed to the cottonwood stump," Jim ordered.

"Sure."

Cody lifted the new Colt pistol from the holster on his left hip, leveled it, thumbed back the hammer, squeezed the trigger, and fired. His shot hit four inches to the right of the board's center.

"How's that, Jim?"

"Not bad. But nowhere near good enough for the Rangers," Jim answered. "You're gonna need a lot of practice. And that's just aimin' at a steady target. Once you've got that down, then I'll have you shootin' at movin' targets, rocks tossed in the air, things like that. Finally, I'll teach you how to get your gun out of your holster, fast. However, that's the last thing you need to know. It doesn't matter how fast you are if you can't shoot straight. You'll be the one lyin' dead, with a bullet in your belly. The man who wins a gunfight is usually the one who takes that extra split second to aim carefully. Now try again. Put the five bullets left in your gun into that target."

"All right."

Cody triggered five more shots. All five hit the target. Three of them were within an inch of the board's middle.

"That's a heckuva lot better," Jim praised. "Now reload. We'll try for those bottles next. I'll go first."

Jim had set up a row of twelve bottles on the fence's top rail. He drew and fired. In quick succession, six of the bottles were shattered by Jim's bullets.

"Wow!" Cody exclaimed.

"Don't be impressed. Just see what you can do," Jim ordered.

"Okay."

Cody took aim at the remaining bottles. When he had emptied his gun, only one remained standing.

"Well?" he smiled.

"Real good shootin'," Jim praised. "But that one bottle still up there could be the hombre who plugs you. I'll set up more targets and you'll try that again. This time see if you can get all six. And don't forget, take your time."

Jim set up six more bottles. As soon as they were in place, Cody drew and fired. This time, he hit four of the six.

"You're rushin' your shots, and tryin' too hard," Jim told him. "You want to squeeze the trigger, not jerk it. Reload. You're gonna try again."

∧∧∧∧∧∧∧∧∧∧∧∧

Jim spent the next week training Cody in the skills needed by a Texas Ranger. Through all the lessons, he kept reminding Cody that, while he would have to be proficient with fists, gun, and knife, his most important weapon as a Ranger would be his brain. No matter how good a Ranger was with Colt and Winchester, he needed to be able to think on his feet, and keep his wits about him at all times.

"Cody, you've gotten about as good as you can with a gun," Jim stated as they finished another session. "You're pretty fast on the draw, too. I can't help you much more. All you need is more practice, and you don't need my help for that."

"I appreciate all you've done for me," Cody replied.

"You're a quick learner," Jim answered. "You also handle a knife well. What I think needs more work is your fist-fightin' ability. I don't believe you're quite ready for a down and dirty saloon brawl. Let's work on that."

"All right," Cody agreed.

They peeled off their shirts and shucked their gunbelts, hanging them from a fencepost. As they turned to face each other, Jim launched a punch at Cody's jaw. Cody ducked under the punch and slugged him hard in the belly. Jim jackknifed. Cody's following blow took Jim on the point of his chin, knocking him flat on his back. Before Jim could react, Cody put his bootheel into the pit of his stomach. Jim lay there for a moment, stunned, then propped himself up on his elbows. He shook his head, attempting to clear the cobwebs. Cody stood over him, grinning.

"How's that, Jim? Am I ready for the Rangers?" he asked.

Jim rubbed his jaw.

"I reckon," he admitted. "You pack quite a punch, Cody. Now, how about lettin' me up?"

"All right."

Cody lifted his foot from Jim's stomach.

Jim slowly came to his feet, then lunged at Cody, slamming a fist into his middle. Cody doubled over, grunting with pain.

"You got careless," Jim said. "Imagine if I'd pulled a knife when you relaxed. I'd've gutted you, Cody. If I'd been some renegade you were after, you'd be dead. Bet a hat on it."

"I guess you're right," Cody gasped.

"It's one more lesson," Jim answered. "Never let your guard down. I learned that the hard way. I'd rather you didn't."

Cody rubbed the sore spot on his belly where Jim's fist had connected.

"I don't think I'll forget," he answered.

"Good," Jim replied. "What now? More practice, or you want to rest a spell and get some cold water?"

"I'd rather the water, but I guess you're right. I need the practice more," Cody conceded.

"I was hopin' you'd say that," Jim approved. "Let's go."

The two men squared off again.

3

Julia looked up from her reading, enjoying the sound of rain hitting the roof. This storm was not a typical midsummer Texas gullywasher, which hit quickly and violently, most of its water running off, but a good rancher's rain, a steady rain which would last for a day or so, sinking deep into the earth. After the recent dry spell, it was just what every farmer and rancher had been praying for.

The rain had kept Jim inside all morning, which he'd spent roughhousing with Charlie. Julia's reading had been interrupted more than once by the sound of shouting and laughter as Charlie and his dad wrestled and chased each other around Charlie's room. Jim would groan in mock pain when Charlie bounced up and down on his stomach. Charlie's giggles became almost hysterical when Jim caught him, pretending to be a "belly monster" who would chomp out Charlie's guts. The boy loved that silly game. The noise of her husband and son playing brought Julia great contentment. All too soon, she knew, the Rangers would have orders for Jim. He would hit the trail once again, Julia not knowing when, or even if, he would return. Still, Julia could never love another man the way she loved her wandering Ranger. His long absences only made their time together that much sweeter.

Julia soon realized the sound of the raindrops and gentle breeze had become so much clearer because of the silence now emanating from Charlie's room. For the past several minutes she had not heard a sound, except that of the rain.

I'd better see what those two are doing, she thought. *When they're this quiet, it usually means they're up to no good.*

Julia set aside her book and went to Charlie's bedroom, following a trail of discarded boots, socks, and finally shirts. She found Jim and Charlie sleeping. Charlie was snuggled against his dad's side, his head resting on Jim's chest. Jim had one arm wrapped protectively around his son.

I guess they finally wore each other out. I'll just let them sleep.

Julia stood in the doorway for quite some time, quietly watching Jim and Charlie while they napped.

If I could stop time, I'd do it right now, she mused. Her reverie was broken by the sound of an approaching horse and rider. Jim stirred at the hoofbeats. He sat up on the edge of the bed.

"Reckon I fell asleep. Someone comin'?" he whispered, not wanting to awaken Charlie.

"Yes, there is," Julia answered.

"Best see who it is." Jim padded barefoot across the floor, retrieved his Winchester from its rack in the kitchen, and opened the door. Todd Jensen, the young clerk from the Western Union office, was just tying his bay mare to the rail.

"Howdy, Todd," Jim greeted him. He placed his rifle against the wall.

"Howdy, Lieutenant Blawcyzk. I've got a wire from Austin for you."

Todd slid from his saddle, climbed the stairs to the porch, and shook water from his dripping Stetson. He reached inside his slicker and removed a telegram from an inside pocket. He handed the message to Jim.

"Thanks, Todd. Why don't you come inside and have a cup of coffee to warm up?"

"I'd appreciate that."

"C'mon in."

"Julia, it's Todd Jensen," Jim called, when they entered. "He's brought a message from Headquarters. I invited him in for some coffee."

"Hello, Todd. I've got some cornbread to go with that coffee, if you'd like," Julia offered.

"That would be fine, Mrs. Blawcyzk," the messenger answered.

While Julia poured a mug of black coffee for Todd, Jim scanned the contents of the yellow flimsy. His blue eyes took on the hue of chips of glittering ice as he read.

"What does Captain Trumbull say, Jim?" Julia asked. "Will you be leaving soon?"

"Yeah," Jim answered. "In fact, as soon as I can get packed and Sam saddled."

"I thought there weren't going to be any funds for the Rangers before next month."

"The legislature came to its senses. They issued an emergency spending order."

"They must have a good reason for that."

"They do. Webb Patton is back in Texas. I'm to take Cody and track Patton down."

4

"We've got to intercept Patton before he reaches Wimberley, Cody. Let me tell you what we'll be up against," Jim explained to the new Ranger. He had left home an hour after receiving the telegram, located Cody, and sworn him into the Rangers. The two had then ridden hard through the rest of the rainy afternoon. The rain had stopped an hour before sunset. Jim and Cody were now camped twenty miles northeast of Bandera.

"Sure, Jim," Cody replied. "Just let me pour myself some more coffee."

Cody lifted the pot from the embers to refill his tin mug.

"Webb Patton and his bunch robbed several banks three years back," Jim began. "They killed four men, including a deputy sheriff. They were caught, tried and convicted. But while they were waitin' to be hanged, they broke out of jail, killin' two more men. They managed to escape Texas. The last anyone knew they were hidin' out up in the Territories."

"But now Patton's back in Texas. Why?" Cody asked.

"Quien sabe?" Jim shrugged. "Probably figures if he can make it back to his home grounds his relatives and friends will protect him. He left a gal behind, so mebbe he's returned for her."

"Seems like he's takin' an awful long chance," Cody noted.

"Maybe. Maybe not," Jim answered. "Patton and his men most likely would have made it home without anyone even realizin' they were back in Texas, if they hadn't robbed the bank in Mason. The marshal there recognized Patton's brother, Jobe. Lucky for us he was able to say so before he died from the slug Jobe put through him."

"Then they hit another bank, in Llano," Cody said.

"So it appears," Jim confirmed. "My guess is they'll now stick to the back country until they reach Blanco. They'll probably stop there to resupply, mebbe even stage another bank holdup, then head for Wimberley. If they make it before we do, we'll have a devil of a time gettin' at 'em. Too many folks there are willin' to hide them."

"Jim, obviously I'm not as familiar with this country as you, but it seems we're cutting this mighty close."

"We are. But I've got a couple of aces up my sleeve."

"What are they? Because it seems to me we might need those."

102

"First, I know this area every bit as well as Patton. I've got a pretty good idea where to find him."

"What's the other?"

"I doubt Patton'll head straight for Wimberley. He's a cautious man. Even with his friends there, he'll want to wait a while for things to quiet down. He might send a man ahead to scout things out before he and the rest of his bunch ride into town. No, Patton'll most likely hole up for a spell, somewhere along the Devil's Backbone."

"What in blue blazes is the Devil's Backbone?" Cody demanded.

"Blue blazes? You're beginning to talk like a Texan, Cody," Jim chuckled. "The Devil's Backbone is a long hogback. It's a razor-back ridge which twists and turns for almost twenty-five miles between Wimberley and Blanco. There's plenty of places for a man to disappear in that stretch. Lots of side ridges and canyons. Patton's used it as a hideout before. I'd imagine he'll use it again."

"That makes sense," Cody conceded. "But why did Captain Trumbull hand this job to you? It seems to me Rangers from Austin could reach Wimberley before us."

"You're right," Jim agreed, "But like I said, I know this country real well, probably better'n any other man in the Rangers. So we've got a better chance of findin' Patton, without gettin' ambushed and a bullet in our backs, than the rest of the outfit."

"That's real comforting," Cody sarcastically replied. "Exactly how many men will we be up against? Or are you saving that as a surprise?"

"Six for certain. Webb and Jobe. Their cousins, Wade and Matt. Two others, Hank Martin and Ed Torneau. There might be one or two more."

"Those are long odds."

"Not for the Rangers. Usually we're outnumbered six or seven to one, even more. Three to one odds aren't much."

"But I haven't even gotten my feet wet," Cody objected. "You're stuck with a raw recruit, Jim. Wouldn't you prefer having an experienced Ranger riding with you?"

"Someone like Jim Huggins?" Huggins was a veteran sergeant who had ridden with Jim on more than one occasion. "Sure, I'd like to have him sidin' me. But you've got to start somewhere, Cody. And I'm not worried. You've got the makin's of a Ranger. You'll do fine. I'd bet my hat on it."

"I appreciate your confidence in me. Sure hope it's justified."

Jim dumped the dregs from his mug.

"Time we turned in. I want to reach Blanco by tomorrow night. That means a full day of hard ridin'. We'll pull out an hour before sunup."

"Why Blanco?"

"Just playin' a hunch. With luck, we'll get there before Patton. If not, we'll trail him down into the Devil's Backbone."

"What if you're wrong, and he's headed straight to Wimberley?"

"Then we'll have two choices. First, try and find him there. That'd be real difficult, since hardly anyone in town would help us. Most likely they'd shoot us instead."

"What's the other option? Any better chance of us finding Patton with that one, and not getting ourselves killed?"

"Yeah. We'd have no trouble at all findin' Patton. In fact, he'd come lookin' for us."

"Why?" Cody asked.

"Because I'm the man who rounded up Patton and his bunch. He vowed to kill me, if he ever got the chance."

"So that's the real reason he's back in Texas," Cody said.

"I'd imagine. And if we don't stop him before he reaches Wimberley, he'll stay there a few days, then head for Bandera."

"Where he'd find you… along with Julia and Charlie," Cody answered.

"That's right. So we've gotta stop Patton before he gets anywhere near my family."

∧∧∧∧∧∧∧∧∧∧∧∧

The Rangers found Blanco with an empty bank vault and dead deputy sheriff, the result of a robbery two days previous. While the outlaws had been masked, the head teller was certain it was Wade Patton's gang which had looted the bank. He also confirmed the robbers had headed in the direction of the Devil's Backbone. Jim and Cody remained in town to rest themselves and their horses overnight. They were again on the trail at the first light of false dawn.

"We don't have a chance of catchin' up with 'em before they reach town if they ride straight for Wimberley, do we, Jim?" Cody questioned. They were keeping Sam and Yankee at a ground-eating lope.

"Not a prayer," Jim confirmed. "But my gut's still tellin' me they'll hole up for a few days first, mebbe even longer. They've stirred up quite a hornet's nest, and if Jobe suspects that marshal talked before he died, they'll know the Rangers'll be after 'em. They'll wait until things settle down a bit. Webb'll send one of his men into town, with word where they'll be. Then, once any lawmen show up in Wimberley, don't find Webb or his men, and leave, one of Webb's kinfolk will ride to their hideout and tell Webb it's safe. That's when he'll finally head for Wimberley."

"Couldn't that lawman kind of hang around outside town, watch for that messenger, then follow him?" Cody asked.

"You're startin' to think like a Ranger," Jim praised. "Yeah, he could, but most likely he'd lose that rider. Either that, or the hombre would bushwhack him. There's not too many lawmen fool enough to ride alone into the Devil's Backbone."

"But I reckon we're two of 'em who are," Cody ruefully chuckled.

"I reckon," Jim agreed. "How you feelin', pardner? Scared at all?"

"Scared? Not a bit," Cody scoffed. "Except for the churning in my guts, the pounding in my head, and my heart racin' a hundred miles an hour, I'm not nervous at all!"

"That's good," Jim replied. "I'd be worried if you weren't scared. Any man facin' a bunch of killers who claims he isn't nervous is either lyin' or loco, or both. And that's the man who'll make a mistake which gets him or his pardner killed."

"Jim, if there's so many hiding places around here, how'll we ever find Patton's bunch?"

"A little bit of skill and a lot of luck. I've got a good idea where to start lookin'. We should come on their tracks sometime today, unless I miss my guess. While

107

there's plenty of hidin' places, there's not that many trails which go clear through to Wimberley. The main one runs right along the ridge top. Patton won't use that one if he can help it. Too hard on the horses, and too many spots where he could be skylined.

"Skylined? What's that?"

"Gotta keep remindin' myself you're still a new recruit," Jim laughed. "A man skylines himself when he's ridin' or standin' on a ridge or the rim of a canyon, with the sky behind him. Makes a real easy target for a drygulcher down below."

"That makes sense," Cody agreed. "Except it seems to me that works both ways. A man up high could spot someone down below real easy."

"You're learnin', Cody."

Jim pulled Sam down to a walk.

"We'll rest the horses for half an hour, once we reach that creek just ahead," he ordered. "After that it'll be slower goin'. I'll start lookin' for signs of Patton."

"All right."

The two men rested for thirty minutes, while the horses had a short drink and cropped at the grass bordering the stream. Once they were back in the saddle, Jim kept their pace alternating between a walk and slow jogtrot, while he searched the ground for any marks of the outlaws' passing. They were now riding along the Devil's Backbone.

It was late that morning when Jim found the first sign. The hoofprints of several horses emerged from a side arroyo. He pulled Sam to a halt.

"Blast it! Hold up a minute, Cody. You see those?"

He pointed at the tracks.

"I sure do," Cody confirmed. "Patton's outfit?"

"I'd bet my hat on it," Jim answered. "That's how he fooled the sheriff and posse, just like he fooled me. I plumb forgot about that old Indian track which runs from the Pedernales south through here. Patton circled north out of town, picked up that trail, and took it. That's why we haven't seen any sign until now."

"But wouldn't circling take longer?"

"Not in this case. That Indian trail does a lot less windin' around and doublin' back on itself than the one we've been followin'. Patton's gained at least half a day on us."

"That doesn't mean we've lost him?"

Jim spat in the dirt.

"Not a chance. And now that we've picked up Patton's trail, there's no way he'll shake us off."

"Even if he tries to cover his trail?"

109

"It's just too hard to hide the signs of eight horses from an experienced tracker," Jim explained. "I might lose them for a bit, but I'll find 'em again. Don't worry about that. Just worry about what we're gonna do when we catch up with 'em."

"How soon'll that be?"

"Tomorrow, or the day after for certain, unless I'm wrong and they are headin' right to Wimberley. In that case, all bets are off. Let's go."

Jim heeled Sam into a lope, Cody and Yankee on their heels.

∧∧∧∧∧∧∧∧∧∧∧∧

They rode until darkness made it impossible to follow the trail any longer. Jim chose a campsite near a small spring. After he was unsaddled, Sam, as always, nuzzled Jim's hip pocket for an ever-present peppermint.

"Sure, you can have one, you ol' beggar," Jim laughed. He slipped Sam a candy, which the paint eagerly took.

"Cody, you want one for your horse?"

"Why not?" Cody answered.

"All right. But once your bronc gets a taste for these, he'll always be lookin' for 'em," Jim warned.

"I suppose. It doesn't matter. Yank's as spoiled as your horse," Cody admitted, as he gave Yankee a peppermint.

"I'm not so sure," Jim disagreed. "But I make no apologies for the way I care for Sam. He's more of a friend than most men."

"I've gotta agree with you," Cody said. "Probably smarter, too. Yankee sure is."

Another thing the two had in common was their affection for horses. After caring for their mounts, they made a cold camp.

"A fire'd stand out for miles around here. It'd be just like a signal beacon," Jim explained to Cody. "We can't chance someone spottin' it, so we'll have settle for jerky, leftover biscuits, and water."

Jim dug the meager meal out of his saddlebags. The two men ate silently, then rolled in their blankets. Jim, as always, said his evening prayers. He noted Cody did the same.

Jim was almost asleep when Cody called him.

"Jim, you asleep?"

"Not quite. Why?"

"I'm just wonderin'. How soon do you think we'll find Patton?" Cody asked.

"If our luck holds out, sooner than you'd imagine," Jim answered. "I've got a pretty good idea where he's at."

"Where?"

"There's an abandoned homestead about a half day's ride from here. It's pretty well hidden, behind a ridge then up a canyon. It's been used by Patton before."

"Is that where you trailed him last time?"

"Not exactly. He'd been there, but already ridden on by the time I discovered the place. I caught up with him a week later."

"Do you really believe he'll go back to the same place, since he must realize you know about it?"

"I'd bet a hat he will. The cabin's pretty large, and in decent shape. There's good water and grazin', and lots of game for meat. Plus the place is well-hidden, and there's plenty of spots in there to hide and pick off anyone snoopin' around."

"That's a real comforting thought," Cody said.

"As long as you ain't dumb enough to step in front of a bullet, you've got nothin' to worry about," Jim laughed. "Now, if you're done with your questions, I'm plumb tired. Good night."

"'Night."

∧∧∧∧∧∧∧∧∧∧∧∧

It was about two the next afternoon when Jim reined up at the almost invisible entrance to a narrow side canyon. Thick brush made the opening nearly impossible to spot.

Patton and his men had made some effort to cover their
trail, but to an experienced tracker like Jim their sign was
still plain. Jim leaned from his saddle to pluck a strand of
sorrel horsehair from a mesquite branch.

"This is it, Cody," Jim said. "Patton's ridin' a sorrel.
They turned in here."

"I never would've found it," Cody admitted. "You've
got some eyesight."

"You'll learn," Jim answered. "Just takes practice.
Let's go. But be careful. And quiet. Does Yank like to call
out to other horses?"

"No. He's not the talkative kind," Cody replied.

"Good. Otherwise you'll have to tie your bandanna
over his muzzle."

Sam snorted a protest when Jim pushed him through
the thorny brush. Once they had gone fifty yards, the
trail widened. The prints of eight horses were plainly
visible in the sandy soil.

"Eight horses went in, none came out. They're in
here all right," Jim stated. "And not even botherin' to
hide their tracks. They must figure no one'd notice that
entrance. Time to check our guns."

They checked the actions of their guns, and put a
bullet into the empty chambers of their Colts. Jim also
removed his Ranger badge from his shirt pocket. He
pinned the silver star on silver circle to his vest.

"All right. That shack's about two miles in. Let's move. Keep a sharp lookout," Jim warned.

They put their horses into a walk, easing them as quietly as possible up the winding path.

About half a mile before the cabin, they rounded a bend and came upon an approaching rider.

"Blawcyzk!" he shouted, recognizing the Ranger. He clawed for his sixgun. Jim pulled his own Peacemaker just as the rider cleared leather, and knocked him from the saddle with a bullet in the chest. The rider pitched to the dirt, rolled onto his face, shuddered, and lay unmoving. His horse trotted a short distance away, then dropped its head to pull at a clump of bunch grass.

Jim swung from his saddle and knelt alongside the dead outlaw. He rolled him onto his back. Cody remained mounted, staring at the body.

"It's Wade Patton," Jim said.

"Is he dead?" Cody asked. His voice shook slightly.

"He sure is," Jim confirmed.

"That's one less to deal with. Only seven of 'em left, Jim."

"Except the rest'll have heard that shot. That'll bring 'em ridin' down on us, unless they figure Wade here was takin' a pot shot at a rabbit."

"So what do we do now?"

Jim gazed at the body of Wade Patton. The dead outlaw was about his size, with blonde hair only slightly darker.

"I've got an idea. Get off your horse and give me a hand," he ordered, then started peeling off his shirt.

Cody dismounted.

"Get the clothes off that hombre," Jim continued. "I'm gonna take his place."

"What?"

"I'm switchin' clothes and horses with him. I'll toss him over Sam's back. With any luck, that'll fool 'em into thinkin' I'm Wade, and that I've just downed an intruder. That might even lure 'em out of the cabin, which'd be a heckuva lot easier than tryin' to blast 'em out of there."

"Wouldn't it be simpler just for me to play dead, with you masquerading as Patton?" Cody questioned. "That way, you wouldn't have to put your clothes on him and load him on your horse."

"It would, except that would put both of us in the line of fire if anything goes wrong. I'd rather keep you hidden, then surprise those renegades when you pop out of the brush. You'll stay behind me, out of sight until I get up to that cabin."

"That won't trick them once you get close enough to be recognized," Cody objected.

"I don't need long, just enough to get a bit of advantage. And don't kid yourself. Patton's not gonna surrender, knowin' he's facing a hangnoose. We're in for a fight. Hurry up and get those duds off."

While Jim swiftly undressed, Cody opened Patton's shirt. He gagged at the sight of the bullet hole in his chest.

"You all right?" Jim asked him.

"I'm a bit queasy," Cody admitted. "First time I've seen a man shot and killed."

"You'll never get used to it," Jim told the young Ranger. "First time I shot a man I puked my guts out. You don't have time for that now. Get sick later."

"Any particular time?" Cody retorted.

"I guess that was a bit harsh. Sorry, pard. I'll give you a hand."

The clothes were stripped off the dead outlaw. Jim redressed in Patton's outfit, then dressed the body in his own clothes. He switched Patton's six-gun with his own Peacemaker.

"Help me get him on Sam," he told Cody.

"Sure."

Patton's body was lifted from the ground. Sam snorted a mild protest when the dead outlaw was draped belly-down over his withers.

"Easy, bud. You've done this before," Jim soothed the gelding. He took Sam's reins and led him to where Patton's bay waited. The bay shied at the scent of blood, but before it could trot off Jim grabbed its reins. His soft voice soon calmed the nervous animal. He exchanged Patton's Winchester for his own, then climbed into Patton's saddle. The Ranger pulled Patton's hat down low, obscuring most of his face.

"How do I look, Cody?"

"Not bad, except for that blood on the shirt."

"Can't do much about that. I hid it as best I could with my bandanna. I just hope none of my blood joins it."

"I have to agree with you there," Cody grinned.

"Appreciate that. Now let's move, before the rest of 'em come up on us."

"One question. How will I know when to come out of the brush?"

"When the shootin' starts," Jim laughed. "No, seriously. You'll know when. You've got good instincts, Cody. I'm trustin' 'em."

"I hope you're right," Cody replied.

With Cody trailing behind, Jim started for the cabin. After a short distance, Wade's fractious bay refused to go any further, dancing sideways and crowhopping.

"Teach this obstinate cuss a lesson, will you, Sam?" Jim asked his horse.

Sam snorted, pinned his ears, and bit the bay viciously on the rump. The gelding squealed in fear of the big paint. Sam nipped him again.

"That's enough, Sam," Jim ordered. He heeled the now-willing bay into a walk once again.

In a short time, Jim came upon the cabin. Hank Martin and Matt Patton were sitting on the porch, while Jobe Patton and Ed Torneau were saddling horses. They looked up at Jim's approach.

"Hey Wade," Martin called. "We heard a shot. Jobe and Ed were just gettin' ready to check on you. Guess there's no need. Who's that you plugged?"

"Ranger," Jim grunted.

"A Ranger! Webb, get out here," Martin shouted. "Wade just killed himself a Texas Ranger."

Jim edged nearer the shack. Webb Patton, along with two men Jim recognized as Steve Sloan and Hal Mellon, both wanted killers, emerged from the cabin.

"What's that? There was a Ranger snoopin' around? You plugged him, Wade?" Webb called.

"Yeah." Jim grunted again, and nodded toward Patton's body.

"That's not Wade!" Webb yelled, as he recognized the Ranger. "That's Jim Blawcyzk! He must've plugged Wade!" Instantly, the outlaws went for their guns.

Jim grabbed his rifle and rolled from the saddle. He fired one quick shot as he dove behind some brush. The bullet tore through Sloan's thigh, dropping him to a knee. Webb and Mellon jumped back inside the shack. Matt followed them, then slammed the door shut.

"Get outta here, Sam!" Jim ordered his horse. The big paint raced for safety. Wade Patton's body tumbled from Sam's back when the horse swerved around the corral.

Bullets were tearing through Jim's meager cover, searching him out. One took the hat from his head.

"Where the devil's Cody?" he muttered. "I sure can't stay here."

Sloan was still on the porch, propped against a post and firing in Jim's direction. Jim rose to one knee and fired. His bullet tore into Sloan's stomach, driving him back. Sloan sagged against the cabin wall, slid to a seated position, and slumped against a chair. Sloan's chin dropped to his chest with his final breaths. Jim rolled back into the brush, then crawled toward a pile of firewood. There was a clearing of some fifty feet between the brush and the wood. Jim halted at the edge of the bushes, waiting his chance.

Cody burst out of the scrub, his horse at a dead run. While Yankee pounded across the yard, Cody swept the corral with bullets. One hit Torneau in the chest, slamming him to the dirt. Jobe Patton screeched in mortal agony when another of Cody's slugs ripped through his belly. Jobe clawed frantically at his bullet-ripped gut, jackknifed, and crumpled. Cody reached the end of the yard, whirled Yankee around, and emptied his rifle at the cabin. One of his shots hit Hank Martin in the neck. Martin clutched his throat, attempting in vain to stem the blood spurting from his severed jugular. He staggered off the porch and pitched to his face. Cody leapt from his saddle and dove behind the well. Yankee scrambled for cover.

While Cody kept the outlaws busy, Jim raced for the firewood. He dove to his belly and slid behind the stacked logs, gasping for breath.

"How many's left, Jim?" Cody called. He pulled out his Colt.

"Three of 'em. They're all inside the shack."

Jim fired the last bullet in his Winchester through one of the front windows. The shot was answered by a volley of gunfire.

" Jim Blawcyzk," Webb called. "Let's talk!"

"There's nothin' to talk about, unless you're givin' yourselves up," Jim answered. He put down his rifle to lift his Colt from its holster.

"Don't be stupid, Ranger," Webb replied. "You'll never be able to get at us, long as we're in here. You know that. Why don't you and your pardner just get on your horses and ride away? I promise we'll let you go, long as you don't cause us any more trouble."

"Your promise ain't worth a plugged nickel, Patton," Jim shot back. "You'd shoot us in the back before we made fifty feet. Far as you gettin' away, I wouldn't bet a hat on it. Five of you are already dead. You wanna join them?"

"The only ones who are gonna join them are you and your pardner," Patton retorted. "You had your chance. Now we're gonna cut you to ribbons."

The three remaining renegades opened fire, pinning the Rangers down.

Jim waved to Cody, signaling that he was going to attempt to flank the cabin and reach the barn, from which he would have a better angle to shoot through the cabin's windows. He pointed toward the porch, indicating that, once he reached the barn, he wanted Cody to try and make the front of the cabin under Jim's covering fire. Cody nodded his understanding.

Jim leapt from his cover and zigzagged toward the barn. Matt Patton opened the door and fired at the Ranger's back. It was a fatal mistake. His bullet missed, whistling past Jim's side. Jim's return snap shot struck Matt square in the chest. Matt fell across the doorsill.

While Jim and Matt exchanged gunshots, Webb Patton took careful aim at the Ranger and fired. His bullet struck Jim high in the left side of the chest. Jim dropped in his tracks.

"They got Jim!" Cody exclaimed. Overcome with anger and grief, he rose from his shelter, grimacing when an outlaw's bullet burned along his ribs. Cody recklessly raced for the cabin, Colt blazing, ignoring the bullets seeking him out. One of his bullets shattered a windowpane, then struck Hal Mellon between the eyes. The slug buried itself deep in his brain.

Cody hurdled the body of Matt Patton, dove into the cabin, and rolled to his knees. As Webb Patton turned to face him, Cody aimed his Colt at Webb's chest, thumbed back the hammer, and squeezed the trigger. It fell on an empty chamber.

Webb laughed harshly. He aimed his gun just above Cody's belt buckle.

"All right, Ranger. I don't know your name, but that don't matter. I'm gonna put a slug in your lousy guts. You're about to die, just like your pardner lyin' out there."

Webb started to thumb back the hammer of his .44 Remington. He hesitated.

"Figure I'll let you think about dyin' for a minute first," he sneered, letting the gun drop to cover Cody's groin. A wicked grin crossed his face.

"I reckon I'll nail you where it hurts a man most, then gut-shoot you," he concluded.

Cody sprang to his feet, pulled the knife from its sheath on his belt, and lunged at the outlaw. He slashed at Webb's forearm, the razor-sharp blade slicing through muscle and tendons. Webb dropped the gun from his paralyzed hand. Cody thrust the Bowie deep into Webb's belly, ripping upward through intestines and stomach. Webb folded over Cody's fist. Cody yanked his knife from the outlaw's gut. A gurgle rose in Webb's throat. He dropped to his hands and knees, then collapsed to his face.

"Like Jim taught me, never relax, Patton," Cody muttered. "It can get a man killed."

"Jim!" Cody's voice caught. A lump rose in his throat. Eyes moist, he left the cabin and headed for his downed partner.

Cody found Sam had returned. The gelding was nuzzling Jim's shoulder, attempting to rouse his rider. When Cody approached, the big paint pinned his ears and whickered a warning.

"Easy, Sam," Cody told the horse. "Let me try'n help your friend."

Sam edged away, still eyeing Cody suspiciously. Cody knelt alongside Jim and rolled him onto his back. Fresh blood was spreading over the shirt he wore. Jim still held his Colt in a death grip.

123

"Jim," Cody murmured.

Jim's eyes flickered open.

"Cody. What happened to Webb?"

"He's dead. They all are."

"Good. You did a fine job, pardner."

"How bad are you hit, Jim?"

"Bad enough. You'll have to..." Jim stopped speaking, lifted his Colt, and fired. Jobe Patton gave a strangled gasp when Jim's bullet punched another hole through his gut. The renegade dropped his gun and crumpled to the dirt. This time, he wouldn't get back up.

"Jobe! He wasn't..."

"Dead," Jim concluded for Cody. "You didn't check those hombres, did you?"

"No," Cody admitted, "I was too worried about you."

"That nearly got you a bullet in the back," Jim said. "Go check those men. Make sure they're dead. And kick their guns away from 'em, just in case."

"What about you?"

"I'll be fine until you're finished. Then you're gonna have to dig this slug outta my chest."

"What? I don't think I can handle that," Cody objected.

"You've got to. Otherwise, I won't live long enough to make it to a doctor. Now stop wastin' time."

"All right."

Cody checked the bodies, then returned.

"They're all done for, Jim. I made sure."

"Fine."

"What now?"

"This bullet has to come out. Open my saddlebags. You'll find a small flask of whiskey and a sack of tobacco. There's also a spare bandanna, and some cloths I use for bandages. Get those. Sam, you let Cody get that stuff," Jim ordered his horse.

"I thought you didn't smoke or drink."

"I don't. They're for treatin' bullet wounds."

Sam pinned his ears at Cody when he approached, but when Jim chided him again, the gelding allowed Cody to open Jim's saddlebags and retrieve the supplies.

"I've got 'em, Jim. Now what?"

"Open my shirt, so you can spot the bullet hole."

"All right." Cody unbuttoned the shirt. He choked slightly at the sight of the bullet hole in Jim's chest, high on the left side.

"You've gotta do this, Cody," Jim urged. "Or else I'm a dead man."

"I'll get through it," Cody promised. "What now?"

"Take that bandanna and tie a knot in it. I'll need somethin' to bite down on while you dig for that bullet."

Cody complied.

"There. What's next?"

"Take my knife and douse it real good with that red-eye."

"Okay."

Cody opened the flask and poured half of its contents over the blade.

"It's soaked, Jim."

"Good. Now comes the hard part. You've gotta take that knife, stick it in my chest, and probe for the slug. You should be able to feel it once you hit it, although it can be tough to tell the difference between a slug and bone. I don't need to tell what'll happen if you're not careful."

"No, you sure don't. You might want to say a prayer before I start."

"That's not a bad idea," Jim agreed. Both men took a moment to ask the Lord's help and mercy.

"I'm ready," Cody said, once he'd concluded his prayer.

"Good. First, take some of that whiskey and pour it over my chest and into the bullet hole."

"Won't that hurt?"

"Like the blazes. That's the reason for the bandanna. But it'll help stop infection."

"You want the bandanna in your mouth now?"

"Yeah."

Cody slid the knotted kerchief between Jim's teeth.

"You ready?"

Jim nodded. When Cody poured the raw liquor into the wound, Jim grimaced with pain, biting down hard.

"I'm goin' after that bullet now," Cody said.

Again, Jim nodded. Carefully, Cody slid the knife blade into the bullet hole.

Sweat broke out on Jim's forehead while Cody probed for the slug. He clamped down on the bandanna.

"I'm bein' as gentle as I can, Jim," Cody assured him.

"Just get that slug outta me," Jim muttered through clenched teeth.

Cody kept probing for the slug. Finally, he felt the blade hit something solid.

"I've got it."

"Good. Now maneuver it outta there. Real carefully."

Cody nodded. He gently manipulated the knife until he was able to get at the slug and remove it."

"It's out." Cody breathed a sigh of relief. "But you're bleedin' more."

Jim pulled the bandanna from his mouth.

"That's all right. It'll help flush the wound."

"What do I do now?"

"Open that sack of tobacco. Pour it right into that hole."

"Tobacco?" Cody was skeptical.

"Yeah. It'll plug the hole, slow the bleedin', and believe it or not helps prevent blood poisoning. Once you've got the hole packed, pour more whiskey over it, then bandage it."

"All right."

Cody did as ordered.

"That's the best I can do," he said, as he tied the last strip of cloth in place.

"You did just fine, Cody," Jim assured him. "Now you'd better take care of yourself."

"You mean this bullet burn along my ribs? It's not much."

"It's not much, but it could kill you if it gets infected. You'd better wash it out, put some whiskey on it, and bandage it. After all, I promised Julia I'd bring you back in one piece. She'd never forgive me if I didn't, since she still plans on hitchin' you up with Sarah Wysocki. I wouldn't want to face those two if you'd gotten yourself killed. In that case, you'd be better off than me," Jim laughed.

"I'm not so sure about that," Cody chuckled. He quickly treated the bullet gash along his side.

"I'm finished."

"Good. I've gotta ask you to do some more work before you can rest, Cody. I can't be much help," Jim apologized.

"Don't worry about that," Cody replied. "What needs to be done?"

"First, check inside that cabin. You should find the money from those robberies. Those renegades didn't have a chance to spend it."

"All right. Then what?"

"Get my clothes off Wade. I'm gonna want my own duds. He's also wearin' my vest. My badge is still pinned to that. I need it back."

"What about the bodies?" Cody asked.

"Not much we can do about them. We'll head back to Blanco, since that's the nearest place to find a doc. I'll have the sheriff return for the bodies. You can drag 'em inside the shack and cover 'em. Even with that the coyotes might still get at 'em. Oh, and turn the horses loose, too. They can fend for themselves until the sheriff gets here. Except Wade's. His is already saddled, so we'll use it to carry the money sacks. And fill our canteens."

"Won't we be stayin' here for the night, at least?" Cody questioned. "You need to rest."

"I need to get to a doc more. There's still a couple hours of daylight left. Soon as you're done, we'll be ridin'."

"Whatever you say." Cody started for the cabin, then turned back to Jim, chuckling.

"What's so funny, Cody?" Jim asked.

"Remember what you told me about not bein' dumb, and steppin' in front of a bullet, Jim?"

"Yeah."

"Next time maybe you'd better take your own advice."

"Havlicek, you'd better…" Jim growled, smiling.

Jim fell asleep once Cody left him. He dozed until Cody shook his shoulder.

"Jim?"

"Yeah, Cody?"

"Everything's set. I found the money, and it's tied to Wade's saddle. The bodies are inside, and the horses are turned out. I've got your clothes, too."

"That's fine. Let me have them."

Jim grinned when he picked up his shirt.

"Now it's my turn," Cody said, "Something strikes you funny, Jim?"

"Yeah. For once my shirt didn't get ruined when I got shot. Switchin' clothes with Wade paid off."

"You might think so, but speakin' for myself I'd rather not get shot at all," Cody retorted.

"I guess you're right," Jim conceded.

131

With some effort, Jim slid out of Wade Patton's clothes and back into his own.

"I'm ready, Cody. You're gonna have to help me onto Sam's back."

"Sure."

Cody helped Jim to his feet, then boosted him into the saddle.

"Will you be able to stay up there?" Cody asked.

"I should. If not, you can tie me in the saddle. Now let's get movin'. We're wastin' daylight."

Cody swung onto Yankee's back. Jim grinned broadly, leaned over from Sam's back, and shook Cody's hand.

"Cody," he said. "Welcome to the Texas Rangers."

Banker's Bluff

1

The sun was setting over the rugged, arid landscape of far west Texas when young Texas Ranger Pete Natowich pulled his horse to a halt, not quite sure his eyes weren't deceiving him.

"Trooper, unless I'm seein' things, that's a lake just ahead, off to the left. Who'd have thought we'd find this much water around here? We'll spend the night here, boy. Can't make Rankin until tomorrow afternoon at the earliest anyway."

Pete put his big bay gelding, with the half-crescent star and strip on his face, into a trot. Sensing water and rest ahead, Trooper responded eagerly. Both man and horse were tired, having been on the trail from Austin for several long, hard days. Pete had been a Ranger for little more than a year. He was barely over eighteen years old, lean, blue-eyed and blonde-haired. This was his first solo assignment, an assignment which would have been handed to one of the more experienced Rangers, if any had been available. The long ride had taken its toll.

A half-hour later, the Ranger reined in at the edge of a large, deep pond.

"Sure enough Troop, it is a lake. Well, a good-sized pond, anyway," Pete stated. "I'm gonna take a nice, cool bath tonight, and so are you, horse. It's time we get some of this dust off our hides."

Pete swung from the saddle, then stripped it and the blanket from his horse's back. Once that was done, he pulled off his boots and socks, then peeled off his sweat-sticky shirt. He placed that on the ground, and next removed his Stetson and bandanna, laying them alongside the shirt. Finally, he unbuckled his gunbelt, leaving it on top of the saddle. He leapt onto Trooper's bare back and urged the Morgan-Quarter cross into the water.

For half-an-hour, Pete swam the muscular bay back and forth, letting the gelding dip his muzzle into the water and snort, allowing him to paw and splash the cool, refreshing liquid. Once he was satisfied the horse had fully cooled off, he rode out of the pond, then took his lariat and picketed Trooper in a patch of lush grass bordering the waterhole.

"You just take it easy and graze a spell, Trooper," Pete told the horse, "I'm gonna take my bath, then swim a bit more." While his horse fell to cropping the grass, the young Ranger dug a bar of yellow soap from his saddlebags and started back to the water. He intended to scrub off ten days' worth of trail grime and sweat.

Pete had begun to unhitch his belt and remove his jeans when a slight sound warned him of danger. Trooper had stopped grazing and lifted his head, ears pricked sharply forward. Pete started to turn, but a sharp voice stopped him in his tracks.

"Don't move, mister!"

Pete froze.

"Get your hands up, and turn around real slow," the voice ordered.

Pete complied. He raised his hands shoulder high, then turned and stared into the dark, malevolent eyes of a heavy-set, bearded man about five years older than himself. He held a Smith and Wesson .44 pointed straight at Pete's belly.

"I don't have much worth takin', if you're intendin' to rob me," Pete said.

"That fine bay horse alone makes killin' you worth it," the gunman retorted. He thumbed back the hammer of his pistol.

Pete's stomach muscles tightened. His own Colt was out of reach, in the gunbelt lying across his saddle. The Ranger was helpless as he faced the man who clearly intended to kill him. He braced himself for the impact of hot lead tearing through his guts.

The hammer clicked in place, and the gunman tightened his finger on the trigger. Just as he fired, Pete, in desperation, threw himself backwards into the water. The bullet pierced the air where his chest had just been. Pete dove under the pond's surface while the gunman fired wildly, his bullets searching out his victim.

Pete stuck his head above water to gasp a quick breath. A bullet whined past his left ear, a second slug just missing when he plunged under the water again.

The young Ranger swam underwater for several yards, until his bursting lungs forced him to surface once more. Instantly, a bullet burned the top of his left shoulder. When the gunman pulled the trigger again, the hammer of his sixgun clicked on an empty chamber.

Sensing his chance, Pete lunged from the pond, leaping at his assailant in a headlong tackle. His head smashed into the gunman's belly, knocking him back, grunting as air was forced from his lungs. The outlaw's gun dropped from his hand. Pete's momentum carried both men to the ground. They rolled several times before scrambling to their feet.

The gunman slammed his right fist to the point of Pete's chin, at the same time driving his left low into the Ranger's gut, catching Pete between his bellybutton and belt buckle. Simultaneously, Pete smashed one fist to the gunman's jaw, the other to the side of the man's head. Both men staggered from the impacts.

The gunman recovered first. He again drove his fist into Pete's stomach, jackknifing the Ranger, then straightening him with a blow to the mouth. He doubled Pete again with another punch in the belly, sinking his fist wrist-deep in the youngster's gut. Pete toppled to the dirt, gasping for breath.

The gunman recovered his pistol and quickly began reloading. Fighting the nausea which threatened to overcome him, Pete lunged for his own Colt, grabbing it just as his assailant finished reloading. Pete rolled to his knees and fired twice, both his bullets striking the renegade in his chest. The man crumpled onto his back, shuddered, gave out a long sigh, and lay unmoving.

Gasping, Pete crawled on hands and knees to the gunman, pulling the sixgun from his hand and tossing it aside. Satisfied the man was dead, Pete collapsed onto his belly, guts churning. He rolled onto his back, head spinning. After a few moments, he managed to drag himself to his feet. Pete pressed a hand to his bruised midsection, then, hunched over, stumbled to his saddle. He dug in his saddlebags for the tin of salve he always carried. He used the ointment to coat the bullet burn along his shoulder. The wound was minor, and had already nearly stopped bleeding. His injuries from the fistfight were more serious. His lips were swollen, blood still trickled from his mouth, and a lump was rising along his jaw. Stabbing pain shot through his belly every time he moved. It would take some time for his battered gut to recover from the vicious blows it had received. He gazed balefully at the body of the outlaw.

"Reckon I'd better check that hombre, to see if I can figure out who he was, and why he was so set on killin' me," he muttered.

Pete knelt beside the dead gunman. He went through his shirt and vest pockets, then the pockets of the man's jeans, finding nothing of interest. He rolled the man onto his stomach, then went through his back pockets, again coming up empty. The entire contents of all the pockets were a few bills, matches, some coins, a sack of tobacco, and a packet of cigarette papers.

"Mebbe there'll be somethin' in his saddlebags that'll help," Pete speculated. "His horse can't be all that far off."

The young Ranger whistled shrilly, and was answered by a whinny from behind a cluster of boulders.

"Least that's one break... his horse answers a whistle," Pete murmured. He headed for the rocks. Rounding them, he came upon a fleabitten gray, ground-hitched. The horse jerked up its head and shied at Pete's approach.

"Easy, boy. It's all right. Easy now," Pete soothed the animal. He ran a hand down the gray's shoulder. His soft voice and gentle touch calmed the anxious mount.

"There. That's a good boy," Pete praised. "You just stand still while I check your saddlebags.

The Ranger went through the alforjas, finding the usual assortment of supplies, a spare shirt, socks, and other sundries. A folded letter in one saddlebag caught his attention. Under the light of the rising nearly full moon, he scanned its contents, then tucked it into his hip pocket.

"Reckon you'll have to carry your rider's body into town, horse," Pete told the gray. He lifted the reins and swung onto the gelding's back, heading it to where Trooper and the outlaw's body waited.

"Got a friend for you, Trooper," Pete called to his horse. The big bay looked up and whinnied, then went back to his grazing. Pete dismounted, stripped the gear from the dead man's gray, and picketed the horse near his own. He took the outlaw's bedroll with him, dragged the body behind some rocks, and covered it with the blankets. That done, he reloaded his pistol and rebuckled his gunbelt around his waist. After pulling on socks and boots and shrugging back into his shirt, he gathered some downed wood and built a small fire. He hunkered alongside the flames to dry his soaked jeans.

Pete suddenly realized he was ravenously hungry. His only food since breaking camp that morning had been a few strips of jerky and a leftover biscuit. While he intended to resupply in Rankin, he still had enough bacon and beans left for one more meal. He retrieved those, his Arbuckle's, frying pan, and coffee pot from his saddlebags. Shortly, the bacon was sizzling in the pan, coffee boiling, and the last of his beans heating.

Pete ate rapidly, lingering only briefly over his coffee. He scrubbed out the tin utensils and plate and doused the fire. He checked both horses, then rolled in his blankets. For some time he gazed up at the stars pinpricking the inky curtain of the sky, their light fading while the moon rose higher.

The young Ranger had trouble falling asleep. Despite the fact he was upwind of a steady breeze, which had kept him from hearing the gunman's approach, and also masked the sound or scent of his horse from Trooper, Pete was angry with himself for allowing the outlaw to sneak up on him undetected.

"I'm lucky it's not me lyin' dead with a chunk of lead in my guts, rather'n that jasper," he muttered. "I'd bet a hat none of the other Rangers would've let him get so close. You're some Ranger, Natowich. Ranger, huh! You wouldn't even make a decent town deputy."

Still berating his carelessness, he finally drifted off to sleep.

2

It took some doing the next morning for Pete to bend the outlaw's rigor mortis stiffened body, so he could drape it belly-down over the gray's saddle, then lash it in place. Once that was accomplished, Pete mounted his own horse and resumed his journey to Rankin. He would reach his destination sometime that afternoon.

As Pete loped along, he mused on how to handle the reaction his arrival in Rankin would stir. A stranger leading a horse carrying a dead man was sure to attract more than the usual share of notice. Add in that stranger's youthful appearance, which belied the fact he was a Texas Ranger, and he was sure to gain some unwanted attention.

"Reckon we might have a bit of trouble explainin' this, Troop," he spoke to his horse. "Well, no point puttin' it off."

He pushed Trooper to a faster pace.

∧∧∧∧∧∧∧∧∧∧∧∧

It was late afternoon when Pete rode into Rankin. The town was busy with folks shopping and conducting business. A crowd soon gathered, following the young Ranger and his grisly burden. Pete ignored their shouted questions until he reined up in front of the marshal's office, which was padlocked and dark.

A burly individual, wearing a white grocer's apron, pushed his way through the mob.

"Hey, you! What's goin' on here?" he demanded.

"Seems pretty obvious, doesn't it?" Pete retorted. "I'm bringin' in a dead man."

"You watch that mouth with me, mister," the grocer snapped. "I'm the mayor of this town, and I'm askin' you a question. Now who are you, and where'd you find that hombre?

"I count that as two questions. Ask 'em politely, and you might get an answer," Pete softly replied.

"He's got you there, Porter," a bystander laughed. "You always did have a big mouth."

"All right. Reckon I did come off a bit gruff," Porter conceded. "I'm Hiram Porter. Like I said, I'm Rankin's mayor. Sorry for spoutin' off like I did, but with our bank bein' robbed and the marshal killed durin' the holdup, we're a bit on edge. We've been waitin' for a Texas Ranger to show up from Austin, but there's been no sign of him. Instead you show up, totin' a body."

"Don't fret it, Mayor," Pete responded. "First, I found this hombre a few miles outside of town. Only he wasn't dead when I came across him. He jumped me, then tried to kill me so he could steal my horse. I shot him instead."

"You killed him?" Porter echoed.

"I sure did. It was him or me. He didn't give me a choice. Now, to answer your other question, I'm the Ranger you're waitin' on. Texas Ranger Pete Natowich."

"You're a Texas Ranger?" Porter exclaimed, looking over the youthful lawman. "Hardly seems likely."

"My papers and orders are in my pocket," Pete answered. "I know I'm a mite young lookin', but I've been a Ranger for some time now. I've been assigned to track down the men who robbed your bank and killed your town marshal. I'm supposed to take care of the law in Rankin until you appoint a new marshal."

"Dunno if a youngster can handle that job," someone muttered.

"You want to try me and find out?" Pete challenged. "Besides, you've got no choice. With all the problems along the border, the Rangers are real short-handed. I'm the only man available."

"I guess beggars can't be choosers," Porter conceded. "You must be all right, if you made the grade as a Ranger. Tell you what. Besides bein' the mayor, I run the general store and do the undertakin' here. Take that body to my store. It's a block down. Mebbe someone'll recognize that jasper."

"Okay," Pete agreed. "Once that's done, I'll want the keys to the marshal's office. Reckon I'll be bunkin' there a spell."

"I've got those at the store," Porter answered. He gestured to an old man, who hovered at the edge of the crowd.

"Hug Prescott here runs the livery stable. He'll take good care of your cayuse."

"That's fine. Trooper here deserves the best."

"He'll get that from me, Ranger," the elderly hostler spoke up. "My stable's right next to the marshal's office, so your bronc'll be handy whenever you need him."

"Gracias," Pete replied. He backed Trooper and the dead outlaw's horse away from the hitchrail and walked them to Porter's Mercantile. The spectators pressed closely behind.

When they reached the store, a tall, well-dressed individual pushed his way through the crowd and walked up to Pete.

"I just heard a dead man was brought in. You the one who found him? Any idea who he is?" he demanded of Pete, not even giving the Ranger a chance to dismount.

"I'm the one who killed him," Pete corrected, "If it's any business of yours, Mister. Is everybody in this town rude?"

"I'm the president of the Rankin Bank, Ebenezer Montrose. I want to know about this body. I thought perhaps he was one of the men who robbed my bank and shot down Marshal Tucker."

"You might want to ask a bit more civilly," Pete replied. "I don't work for you."

"This man's a Texas Ranger, Ebenezer," Porter interjected. "The dead hombre tried to kill him for his horse. As you can see, the Ranger shot straighter."

"I apologize for being so abrupt, Ranger," Montrose said to Pete. "It's just that I'm anxious to find those outlaws and murderers."

The banker had dark eyes, which seemed to Pete to glitter like a snake's. His black hair was carefully pomaded in place, his mustache crisply trimmed. His well-tailored suit was carefully cut to fit his slim figure. Montrose held a thin, unlit cigar.

"I understand," Pete answered. "Let's get him off his horse and inside, then you folks can take a look at him."

"Makes sense," the banker agreed.

Pete dismounted, and looped Trooper's and the outlaw's horse's reins around the rail. The dead man was lifted from his horse and carried into the back room of the store, where he was laid out on the floor.

"He doesn't look familiar to me," Porter observed. "Any of you ever seen this man?"

His question was met with a murmur of negatives.

"Those robbers were masked, so he could've been one of 'em," Jake Butler, the saloonkeeper, noted.

"Could've been, but I've never seen his horse in town. That animal was never put up at my stable, either," Prescott noted.

"Ranger, where'd you say you shot this man?" Montrose questioned.

"A few miles outside of town. My horse was tired, so I decided to rest him a spell. I was lettin' Trooper graze and gettin' some shut-eye for myself when he came up on me."

"You didn't find any identification on him?"

"Nope."

"Nothing in his saddlebags which might indicate who he was? No letters, papers, anything like that?" Montrose insisted.

"Not a thing," Pete replied. "Reckon he was just a driftin' renegade. Once I get settled in, I'll check my

Fugitive List to see if he matches any descriptions in that."

"The Ranger here's gonna be the law in town until we appoint a new marshal," Porter explained.

"Fine, fine. If anyone can track down those murderers, a Ranger can," Montrose answered.

"Let's cover this hombre for now. Soon as I can nail a few boards together for a coffin, we'll bury him," Porter said. He lifted a ring of keys from a peg over his desk and handed them to Pete.

"Ranger, here's the keys to the marshal's office."

"Thanks," Pete answered. "Guess I'll mosey over there and make myself comfortable. Mister Montrose, once I get some rest, I'd like to question you about the robbery."

"Certainly," Montrose agreed. "I'm at your disposal, Ranger."

Once the body was covered, Pete and the others headed back outside.

"Trooper!" Pete exclaimed. "What are you doin', horse?"

Trooper merely looked up from munching on a split open watermelon and nickered, then again buried his muzzle in the sweet fruit. The big bay had stretched his reins to the limit, in order to reach a display of watermelons on the boardwalk in front of Porter's. He had knocked several from the display, and was happily chowing down. The outlaw's gray was also working on a melon which had rolled within his reach.

"I'm sorry, Mister Porter," Pete apologized. "I should've known enough not to tie my horse so close to those watermelons. He dotes on 'em. I'll pay you for them."

"Don't worry about that," Porter offered. "It's worth losing a few melons to have a Ranger here. Your horse is welcome to them. Just don't let him make a habit of stealin' 'em."

"I promise you that," Pete said. He untied Trooper, while Hug Prescott took the gray's reins.

"C'mon, Troop. Time you had a good feed and rubdown," Pete told the gelding.

Pete left Trooper and the outlaw's gray at Prescott's Livery. Satisfied they would be well cared for, he took his saddlebags and Winchester, then headed for the marshal's office.

"This isn't too bad," the Ranger murmured, after he entered the office and shut the door behind him. While the room was coated with a layer of dust, it was otherwise in decent shape. Two cells were at the back of the office, and a bunk for the marshal was in a far corner, while a coffeepot sat on a stove opposite. Pete removed his gunbelt and hung it from a peg over the cot. He sat on the edge of the mattress, pulled off his boots, and slipped out of his shirt. Pete stretched out on the bunk. Within minutes, the exhausted Ranger was sleeping soundly.

∧∧∧∧∧∧∧∧∧∧∧∧

While Pete slept the afternoon away, Ebenezer Montrose was busy. It wasn't an hour after Pete had reached town when two men dressed in cowpuncher's outfits arrived at the Rankin Bank, in answer to the banker's summons. Montrose ushered them into his private office, shutting the door behind them.

"What's the problem, Montrose?" Ben Reed asked. "You interrupted my visit with a very willing young lady. I don't appreciate that."

"Yeah, and I was in the midst of a winning streak," Tom Pardee complained.

"Just sit down. We have a problem," Montrose answered. "Light up if you want. This is going to take awhile."

Both men took seats. Montrose waited while they rolled and lit quirlies before continuing. He lit a cigar, poured a glass of whiskey for himself, and two for the others.

"All right. You saw the body that Ranger brought in this afternoon."

"Yeah. So what?" Reed grunted.

"That dead man's John Hunter."

"Hunter? You mean the hombre who was supposed to retrieve the money we stole and bring it back for us to split?" Pardee demanded.

"The same," Montrose confirmed.

"Did the Ranger mention findin' any money on Hunter?" Reed asked.

"No, he didn't," Montrose answered. "He claims there was no identification on Hunter's body, either. I don't believe him."

"You mean you think the Ranger is plannin' on keeping that cash for himself?" Reed questioned.

"That's a possibility. But I have a feelin' he's too honest to do that," Montrose replied. "Besides, he most likely would have made a run for the border with that money by now if he intended to take off with it."

"I dunno. Over forty thousand dollars is enough dinero to tempt any man," Pardee disagreed.

"That's true," Montrose admitted. "But let's assume he's not keeping the money. That means one of two things. Either, as he claims, there wasn't anything on Hunter to give us away. More likely, that Ranger went through Hunter's clothes and saddlebags. He found my letter with the directions to where the money is stashed, and is going to play things close to his vest. He'll wait to see if anyone else goes after the cache."

"For that matter, he might've killed Hunter right where the money's hidden," Reed speculated. "Mebbe he came up on Hunter diggin' up the loot, surprised him, they shot it out, and Hunter came out on the short end. Now the Ranger's just bidin' his time until he can grab the money for himself."

"Or will wait until someone goes for it, like Montrose says," Pardee stated. "So what do we do now, Montrose?"

"We'll wait a bit, perhaps a couple of days," Montrose answered. "Then you'll get Stanton, Lennox, and Jackson. You'll go after that money."

"What about the Ranger?" Pardee protested. "If you're right, he'll be watchin' for someone to make a move."

"I want him to follow you," Montrose explained. "Once you reach the right spot, kill him."

"Should be easy enough," Pardee agreed.

"Don't ever underestimate a Ranger," Montrose warned.

"I wouldn't, but this one's hardly a Ranger," Pardee sneered.

"Tom's right," Reed concurred. "We all heard that kid tell Porter he was the only man Austin could send. He's still wet behind the ears. I think it'd be a good idea to find out just how tough he really is."

"He killed Hunter, and Hunter was real good with a gun," Montrose noted.

"Yeah, but the Ranger must've taken him by surprise," Reed answered. "Let me try'n take him on here in town. Mebbe he'll turn yellow and run, if he's up against a real challenge. That'll solve our problem."

"You can try if you want," Montrose answered. "Just remember one thing. Don't kill him, at least not in town. The last thing we'd need is more Rangers snoopin' around because one of their own got killed. It's better to wait until you've got that Ranger where no one will ever find his body."

"We should keep an eye on him, just in case he does leave town real sudden-like," Pardee advised. "He might just have left the money where it's at until things have quieted down. That'd be the smart thing to do. After a spell, he could pick up the money and just keep ridin'."

"That's a possibility I hadn't considered," the banker admitted.

"Don't worry, Montrose. We'll take care of the Ranger, one way or another," Reed assured the banker.

"Good. Now, let's figure out how to make sure he follows you when you ride out although, I doubt that will be much of a problem. If the Ranger found my letter in Hunter's possession, he'll be watching me real closely. Then both of you get out of here. I'll get word to you when it's time to make our move. And remember, don't think of double-crossin' me. You'll regret it."

∧∧∧∧∧∧∧∧∧∧∧∧

Pete awoke just before sundown.

"Slept longer'n I planned," he muttered. "Reckon I'll have to wait 'til tomorrow to talk with that banker. 'Sides, my belly's growlin'. Been too long since I've had a decent meal."

He found a pitcher and basin on a shelf, and filled these from the pump out back. He washed up, pouring the water over his blonde hair, letting it run down his chest and shoulders. That done, he redressed and headed for the nearest café. There, he ate a meal of steak, boiled potatoes, and green beans, following up with a huge slab of dried-apple pie and several cups of strong black coffee. After supper, Pete spent the next two hours making the rounds of Rankin. He finished his first watch at Jake Butler's Red Rooster saloon, intending to take a break over a beer or two.

"Howdy, Ranger!" Butler boomed a greeting. "Step right up to the bar. What can I get for you?"

"Evenin', Mister Butler," Pete answered. "I'll have a beer."

"Comin' right up, Ranger. And call me Jake."

Butler filled a mug and placed it in front of Pete, who tossed a dime on the bar.

"That's for a refill," he said, then took a swallow of the brew, which, to his surprise, was chilled, unlike the warm beer served in most frontier barrooms.

"Good beer, Jake. It's even cold."

"That's 'cause I keep the kegs in my cellar. I get ice in the winter, cover it with sawdust, and it lasts most of the summer," Jake explained.

"Well, it sure tastes good," Pete replied. He took another swallow.

"Now's our chance," Ben Reed hissed to his partner. "Let's go."

He and Tom Pardee left their place at the far end of the bar and took up positions on either side of Pete. They didn't waste any time in taunting the young lawman.

"You must've been real lucky, kid, to gun down that hombre," Reed said.

"Might've been," Pete shrugged, not rising to the bait.

"I'd bet he wasn't lucky, Ben," Pardee piped up. "Just sneaky. I'd hazard he drilled that jasper from ambush. A young'n'll do that, tryin' to make a reputation for himself."

"Mebbe we should try and find out," Reed answered. "What d'ya say, kid?"

"I wouldn't try it," Pete warned, his voice low and menacing.

"You gonna let this young pup order you around, Ben?" Pardee sneered.

"No wet behind the ears lawman'll ever tell me what to do," Reed replied. He grabbed for his gun.

Instantly, Pete's hand slashed down and up, jerking his Colt from its holster. He jabbed the barrel deep into Reed's gut. Reed doubled over, air whooshing from his lungs. Pete brought his pistol down in a streaking arc, slamming it into the base of Reed's skull. The gunman collapsed, out cold.

Before Pardee could even react, Pete whirled and drove his knee into Pardee's groin. With a howl of agony, Pardee went to his knees. Pete clubbed his gun barrel onto the top of Pardee's head. Pardee toppled to the sawdust-covered floor.

"Anyone else want to try something?" Pete challenged, the gun in his hand and the glint in his blue eyes seeming to mark every man in that room for death.

Butler's voice cut through the dead silence.

"I reckon not, Ranger."

"Bueno," Pete said. "I figure a night in a cell will cool these two off. Couple of you help me carry 'em to the jail. Keep my beer waitin', Jake. I'll be back shortly."

"Will do, Ranger," Butler grinned. "Morrissey, Hughes, give the Ranger some help."

Reed and Pardee were hauled to the jail and dumped unceremoniously into one of the cells. They were still lying on the floor, unconscious, when Pete finished his rounds, well after midnight.

3

Three days later, two hours past sundown, Pete followed
Reed and Pardee, along with three others, Judd Stanton,
Sam Lennox, and Mick Jackson, as they rode out of
Rankin. He'd released the pair the morning after the
incident in the Red Rooster. Instead of riding out of
town, they had remained, hanging around the saloon
and nursing their bruises. Then, last night, they had paid
a visit to Ebenezer Montrose at his home. Now, they
were heading out of town. Pete's patience in keeping tabs
on the banker could be paying off.

"Easy, Trooper," Pete cautioned the bay. "If my hunch
is right, we know where those hombres are headed. No
need in chancin' them spottin' us. We'll stay back a ways.
Besides, if they do change direction, there's enough of a
moon we can follow their tracks.

Trooper had rested the past several days and was
eager to run, but Pete held him to a slow trot. They had
gone about five miles when Pete reined in. Even at this
slow pace, the Morgan-Quarter cross's steady gait was
bringing them ever closer to the renegades.

"We're still gainin' on 'em, pal," he told the big gelding. "You might as well take a breather. I have a feelin' we'll be seein' a bellyful of action before long."

He dug his heels into Trooper's ribs, putting the horse into a walk.

An hour later, they approached the pond where Pete had been accosted by John Hunter. Pete halted Trooper, then swung out of the saddle.

"Like I figured, those hombres are headed straight for the pond, Troop," he told his horse. "Reckon I might as well let them dig up that money, and save me the trouble. You wait here while I scout around a bit. I have a feelin' one or two of those renegades'll circle around and keep watch for me. It'd sure simplify things for them if they could put a bullet in my back."

Pete looped Trooper's reins loosely around a mesquite. The bay could pull free and come at his rider's whistle.

"You keep quiet," Pete ordered his horse. "I'll be back shortly."

Trooper nuzzled Pete's shoulder, then fell to munching on the mesquite pods. Pete slipped into the dark. A few moments later, he was overlooking the pond.

"Just where I figured they'd be," he muttered. Three of the men were digging alongside a large boulder, while the fourth stood guard. A good-sized fire illuminated their work area.

"Don't see the fifth hombre, though. Sure wish I knew where he's at. I'd feel a heap more comfortable knowin' he's not linin' his gunsights on my spine."

Pete lifted his Colt from its holster and settled behind a fallen log, to watch and wait until the stolen money was unearthed.

It was half-an-hour later when Judd Stanton grunted in satisfaction.

"Got it."

He lifted several canvas sacks from the hole.

"We could just take this cash and head for Mexico," Mike Jackson suggested.

"I wouldn't chance it," Ben Reed advised. "Montrose has a long reach. He'd track us down for certain."

"Sam's right," Tom Pardee agreed. "Let's not get greedy. Our shares are still plenty."

"Speaking of long reaches, I wonder what happened to the Ranger," Stanton mentioned.

"Mebbe he didn't find our tracks, or wasn't clever enough to follow us after all," Reed speculated. "Sam's out there watchin' for him, and I haven't heard any gunshots. Let's just get this money on our saddles and head back to town. With any luck we'll run into the Ranger on our way."

Pete's voice cracked like a whip.

"You won't have to look for me. I'm right here, Reed. All of you get your hands up."

"It's the Ranger!" Jackson exclaimed. He went for his gun. Pete dropped him with a bullet in the chest.

The others scattered, yanking guns from holsters. Pete's next shot grazed Pardee before the outlaw could dive out of the circle of firelight.

The outlaws fired blindly, unable to see Pete in the darkness. He had rolled to a new spot by the time they were able to locate his gun flashes.

A shot from behind him plunked into Pete's lower ribs. He grunted from the impact, flopped onto his back, and returned fire. Another shot rang out, digging into the log. Pete aimed just to the left of the gun flash, and was rewarded with a yelp of agony. Sam Lennox, hands pressed to his middle, stumbled out of the dark and collapsed onto the fire. The acrid odors of singed fabric and flesh filled the air, while the clearing was plunged into darkness.

The three remaining outlaws had now determined Pete's location. They concentrated their fire on the fallen log. Fighting the pain from the bullet in his back, Pete kept shifting positions. When he aimed at another powder flash, his bullet hit Tom Pardee, who jackknifed and pitched to the dirt.

"I'm hit in the belly, Ben," Pardee screamed. "Gimme a hand, will ya?"

"Hang on, Tom," Reed called back. "Soon as we finish this Ranger, we'll get to you."

Reed's next shot just missed Pete's chest. Pete returned fire, but missed. He quickly reloaded.

Judd Sutton's shot ricocheted off the boulder where Pete had taken cover. Pete screeched, fell, and lay groaning.

"I think I got him, Ben," Sutton called.

"Be careful, Judd," Reed warned.

"That Ranger sounds like he's in bad shape. I'm gonna finish him," Sutton answered. He crept closer to where Pete was stretched out against the boulder. Taking no chances, Sutton circled the rocks. He climbed onto the one sheltering Pete.

"Ranger. You hit bad?" he called.

"I'm... done for," Pete gasped. "You got me... in my... guts. Hurts... somethin' fierce. Reckon... you win."

"Aw, gee. That's a real shame, lawman."

"Just... finish me off, will... ya?" Pete pleaded.

"With pleasure, Ranger."

Sutton stuck his head over the boulder. Pete shot him between the eyes. Sutton plunged off the rock and thudded to the ground, alongside the Ranger.

"Judd?" Reed called. "Judd?"

"He's dead," Pete answered. "So are you, Reed, unless you throw down your gun, right now."

"Not a chance, Ranger," Reed screamed. He raced toward Pete, firing wildly. One bullet grazed Pete's scalp, then Pete aimed carefully as Reed loomed above him. He fired twice, his first shot taking Reed in the stomach, the second in his left breast. Reed spun, then crashed face-down. Silence descended. The only sounds were Pete's labored breathing and the moaning of the badly wounded Pardee.

Pete reloaded his gun, then pushed himself to his feet. He staggered to where Pardee lay, hands clamped to his gut. Pete kicked Pardee's gun out of reach.

"You gotta help me," Pardee begged.

"Soon as I check your pardners, I'll see what I can do for you," Pete promised. He checked the other men, making sure they were dead. That done, he whistled for Trooper. A moment later, the big bay trotted up to the Ranger and nuzzled his shoulder.

"Good boy, Troop," Pete praised. He dug in his saddlebags for his medical kit and a clean cloth, then returned to Pardee.

"Lemme see what I can do for you," he said.

"Dunno if you can do anythin'," Pardee answered. "You gut-shot me, Ranger. Figure I've had it, but at least takin a slug's better'n hangin'."

"Let me take a look."

Pete opened Pardee's shirt.

"You're hit bad, all right," he said. He placed the cloth over the bullet hole in Pardee's middle.

"Be right back." Pete pulled the shirt off Ben Reed, tore it into strips, then used those to tie the bandage in place.

"Best I can do for you until we reach town and I get you to the doc," Pete noted.

"Ranger, all my pardners are dead, ain't they?"

"They sure are."

"Listen to me. I'm not gonna die and let Montrose get away with his scheme. That banker was behind the whole thing. It was his idea to have his own bank robbed, then after a few weeks, when things had quieted down, get the money back. He'd been embezzling from his customers for quite a spell. Needed some way to cover that up."

"I know," Pete answered. "I found his letter in Hunter's saddlebags. Figured if I didn't let on Montrose'd trip himself up."

"You ruined everythin' when you shot Hunter," Pardee complained.

"We'd better get movin'. I'll load up your pards, get you in the saddle, and we'll head for town," Pete said.

"I'm not goin' anywhere, except mebbe to Hell," Pardee replied.

The bullet in Pete's back was out of his reach. It would have to remain where it was until he could get to a doctor. Fighting the pain and nausea which threatened to overcome him, he retrieved the outlaws' horses, draped the dead men belly-down over their saddles, then got Pardee onto his horse. He tied the wounded man in place.

"Try'n hold on until we reach Rankin," Pete told him.

"I'll do my best," Pardee answered, then slumped over his horse's neck.

4

Pete rode hunched in the saddle until he reached town. Once there, he forced himself upright. A crowd quickly gathered when he reined up in front of the marshal's office. Hiram Porter was at the forefront.

"What happened, Ranger? These the jaspers who robbed the bank?" he questioned

"They are," Pete confirmed.

"You got all of 'em?"

Before Pete could answer, Ebenezer Montrose joined Porter.

"You caught those outlaws? Good work, Ranger. Did you retrieve the stolen money?"

"I didn't get all of 'em. Not quite yet," Pete answered.

Tom Pardee roused himself.

"That's right," he gasped. "Montrose, I'm gonna make sure you go to Hell along with the rest of us. I'm sayin' right here you planned the entire thing. You had your own bank robbed."

"That's preposterous," Montrose snapped.

"No, it's not." Pete growled. "I found your letter in Hunter's saddlebags. You're under arrest for robbery and murder, Montrose."

With an oath, the banker pulled a short-barreled revolver from inside his coat. Before he could shoot, Pete yanked his Colt from its holster and fired. His bullet struck Montrose in the heart. The banker took two stumbling steps, then crumpled.

"Reckon I'll be seein' Montrose and ol' Satan in a few minutes," Pardee muttered. He sagged over his horse's side.

"What in the blue blazes happened here, Ranger?" Porter demanded.

"I'll explain it all after I see the doc," Pete answered. "I need to get a slug outta my back."

With that, Pete slid off Trooper and fell to the road. Once the bullet was removed, he would take several weeks to recover, before he returned to his duties as a Texas Ranger.

The Wind

1

I awoke with a scream loud enough to wake the dead. I started to leap from my bunk, but instead settled back down, shaking with fear and covered with sweat. The full moon sent its vivid light through the bunkhouse window and directly onto my bed, while a steady wind moaned through the pines. That wind had blown open the door and slammed it against the wall.

"What in blue blazes was that all about, Bob? You all right?" Thad Coburn, one of the other new men here at the Rafter K Ranch, called. I'd awakened everyone in the bunkhouse. They were staring at me questioningly.

"Yeah. Yeah, I'm fine. Just had a real bad nightmare, that's all," I explained.

"You must've been dreamin' that the devil himself was after you to let out a holler like that. Sent shivers up

167

my spine," Jake Bennett, the Rafter K's segundo, added. "Sure hope you don't wake up like that again."

"I won't," I promised him. I'd arrived at the Rafter K only a few days previously, and had talked them into taking a chance on this grubline-riding cowboy named Bob Lydell. I sure didn't want to lose the job by scaring everyone out of their wits, ruining their sleep. And I liked what I'd seen of the place so far. The Rafter K was set high in the foothills of the Colorado Rockies, with fantastic scenery and crisp, clear air. The bunkhouse was sturdily built and cleaner than most, the other buildings in good repair, while the chuck was the best I'd had on any of the spreads where I'd worked. The cattle were all nice and fat from grazing on that thick Colorado grass. Best of all from a working cowboy's standpoint, every horse in the string I'd been assigned was a superior mount. Each of them was a hardworking cowpony, trustworthy and true. I felt I had finally found a place where I could be content for the rest of my life, and perhaps drive the demons from my mind for good.

"Good. Then I'd recommend we all get back to our shut-eye. We've got an early start and a long day ahead of us," Bennett ordered.

"As for me, if I'm gonna dream, it's gonna be about Betsy, that cute blonde filly down at the Drover's Bar," Coburn commented.

"Dreamin' about her's about all you'll do," Hank Mayburn retorted. "That gal ain't ever gonna give you the time of day."

The others were soon back asleep, snoring softly under their blankets. However, I couldn't shake the terrifying image of that nightmare from my mind.

I tossed and turned for a spell, then gave up trying to get back to sleep as a lost cause. I swung my legs over the edge of the mattress and sat up, then picked up my shirt and jeans from the floor alongside my bunk. I used the shirt to wipe the sweat from my face and chest, tossed it aside and pulled on the jeans. I reached for my vest, hanging from a peg over my bunk, and removed my matches, cigarette papers, and sack of Durham from the left breast pocket. Not wanting to again disturb my bunkmates, I didn't pull on my boots, but quietly as possible padded barefoot to the door. My hands were shaking so violently it took me several tries to build a smoke. I spilled half my sack of tobacco before I managed to sprinkle enough on a paper to roll a quirly. When at last I succeeded, I scratched a lucifer to life on the wall, then touched it to the end of the cigarette.

Dark, puffy clouds were scudding across the sky, alternately obscuring then revealing the full late September harvest moon. The interplay of light and dark sent eerie shadows across the rolling foothills. The tall pines seemed to bend threateningly toward the bunkhouse with each fitful gust. Inside the stable the horses were restless, nickering and stamping. And somewhere in the hills a wolf howled mournfully, its chilling call echoing off the hills and over the prairie. The animal's high-pitched wail sent shudders up my spine.

That wind, the moon, the shadows, and the wolf's cries brought back memories of another night a year ago. A night on the Wyoming high plains, much like this one. A night that, try as I might, I would never forget.

2

One Year Previous

I'd spent most of my twenty-eight years on this earth as a drifting cowpoke, starting in Texas at the age of sixteen, following the herds north to the Kansas railheads. Since then I had cowboyed from Texas west to the Arizona Territory, then north to the Dakotas and Montana, with jobs just about everywhere in between. Just plain fiddlefooted, I'd stay in one place for a time, then move on. I'd finally wound up working for the Diamond M in Wyoming.

The Diamond M was a huge operation, big even by Wyoming standards. It sat south of the Bighorn Mountains, east of Wind River Canyon and the Owl Creek Range. Its range spread all the way from Badwater Creek to the South Fork of the Powder River. Besides being mighty good grazing land, the Diamond M took in some of the prettiest scenery in the West. I had been working there for six months, as long as I'd ever stayed in one place. Now, in early September, I was seriously considering remaining through the winter.

However, right now I was sick of the whole place. I'd been assigned one of the most distasteful tasks a cowboy could have, aside from digging postholes. I'd been sent to check and repair miles of fenceline along Badwater Creek, from its headwaters south for thirty miles. While I would ordinarily welcome the solitude of such a job, after two weeks of mending fence I just wanted to get back to the Diamond M's headquarters, then head for town and blow off some steam. But with sunset coming on, all I had to look forward to was yet another night sleeping on the hard ground, the only warmth to ward off the autumn chill that of a sagebrush fire.

"C'mon, Laramie, let's find a spot to hole up for the night," I told my paint gelding. Rather than using one of the horses from my assigned string, I'd taken Laramie, my personal mount. At this point I even envied that horse. He'd spent a good part of the last two weeks loafing and grazing while I stretched and patched wire and straightened fence posts.

It took me until well after dusk to find the spot I wanted, a hollow which would shelter me from the almost constant north wind. That wind had been blowing just about every day since I'd left the ranch headquarters, and truthfully it was making me a bit jumpy. For the past two days it had been gradually increasing in speed, the gusts becoming more intense. I didn't want to spend another night out in the open, but on those desolate high plains

I didn't have much choice. At least the hollow would provide a bit of protection from that chilling wind.

I unsaddled Laramie, let him drink from the small waterhole in the center of the hollow, then rubbed him down and picketed him to graze. Once he was settled, I gathered sagebrush for my fire, made my bacon, biscuits, beans, and coffee, then quickly downed my supper.

After cleaning the frying pan and tin eating utensils, I lingered over a final smoke and cup of coffee, watching the sky as it faded from indigo to black, and the countless stars pinpricking its inky curtain. A dim light on the eastern horizon promised the nearly full moon would soon be rising. The wind was moaning overhead, but down here in this hollow it was merely a light breeze.

I drained the last of my coffee and stubbed out my cigarette. This night promised to be even chillier than the last several, so I collected more sagebrush and tossed it on the fire.

I walked over to Laramie, scratched his ears, bade him goodnight, then checked his picket rope. Satisfied he was secured for the night, I retrieved my blankets and spread them out. I pulled off my hat, boots, and gunbelt, slid under the blankets, and soon fell asleep.

3

The next day dawned much the same as the last several. The sun rose brassily in the chilly air, doing little to take the edge off the frosty morning. However, by noon I'd be sweating under that same sun. The wind, which had died down during the night, was once again picking up from the northwest. It was certain to torment me all day.

I rekindled my fire, cooked my breakfast, and wolfed it down. Once I was finished, I didn't even bother to take the time for a smoke. I cleaned up my campsite, tied my bedroll behind my saddle, pulled on my leather gloves, and retrieved Laramie. The sun was barely a half-hour above the eastern horizon when I was back in the saddle, facing another long day of drudgery.

The next several hours were a repeat of the past two weeks. It was ride along the fence until I found a break. Then I'd dismount and ground-hitch Laramie. I'd take my pliers, pull the wire taut, and splice it back together. If a post were down, I'd straighten it back up, tamp down the soil at its base, then hammer the wire back in place. Occasionally I would have to employ wire cutters to break through a tangle of downed wire, cutting and splicing until I had the snarl cleared and the fence back in place.

By late afternoon I was wistfully reflecting on the days of the open range, before this cussed "devil's wire" had been invented. Several times the sharp barbs had ripped through the protection of my thick leather gloves to slice my hands. My language had been reduced to swearing every time I felt another sting from that wire. I was almost convinced it was a thing alive, malevolently attempting to tear me to shreds. When the wire in a particularly nasty snag snapped without warning and slashed across my face I went to my knees in pain, violently cursing Joseph Glidden, the hombre who'd perfected barbed wire. If I'd had him in front of me at that moment I'd have cheerfully gut-shot him. However, all I could do was curse Glidden roundly, put my bandanna to my ripped cheek until the bleeding stopped, then resume my task.

But much as I hated it, that blasted wire wasn't the worst of my troubles, at least not to my mind. That accursed northwest wind had been steadily increasing all day. I'd had to tie my bandanna over my nose and mouth to keep out the dust it carried. Nonetheless, bits of sand and grit stung my eyes and blurred my vision. With evening coming on, that wind carried the chill of the faraway snow-capped peaks where it was born. It had rolled out of those mountains, tumbled over their foothills, and worked its way through the canyons and river breaks, picking up speed all along its journey. By now it had been blowing for miles over the high prairies, unimpeded except for the occasional coulee or draw. Where it funneled through those defiles that wind shrieked with the voices of a thousand demons. It was even affecting Laramie, my normally unflappable paint. The gelding kept tossing his head, snorting anxiously, his nostrils flaring as he scented the air and stamped nervously. He finally came up to me and nuzzled my shoulder.

"I reckon you're right, boy," I tried to soothe him. "It's time to call it a day and try'n find some cover from this gale."

I jammed my tools into the saddlebags and climbed onto Laramie's back. Once mounted, I scanned the surrounding prairie for any sign of shelter. The only place I spotted was a high ridge. With luck, once I topped that rise and headed down the other side, it would provide a bit of cover from the unceasing wind.

"Let's go, boy," I urged my horse. He gave a snort of protest when a particularly fierce gust stung his hide with fragments of gravel. It ruffled Laramie's mane and blew his tail nearly perpendicular to his body.

"It's gettin' worse," I muttered, "And there's nowhere to hide."

Here on the high plains, that wind could blow for days, even weeks. It had been known to drive men insane.

If I didn't escape from its grasp, I could very well meet the same fate.

I heeled Laramie into a slow jogtrot.

4

At the crest of the ridge, the ceaseless wind reached its full fury, tossing sand into my face. I wiped a hand across my eyes and squinted into the distance, searching for a safe path down the steep slope.

I don't believe it!

My mind refused to consider what I'd seen was real. I blinked, and gazed down the ridge again.

It is a soddy! I will have a place to spend the night!

In a little hollow below the ridge stood a small sod cabin, apparently long abandoned. Nonetheless, it still appeared sturdy, despite years of neglect.

"C'mon, Laramie. We'll both sleep comfortable tonight."

I pushed my gelding down the grade, then rode slowly up to the sod shack. Dried grass and weeds overgrew the roof, and the door hung by one leather hinge. It banged open and shut in the wind. However, the soddy was firmly built and solid, an inviting shelter from the elements. Even the small corral alongside it was still in good shape, and overgrown with frost-killed grass it would provide my horse with fodder for the night. All I'd have to do was nail a couple of the rails back in place and it would hold Laramie quite nicely.

I dismounted, led my horse inside the corral, and removed the saddle and bridle. Laramie rolled, then fell to cropping at the dry grass. While he grazed I hammered those fallen rails into place.

There was an old rusted bucket lying in one corner of the enclosure. I carried it to the small pond behind the cabin, filled it, and left it in the corral for Laramie. Satisfied I had settled my paint as well as possible under the circumstances, I scratched his ears.

"You take it easy, fella. Get a good night's rest," I told him.

I untied my bedroll from the cantle of my saddle, shouldered my saddlebags, and headed inside the dirt shanty.

The air inside the soddy was thick and musty. There was no furniture, except for a rusted stove in one corner, tipped on its side. Previous passersby must have stripped the place clean. Apparently even the mice had abandoned this sorry place, for there wasn't a sign of those rodents anywhere. A thick coating of dust covered every surface. With the wind, more dust drifted from the roof in a thin brown haze. The soddy's dank interior would be dreary enough on a sunny day. Now, with clouds thickening and night coming on, it was downright depressing.

The wind moaning overhead and pushing in fitful gusts through chinks in the walls made the dirt-walled shack seem almost threatening.

Worn-out, I didn't attempt to find fuel and build a fire. I gulped down some hardtack, washing it down with tepid water from my canteen.

Too dog-tired to even pull off my boots and gunbelt, I rolled out my blankets on the packed earth floor and slid under them. That soddy might have been gloomy, the atmosphere inside oppressing, but I was grateful for the shelter it provided from the maelstrom.

I curled up on my side and fell asleep to the accompaniment of that ceaseless, howling wind.

ΛΛΛΛΛΛΛΛΛΛΛΛ

I had no idea how long I'd been sleeping when I became aware of a presence in the room. The soddy seemed dimly illuminated by the mid-morning sun, but a brown haze still hung in the air, and the wind still moaned.

The door had been blown open, and outside the shack stood a woman, along with two young children. They were standing in front of a freshly dug grave. A crude wooden cross stood at its head, while the wind lifted dirt from the loose earth mounded over the grave and carried it off. The family stood with heads bowed for a time, then turned toward the cabin. Just before they reached the door the wind swept them away, to disappear in a cloud of dust.

I jerked awake, gasping for breath, my heart pounding. Groggily, I reached for a match, then realized there was no lamp. I settled back. The door was still closed, the only illumination a few streaks of light from the rising full moon working their way through cracks in the door.

It was only a dream, I thought. *That wind's got you spooked.*

I reached into my vest pocket, took out the makings, and built a cigarette. I struck a match and lit the smoke, taking a long drag. I lay there in that shack smoking and listening to the wind. By the time I'd smoked that quirly to the butt, the tobacco had calmed my jangled nerves. I stubbed out the cigarette, rolled back up in my blankets, and drifted back to sleep.

Once again, that vision interrupted my slumber. As before ,the wind had awakened me. I now saw that same woman holding two pillowcases, cases which had once been white, but were now yellowed with age. She dipped the pillowcases in a basin of water, then carried them to the bed where her children lay sleeping. She tenderly placed the moistened clothes over their faces to protect them from the dust filtering from the dirt roof. That done, she tied another wet cloth over her own mouth and nose. She stood watching the slumbering children, then turned toward the door, listening. A look of utter despair crossed her face when the wind's soft moan increased to a full-throated shriek.

The woman turned from the door and threw herself down alongside her children. The howling wind drowned out her hopeless sobs.

I was jolted to full wakefulness, my blood racing. Despite the night's chill, sweat was pouring from my brow.

I rolled onto my belly and reached for my saddlebags. I pulled out the small bottle of whiskey I carried, uncorked it, and stared at it for a long while. Reluctantly, I recorked the flask, put it away, and fell back on my blankets. I sure didn't need that liquor's effect on my already heightened imagination.

I somehow slept a bit longer, but the dream soon returned. This time the woman had a long-handled spade in her hands. There were now three graves, the two brand new ones smaller than the other. The woman tossed a final shovelful of dirt on one grave, her shoulders slumped in defeat, her eyes dull and lifeless.

The soddy's door burst open. I scrambled from my bedroll, trying to clear the cobwebs from my mind. Upon the ridge above the shack stood the emaciated figure of that woman, pale as death, her features white as bone in the moonlight, the wind whipping her tattered dress.

Unable to pull my gaze from that specter, I watched in dread while she raised her withered arms as if in supplication. Then, with a shriek of such despair it turned my blood cold, she vanished before the wind.

In abject horror, I dashed from that shanty and for my horse, with the wind screaming all around. Laramie was pacing back and forth in the corral, trumpeting his fear. I jumped the fence and grabbed my gear. Somehow I managed to calm my terrified gelding enough to throw blanket and saddle on his back and get the bridle over his head.

I jumped into the saddle, realizing in my panic I had neglected to open the gate. I dug my spurs into Laramie's flanks, sending the frenzied horse directly at the rails I'd just repaired. He broke through those boards as if they were straw.

My paint needed no urging to flee that hollow. He bounded away from there at a full gallop.

I kept Laramie at that pace, heedless of any obstacles in our path, my only thought to put as much distance between myself and that terrifying vision as possible. I never looked back as I raced for my life, with the merciless wind shrieking at my horse's heels and the woman's banshee wail echoing in my ears.

By first light, we were miles from that dirt shack. Laramie came to a stop alongside a small creek. He was completely exhausted. I slid from the saddle. He stood spraddle-legged, his head hanging. I pulled the saddle from his back and dropped it to the ground, then collapsed alongside it.

Fatigue finally overcame my fear. Sleep claimed me, and in the daylight I slept soundly for several hours. I awakened feeling greatly relieved I'd managed to escape from that wraith. Laramie had recovered somewhat also, for when I awoke he greeted me with a cheerful nicker. He'd drunk and grazed while I dozed.

"I'm sorry, pal," I apologized to my paint. I pulled a currycomb from the saddlebags to brush the dried sweat from his hide. By the time I had finished, the sun was well on its descent toward the western horizon. I shivered when a chance breeze brushed my cheek. Dread at the thought of spending another night out on that prairie churned in my belly. Besides, in my panic I'd left my blankets in that soddy. I would be mighty chilly without them.

"Let's try for town, pardner," I whispered to Laramie.

I quickly saddled my horse and climbed onto his back. He broke into an eager trot without hesitation.

Darkness came well before we reached the nearest settlement, Aminto, a collection of a few shacks, a general store, a livery stable, and a saloon. I settled my horse in the stable and headed for that saloon. I would spend a week in that town trying to drink the horrific vision of that woman out of my mind. And the Diamond M would never learn what had happened to me. I never went back.

The Youngest Rangers

1

Texas Ranger Clay Taggart reined his black and white overo to a halt atop a low hill. The view took in the settlement a short distance south. Taggart swung out of the saddle and pulled off his Stetson. He lifted his canteen from the saddlehorn, opened it, and poured most of the contents into the hat. He placed the hat in front of his horse's muzzle. The gelding drank greedily.

"That'll be Uvalde just ahead, Mike," he told the horse. "We're headin' into Travis Burnham's home grounds. Mebbe we'll finally catch up with him. Boy howdy, he's led us a chase for fair."

Taggart had been trailing the renegade for almost two months, from San Marcos, where Burnham had robbed and killed two cattle buyers, through Boerne, where he'd robbed the bank, badly wounding the clerk, to Kerrville. Taggart had missed finding the outlaw in that town by two days. Word had reached Burnham a Ranger was on his trail, so he left town on the run.

From Kerrville, Burnham had headed almost due south to Bandera, where he'd robbed another bank, this time killing a deputy. When Taggart reached Bandera, he was informed Burnham was evidently continuing south toward Uvalde, where he had kin.

Taggart allowed his pinto to finish drinking, then took a swallow from the canteen for himself. He climbed back into the saddle.

"Let's go, boy."

He kicked the horse into a lope.

Twenty minutes later, Taggart rode into Uvalde. He drew abreast of the school just as a group of boys boiled out from behind the building, several of them yelling encouragement to a pair of ten year olds, who were fighting. One landed a blow to his opponent's chin, knocking him backwards. He wrapped his arms around his adversary's waist and drove his head into his stomach. The two boys rolled in the dirt, fists flailing.

Taggart spun Mike and leapt from the saddle. He reached the combatants in two strides, grabbed them by the shoulders, and pulled them to their feet.

"Whoa, take it easy. You're stirrin' up quite a commotion. Settle down," he ordered.

"Lemme go, Mister!" the smaller boy, towheaded, with light blue eyes, ordered.

"Not until you quiet down!" Taggart reiterated. "That goes for both of you," he added, when the other boy tried to twist out of his grasp.

Realizing the futility of further attempts to break free of Taggart's grip, the boys quit their squirming. They gazed up sullenly at the Ranger.

"Now, what's this all about?" Taggart asked.

"Nothin'," one muttered.

"It didn't look like nothin' to me," Taggart responded. "In fact, it appeared you two were tryin' your darndest to kill each other. Let's try this again. If I let you loose, will you behave?"

"I reckon," the towhead replied.

"Same here," the second, lankier, with dark brown hair and eyes, conceded.

"That's more like it."

Taggart released the pair.

"What's your names?"

"Bobby. Bobby Madison," the taller boy answered.

"Jesse Collins," the towhead responded.

"Good. Now we're gettin' somewhere. So what was that ruckus all about?"

"Bobby claims Freckles is no good!" Jesse exclaimed.

"You'd better make that a mite clearer," Taggart urged. "Who's Freckles?"

"My horse. That's him over there."

Jesse pointed to a scrubby bay pinto cowpony tied to the school's hitchrail.

"Bobby said Freckles isn't good for anything just because he's spotted. I couldn't let him say that about my horse!"

"I'm tellin' the truth," Bobby insisted. "My dad's the smartest rancher in these parts, and he says pintos ain't good for nothin'! Only Indians think they're worth anything."

"That's not true! You take that back, Bobby!" Jesse demanded.

"Just simmer down," Taggart ordered. He turned to Bobby.

"You claim pintos are worthless, Bobby?"

"That's right. Everyone know it," Bobby retorted.

"You're wrong, son. I'll show you," Taggart answered. He gave a soft whistle. Mike trotted up to him and nuzzled his hand.

"You see this pinto? This is my horse, Mike. He and I've been trail pards a long time. He's one of the smartest broncs you'll ever meet. Watch. Give Bobby a kiss, Mike."

The big gelding lowered his head and licked the boy's face.

"Yuck!" Bobby exclaimed, wiping his cheek. The other boys laughed.

"Now give Jesse a hug, Mike."

Mike twisted his head to the side, then laid it on Jesse's shoulder.

"Good boy, Mike," Taggart praised. He dug in his pocket for a peppermint, which he gave to the horse.

"Mike'll also shake hands," Taggart added.

"Almost any cayuse can learn tricks, but that doesn't mean he's worth much, Mister," one of the other boys objected.

"What might your name be, son?" Taggart asked him.

"Joe Perkins."

"You're right, Joe," Taggart agreed. "But anyone who says the color or pattern of a horse's coat determines whether he's a good mount is dead wrong. Mike's the finest horse I've ever owned. He's saved my life more than once. Besides, a Texas Ranger has to ride the best horse he can possibly find."

"You're a Texas Ranger, Mister?" Jesse echoed.

"That's right. Ranger Clay Taggart. Been a Ranger for quite a few years. Mike's been with me for most of them. He's taught me the color of a horse's hide doesn't matter. It's the heart and guts under that hide which counts, just like with men. Mike's got both. And a Ranger sure needs that, since his life often depends on his horse."

"Well, mebbe I was wrong about all pintos," Bobby admitted, "But that still doesn't mean Jesse's horse is a good one."

"We'll have to see about that," Taggart replied. "Jess, bring your horse over here."

"Sure thing, Mister Taggart!"

Jesse hurried to his horse, untied him, and brought him to the Ranger.

"Let me take a look at him," Taggart said.

Taggart circled the small horse, studying him from every angle, picking up Freckles' feet to examine his hooves, all the while speaking soothingly to the gelding. He stroked the horse's neck, then looked into his eyes.

"Well, Mister Taggart?" Jesse demanded.

"Call me Clay, Jess. Or Ranger Clay. That goes for all of you."

"But what about Freckles?" Jesse insisted.

"Yeah. Is he any good?" Bobby added. "Sure don't look like much."

"Freckles isn't the best lookin' bronc in Texas, that's for certain," Taggart answered. "But he's got good legs and feet. Pretty deep chest, too. Most of all, he's got a kindly eye. To me, that's the most important thing in a horse. Jess, Freckles is a mount you can depend on. I'd bet my hat on it."

"Gee, thanks, Ranger Clay. See, Bobby. I told you."

"I guess I was wrong," Bobby conceded. "Reckon I own you an apology, Jess… for what I said about your horse, and the fight."

"Heck, I started that fight," Jesse admitted. "Wasn't all your fault, Bobby."

He retied Freckles to the rail.

"I'd say neither of you needs to apologize," Taggart told them. "Men disagree about horses all the time. Long as you shake hands you can put this behind you. How about it?"

"I reckon we can," Jesse answered. "Friends again, Bobby?"

"Sure. Friends again."

The boys shook hands.

"That's settled. Now, I noticed a general store just up the road. Why don't all of you skedaddle down there for some licorice? I'm buyin'," Taggart grinned.

"You bet, Ranger Clay! Bobby exclaimed. "Let's go!"

The boys headed for the store on the run.

"You handled that situation quite well, sir."

Taggart looked around at the sound of that feminine voice. For the first time he noticed the schoolmarm. She was standing on the school's porch, gazing with admiration at the Ranger.

"Why, thank you, ma'am," Clay replied. "I was just tryin' to break up that fight."

"I appreciate what you did. That's why I didn't interfere. You had everything under control. And they're not really bad boys. It's just that Jesse's family doesn't have much, except their hardscrabble ranch, while Bobby's family is fairly well-off. They own a large spread just outside town. But despite the impression you might have gotten from that fight, Bobby and Jesse are best friends."

"Well, I was a boy myself once," Taggart answered.

"I would imagine you were," the teacher laughed.

"I guess that did sound pretty silly," Taggart admitted. Without realizing it, he was staring at the pretty young woman. She was petite and blonde, with blue eyes the shade of cornflowers, her complexion the color of cream.

The conservative dark gray dress she wore couldn't quite managed to conceal the curves of her well-formed figure. Her appearance contrasted with, yet perfectly complemented, the tall, brown-eyed, brown haired Taggart's rugged looks.

"Are you going to introduce yourself, or stand there staring all afternoon?" she asked.

"I… I'm sorry, ma'am," Taggart stammered, flushing with embarrassment. "I'm Texas Ranger Clay Taggart."

"So I heard you tell the boys. I just wanted to hear your name again," she teased. "My name is Lucy Squires."

"I'm pleased to make your acquaintance, Miss Squires."

"Please. Call me Lucy. Would you mind if I take a closer look at your horse? He's quite beautiful."

"Not at all. I'll get him."

Taggart picked up Mike's reins and led his pinto to the teacher.

"He's everything you said he is. He's magnificent," Lucy praised.

Mike stuck his nose in the middle of Clay's back and shoved hard, knocking the Ranger off balance. Struggling to keep his feet, Taggart toppled against the schoolmarm, wrapping his arms around her to maintain his equilibrium. He remained leaning against her a moment longer than necessary.

"I'm sorry again," Taggart apologized, when he pulled himself back. "I don't know what got into Mike. He knows better'n that."

"He was just being fresh. I don't mind," Lucy smiled.

"He still needs to apologize. Tell the lady you're sorry, Mike."

Mike snorted.

"I mean it, boy."

Mike nuzzled the teacher's cheek.

"Thank you, Michael. I know you didn't intend any harm. You're a gentleman."

Lucy patted the horse's nose.

"He seems to like you," Taggart observed. "But his name's Mike."

"I prefer to call him Michael. It fits him better. And the feeling is mutual. I like him a lot. I think I also like his owner," Lucy answered. She gave Clay a smile which warmed his insides.

Taggart flushed, and changed the subject.

"I… figure I'd better get down to the store before those boys get in trouble."

"Yes, you probably should," Lucy agreed. "But perhaps we can visit again. Will you be in Uvalde long?"

"That depends on how long it takes to find the hombre I'm after. I'll be here as long as it takes to corral him."

"Who is that?"

"Travis Burnham."

Lucy gasped.

"Travis Burnham?"

"Yes. Do you know him? He has kin in this area."

"I've never met him, but I know his family. His mother died some time ago. His father and younger brother have a place south of here. They're decent people. Travis supposedly isn't anything like his relatives. I understand he's an outlaw and killer. Please be careful, Clay."

"Always am," Taggart grinned. "Besides, I would like to have that visit you mentioned. Wouldn't do to get my hide punctured before we can."

Clay lingered for a moment.

"You should get to the store," Lucy urged. "Those boys are expecting their licorice."

"You're right," Taggart conceded. "I'll be on my way."

"Just remember that invitation stands. I expect to see you again, Ranger Clay Taggart."

"You can count on that, Miss Lucy Squires," Taggart promised. He swung into the saddle and heeled Mike into a slow jogtrot.

∧∧∧∧∧∧∧∧∧∧∧∧

"I wonder what's taking that Ranger so long?" Tad Martin questioned. "Bet he's not gonna buy us any licorice after all."

"He'll be along," Bobby assured him. "Appears to me he's makin' calf eyes at Miss Squires."

"Don't be dumb, Bobby," Tad objected. "Rangers ain't interested in gals. They're too busy chasin' renegades and Comanches."

"You're wrong about that," Bobby retorted. "Rangers like gals as well as the next man. And Miss Squires sure is pretty. We've all said that. I reckon she caught Ranger Clay's eye, all right."

"Don't matter," Jesse said. "He's comin' now."

Taggart walked Mike up to the store, dismounted, and looped the gelding's reins over the hitchrail. He gave his horse another peppermint.

"You boys still waitin' on that licorice?" he grinned.

"You bet'cha!" they exclaimed, in unison.

"Let's go."

Taggart led the group into the establishment. The storekeeper fixed him with a steady gaze.

"Howdy, stranger. I was about to chase these ruffians from in front of my store, but they told me a Texas Ranger was in town and had promised them some candy. I wasn't sure whether to believe them, but I reckon you're him. I'm Ezekiel Haskins, at your service."

The sparkle in his hazel eyes and the broad smile on his face belied his harsh words.

"That's right. I'm Ranger Clay Taggart. Howdy yourself."

"Pleased to meet you. What type of candy would these boys like?"

"Licorice. Give me two sticks apiece for them, and two for myself. I'd also like about half that jar of peppermints for Mike."

"Sure thing. Mike's your pardner?" Haskins queried.

"I guess you could say that. Mike's my horse," Taggart explained. "He loves peppermints."

"He's not the first cayuse I've heard of who likes 'em," Haskins smiled. "I would imagine a Ranger's horse is as much a partner to him as any human."

"You'd be right," Taggart agreed.

Haskins handed two licorice sticks to each of the boys and the Ranger, then filled a paper sack with peppermints.

"That will be sixteen cents for the licorice, and five cents for the peppermints. You owe me twenty-one cents, Ranger."

"That's fair."

Taggart dug in his pocket, came up with a quarter, and handed it to the storekeeper. He received a pair of two cent pieces as change.

"Thank you. And please come again," Haskins said.

"I'll be by later for some supplies," Taggart promised.

After the candies were paid for, Taggart herded the boys onto the porch. They gathered around him, gnawing on licorice.

"You're a real Texas Ranger, right Clay?" Bobby asked.

"I sure am," Taggart confirmed.

"Then you must've killed a whole lotta owlhoots."

"Not that many," Taggart replied. "I don't like killin' a man unless he forces my hand."

"Bet you've got a real fast draw, too," Bobby continued.

"Yeah. You've gotta be real fast with a sixgun to be a Ranger," Jesse added. "I'll wager you've outdrawn a lot of gunslingers, Ranger Clay."

"Not at all," Taggart demurred. "I've never drawn on a man yet."

"You must've," Jesse persisted. "Lawmen have to face down gunfighters all the time."

"Jesse's right," Joe agreed. "So tell us how many, Clay."

"Not one," Taggart reiterated.

"You're joshin' us," Bobby complained.

"I'm not joshin' at all. You boys have been readin' too many dime novels," Taggart answered. "Gunfights like you're talkin' about mostly take place in the pages of cheap fiction. Sure, there's been a few of them, but nowhere near as many as folks believe. As for me, when I'm attemptin' to arrest a man I've already got my gun out and aimed at him. I'm sure not gonna chance a killer getting the drop on me and puttin' a slug through my guts. That goes for all of the Rangers."

"You mean you've never killed an outlaw or Indian?" Jesse asked.

"I didn't say that," Taggart clarified. "I've had to shoot raidin' Indians, and I've had to kill some white desperadoes too. But I don't like doin' it. Most of the hombres I've plugged I shot in self defense, when they wouldn't surrender."

"I don't care what you claim, I say you're real quick," Jesse insisted. "Please show us how fast."

"Yeah," Bobby added, "Let's see how fast you are, Ranger Clay. I'd bet if we were outlaws you could outdraw and shoot down the whole bunch of us."

"I doubt that," Taggart chuckled. "Think about it."

"What do you mean?" Jesse asked.

"Well, there's seven of you, and I'm only wearin' a sixgun, so I'd be one bullet short. One of you'd be certain to plug me. Besides, there ain't a man anywhere who could outdraw and shoot more'n two or three men before he took a bullet."

"I guess you're right," Jesse conceded.

"We'd still like to see how fast you are," Bobby said. "How about it? Bet you can't outdraw me!"

"I wouldn't even try," Taggart grinned. "I wouldn't have a chance against a dead shot like you."

"C'mon, try me," Bobby pleaded.

"Nah. Wouldn't want to have you gut-shoot me, kid."

"What's the matter, Ranger? You scared of me?"

Bobby dropped his hands to his sides and settled into a half-crouch.

"Nope. But I know when I'm up against a faster gun," Taggart answered.

"Show him you're faster'n he is, Clay," Tad urged.

Taggart gave in.

"All right. Reckon you're givin' me no choice."

The Ranger dropped his right hand to his hip and nodded.

"Whenever you're ready, kid!"

"Now, Ranger!"

Bobby and Taggart jerked their hands upward, index fingers and thumbs forming "pistols". Bobby aimed and "fired". Taggart grabbed his middle, spun, and toppled across the porch rail.

"Said I was faster than that Ranger!" Bobby shouted triumphantly. "Got him in the belly!"

"You nailed him all right," Tad exclaimed.

"Right in the guts!" Jake Slocomb added.

Jesse nudged Taggart's ribs.

"Clay? Was Bobby really faster'n you?"

Taggart pulled himself upright.

"He sure was," he confirmed. "If we'd been facin' each other for real I'd be dead right now. Nice shootin', Bobby. The Rangers'll sign you on whenever you're ready. That goes for all of you jaspers."

"Thanks," Bobby replied. "Since I plugged you doesn't that mean I get your last licorice stick?"

"I reckon it does, long as you share it with your pards," Taggart laughed. He handed Bobby the candy. "By the way, don't ever point a real gun at another man, less'n you mean it. Guns aren't toys."

"Ranger, how about telling us some stories about the outlaws you've faced?" Tad requested.

"Mebbe another time. Right now I've got to get Mike stabled and head for the sheriff's office. I need to check in with him. You boys better head on home."

Taggart checked the bruise which had risen on Jesse's chin.

"Dunno how you're gonna explain that. Your mom sure won't be happy when she sees it."

"Aw, she won't mind that much," Jesse said. "This isn't the first lump I've got scrappin', and it won't be the last."

"Are we gonna see you again, Ranger Clay?" Bobby asked.

"I'll be around for awhile," Taggart answered. "I reckon our paths will cross. Now scoot, all of you. Get on home."

"Yes sir, Ranger!" Jesse answered. "G'night."

"'Night, boys. And no more fightin'!"

∧∧∧∧∧∧∧∧∧∧∧∧

After the boys departed, Taggart settled Mike at the livery stable, with instructions to the hostler to make sure the pinto had a thorough rubdown and hearty feeding. Assured his horse would receive the best of care, Taggart headed for the sheriff's office. When he entered, the man behind the desk looked up from the stack of wanted notices he was perusing.

"Can I help you, Mister?" he asked.

"Maybe. I'm Texas Ranger Clay Taggart."

"A Ranger?" The sheriff leapt to his feet.

"We haven't had a Ranger around here for way too long. I'm Bill Moran, Uvalde County Sheriff. What can I do for the Rangers?"

Moran was over fifty, but still had the look of a man who could hold his own in any brawl or gunfight.

"I'm trailin' a killer who headed this way. He's originally from these parts."

"You don't have to give me a name," Moran answered. "Bet he's the man named on this wanted dodger."

He took the notice and handed it to Taggart. It carried a description of Travis Burnham, and offered a one thousand dollar reward for his capture.

"That's the hombre I want. You have any idea where he might be holed up?"

"He'd be a fool to show his face around Uvalde," Moran declared. "Too many people know him. I think you're on the wrong track, Ranger."

"I've gotta disagree with you, Sheriff," Taggart replied. "I've been trailin' Burnham for nearly two months. I know he's got folks around here. After he robbed the Bandera bank and killed a deputy there, he headed due south. He's probably makin' for Mexico, but figures on stopping by his home place for supplies and rest before continuing on. Probably countin' on pickin' up a fresh horse there, too."

Moran shoved back his Stetson and scratched his head.

"You might be right at that. But it wouldn't be likely he'd get any help from his pa or kid brother," he observed. "Troy Burnham's a real decent sort. His boy Tom's the same. Neither of 'em hold much truck with Travis. That boy was never anythin' but trouble."

"I understand Mrs. Burnham died a few years back. Did that have something to do with Travis becoming an outlaw?"

"Not a thing. Travis left home three years before his ma died. In fact, everybody feels Travis's goin' bad is what killed Molly. She and Troy did everything they could to raise their boys right, but it just didn't stick with Travis. You know how it is. Some kids just turn out mean, no matter how good they're raised. A few of them learn their lessons and change their ways, but most don't. Travis is one of those."

"I know," Taggart concurred. "But kin is still kin. Burnham is probably countin' on that. His folks might not give him any help, but they'd most likely never turn him in. And if he decided to only take some supplies from 'em they sure wouldn't object."

"I guess that could be," Moran agreed. "So you'll be needin' directions to the Burnham place."

"That's right."

"It's not hard to find. It's fifteen miles south of town. Take the south road until you come to a fork marked by a rock cairn. Take the left fork, and the Rocking B's two miles down that road. There's a signpost nailed to a big mesquite that marks the place. Take a right there and go another quarter mile. The Burnham cabin's at the end of that lane."

"Bueno. I appreciate your help, Sheriff."

"You gonna head out tonight? And you want me to ride along with you?" Moran asked.

"No on both counts," Taggart replied. "It's gettin' late. It'd be after dark before I could reach the Burnham ranch. Besides, I need a rest, and more importantly so does my horse. I'll get a room at the hotel, grab supper, and get a good night's sleep, then leave at first light. Travis Burnham is only one man. I can handle him."

"He's probably already ridden on to Mexico by now," Moran pointed out.

"Possibly," Taggart agreed. "But I'll keep on his trail until I run him down."

"Even if it means crossin' the border?"

"Even if it means crossin' the border."

"Well, I wish you luck," Moran said. "You'll need it."

"Thanks. I appreciate that, Sheriff. Adios."

"Vaya con Dios, Ranger."

2

Two hours after sunup the next morning found the Ranger at the gate of the Rocking B Ranch. Two men were working a colt in one of the corrals. They stopped to watch Taggart while he eased Mike through the gate and into the yard. The younger of the pair kept his hand on the butt of an old Navy Colt hanging at his hip.

"What can we do for you, Mister?" the older man asked.

"Are you Troy Burnham?

"I am," Burnham confirmed. "This is my boy, Tom."

"We don't care for strangers comin' around," Tom snapped. "The smartest thing for you would be to turn that fancy pinto of yours around and ride on outta here. Make sure you close the gate on your way out."

"I'm afraid I can't do that," Taggart replied. "I'm not here to cause you or your pa any trouble, but I do have to ask you some questions. My name's Clay Taggart. I'm a Texas Ranger, and I'm after your brother Travis. Been on his trail for quite awhile now."

"You ain't gonna find him here," Tom growled.

"I'd rather speak with your pa, son," Taggart answered. "Mr. Burnham, would you mind if I got off my horse?"

"No, I don't mind," Troy replied. "Reckon I couldn't stop you anyhow."

"Thanks. I won't take up much of your time."

Taggart swung from his saddle.

"Now you're dismounted. Speak your piece," Troy said.

"All right. Is Travis here?"

"No, he ain't!" Tom snarled.

"I was speakin' to your father, not you," Taggart retorted. "Mr. Burnham, is your boy here, or has he been here recently?"

The elder Burnham shrugged. A look of utter hopelessness crossed his face.

"There's no point in lyin' to you. You'd figure it out soon enough anyway," he sighed. "Travis was here. Arrived the night before last. Took some grub, ammunition, and a fresh bronc. He lit out just after dark last night."

"He say which way he was headed?"

"Don't tell this lawman anythin' more, Pa," Tom urged.

"Son, I know you love your brother. So do I," Troy responded. "But he's no good. Hasn't been since he growed

210

up. If this man doesn't stop him, he'll rob and murder more innocent folks. Sooner or later Travis is bound to die with a bellyful of lead, or hangin' from a cottonwood limb. I'm not gonna protect him any longer."

To Taggart he continued, "Travis didn't say where he was goin'. He headed south from here. My guess is Mexico."

"That's what I figure too," Taggart answered. "What's he ridin' now?"

"A big-chested bay gelding with a sock on his near forefoot," Troy answered.

"That's one good horse," Tom broke in. "You'll have a heckuva time catchin' up to my brother with that pinto of yours. He's pretty, but I've never seen a spotted horse with much bottom."

"Well, you're lookin' at one now," Taggart said. "Mike'll outlast just about any other horse in Texas. But I won't catch Travis standin' here palaverin'. I'd best get ridin'."

"You want some coffee or chuck, Ranger?" Troy asked.

"Can't take the time. I've got plenty of grub in my saddlebags. But thank you for the offer, and the information. I know it wasn't easy for you to answer my questions. I'll try and take your boy alive if at all possible."

"Don't matter none." Troy's voice was thick with despair. "Travis made his choice a long time ago. I reckon it'd be best if you kill him with a bullet, rather'n him bein' jailed and dyin' at the end of a rope."

"That'll be his decision," Taggart answered. "Tom, Mr. Burnham, again, muchas gracias. Adios."

3

It only took a few moments for Taggart to find the tracks of Travis Burnham's horse. As his father had said, the renegade had headed south from the Rocking B.

"He ain't tryin' to cover his tracks," Taggart told his horse, "Appears he's makin' a beeline for Mexico. It's up to us to stop him before he gets there. C'mon, boy. Pick up the pace."

He spurred Mike into a ground-eating lope, a pace the gelding could maintain all day without tiring.

Two miles later, the hoofprints of Burnham's horse turned right, into a brush-choked ravine. Taggart reined Mike to a halt. He took a drink from his canteen while he examined the tracks.

"Looks like Burnham decided to try and shake off any pursuit after all," Taggart muttered. "And that draw's the perfect spot for an ambush. We go in there and I'm liable to end up with a bullet in my back, horse. Reckon we don't have any choice, though. Besides, those prints are several hours old. My guess is Burnham ducked in there hopin' no one'd follow, and just kept on goin'. Well, let's find out."

Taggart pushed his mount into the thick growth. Mike snorted a protest when the thorny vegetation jabbed his hide.

Taggart's pace was slowed to a walk while he worked his way through the winding ravine. Several times, he had to stop Mike and dismount, to force his way through the dense underbrush. Both man and horse had blood flowing from deep scratches gouged out of their flesh by spiny needles and thorns before they finally emerged from the draw.

"Burnham accomplished what he set out to do. We lost considerable time tryin' to follow his tracks through there. But soon's I find some water we're gonna take a few minutes and rest. You need a drink and I want to rub some salve on your scrapes, Mike."

The Ranger followed Burnham's trail for another twenty minutes, until he reached a small cienega.

"Burnham stopped here to rest his horse. We're gonna do the same."

Taggart swung from the saddle and loosened the cinches. He slipped the bit from Mike's mouth and gave him a peppermint. He let the overo drink, then while Mike cropped at the lush grass surrounding the seep, dug a tin of salve from his saddlebags. He coated his horse's wounds with the ointment, then did the same to the scratches marring his own face and hands.

214

Taggart removed some jerky and hardtack from his saddlebag. He ate a quick meal while Mike grazed. He washed down the stringy meat and dry biscuits with water from the seep, then refilled his canteen.

"Enough relaxin' for you, bud," he told his horse, with a fond slap on the neck. "Burnham's puttin' miles between us, and we're burnin' daylight. Time to get movin'."

Taggart slid Mike's bridle back in place and retightened his cinches. Once he was in the saddle, he again pushed the pinto into his tireless lope.

After several miles, Taggart again reined to a stop. He thumbed back his Stetson and scratched his head in puzzlement.

"This doesn't make any sense, Mike. If I didn't know better, I'd swear Burnham is circlin' back north, mebbe even headin' back to Uvalde itself. What the devil is he up to?"

Instead of heading directly south toward Mexico, once he'd emerged from the ravine Burnham had set a twisted trail, which switched back on itself several times, but which was unmistakably gradually turning back north.

"Well, there's nothing we can do but keep followin' these tracks," Taggart continued. "At least we're gainin' on him some. Long as daylight holds out we've got a chance of catchin' up to him."

He heeled the gelding into motion once again.

To Taggart's frustration, dusk found him apparently still several miles behind his quarry. Clouds had covered the sky during the course of the afternoon, and with a new moon there would be no chance of continuing on Burnham's trail until morning.

"I reckon we'll have to find a place to hole up for the night, Mike," he said to his horse. "Well, at least you'll get some rest. You could use it. We both can. We'll start out fresh at sunup."

The Ranger rode two more miles, until he came upon a clear stream. The creek tumbled over a steep bluff, widened into a deep pool, then flowed into a series of rapids, which cascaded over a bank on the opposite side of the trail. From there it disappeared into dense undergrowth.

"This looks like as good a place as any to set up camp, Mike. We'll spend the night here."

Taggart dismounted, unsaddled his horse, and rubbed him down. That done, he let Mike have a long drink, then picketed the pinto for the night on a section of thick grama grass.

"Reckon you're all set, pardner," he noted. "Now that you're settled, that water looks mighty good to me. Reckon I'll take a swim before I make my supper."

Taggart stripped off his sweat and dirt stained clothes, and tossed them on the stream bank. He plunged into the water.

The Ranger spent several minutes swimming, then several more relaxing in the creek, allowing the cool water to soak away some of the grime and aches of the trail. Once he felt thoroughly refreshed Taggart emerged from the stream. He allowed the evening breeze to dry him off, then redressed.

"Time to eat."

Taggart pulled his frying pan and coffeepot from his saddlebags. He hunkered alongside the creek to fill the pot. Just as he pulled it from the water, excruciating pain exploded through his head. The last things Taggart remembered were the crack of a rifle shot, then a distant thud as his body struck the ground. He rolled over the embankment, slid to the bottom, and lay unmoving.

4

"I'm sure glad it's Saturday, so we can go fishin' rather'n wastin' the day in school," Bobby remarked to Jesse. "You about ready there?"

"Just about." Jesse picked up his fishing pole and climbed onto Freckles' back.

"Now I'm set. Let's go."

The boys put their horses, Jesse's pinto and Bobby's blaze-faced chestnut gelding, into a shuffling walk. With the entire day ahead of them, they were in no particular hurry.

"Where do you want to head, Bobby?"

"How about that spot on Agua Verde Creek? The fish are usually bitin' there," Bobby suggested.

"That's fine with me. And if they're not, we can go swimmin'," Jesse agreed.

Walking along in the warm sunshine, the horses were almost as lethargic as their young riders. They meandered up the trail, the boys letting them set their own pace. After about three miles, Freckles suddenly stopped. He stood stock-still, head high and ears pricked sharply forward. The little pinto's nostrils flared as he keened the air.

"C'mon, Freckles. Get goin'!" Jesse urged. He drummed his heels on the horse's ribs. His gelding merely danced sideways, still staring into the distance.

"What's the matter with your horse?" Bobby asked.

"I don't know what's gotten into him," Jesse replied, again kicking the pinto in his sides. "Let's go, Freckles!"

"Somethin's botherin' him, that's for certain," Bobby said. "Either that, or he's just bein' stubborn."

"Maybe. Or dumb," Jesse answered. He tried to push his horse into motion. Freckles spun sideways, fighting the reins. He let out a loud neigh, then stood nickering.

"Seems like he wants to head up that old side trail to Peter's Bluff," Bobby observed. "Maybe we should see why."

"There's nothin' much up there," Jesse protested. "The fishin' hole's straight ahead."

"I know that, but your horse insists on takin' that trail. Wait a minute. Listen, Jess!"

"I don't hear anything," Jesse complained.

Freckles gave out another neigh. It was answered by a return whinny. Freckles trumpeted again, this time joined by Bobby's chestnut.

"There's a horse up there! Monte hears it too!" Bobby exclaimed.

"You're right! Maybe it's hurt," Jesse answered. "We'd better go and find out."

Jesse released the pressure on his reins. Instantly, Freckles shot up the narrow side trail at a dead run, Bobby's chestnut at his heels.

They reached the summit of the rise, racing along the base of the bluff. Freckles rounded a bend, then stopped so abruptly Jesse was tossed over his head and thudded to the ground.

Bobby leapt from Monte's back and hurried to his friend's side.

"Jesse, you all right?"

"Yeah," Jesse gasped. "But you were right about pintos bein' stupid. Dumb horse."

"He's not so dumb. Look there!"

Bobby pointed to a black and white gelding, straining at the end of its picket rope. The horse was pawing the ground and whickering frantically.

"That's Mike! Ranger Clay's horse!" Jesse exclaimed.

"It sure is. Clay must be in trouble," Bobby answered.

"We've gotta help him. But where's he at?" Jesse wondered.

"He can't be too far off. Not without his horse." Bobby replied.

"Maybe Mike can help us."

Jesse hurried to the Ranger's horse.

"Can you show us where Clay is, Mike?"

"Turn him loose," Bobby suggested. "He might lead us to Clay."

"Good idea."

Jesse untied the rope from Mike's halter. The overo trotted to the embankment, where he stood pawing the dirt and whinnying.

"Down there!" Bobby exclaimed, following the gelding's gaze.

"Where? I don't see anything," Jesse answered.

"There. Half-hidden in the scrub. You can hardly see him."

Bobby pointed to the still form of a man, barely visible through the thick underbrush.

"I've spotted him. Clay!" Jesse shouted.

"He's not movin'," Bobby said. "Ranger!"

"Ranger! Hey, Ranger Clay! Ranger Clay!" both boys shouted.

"It's no use," Bobby muttered. "He doesn't hear us."

"We've gotta get him outta there," Jesse insisted.

"But how?" Bobby answered. "We might be able to climb down that bank, but we'd never be able to pull Clay back up. He's way too heavy. Besides, what if he's… dead?"

"We can't know that until one of us goes down there. You afraid of a dead man?" Jesse asked.

"I… I guess not," Bobby stammered. "It's just that, well, I ain't never seen a corpse up close before."

"If you're scared, I'll go down that bank," Jesse offered.

"We've still gotta figure out how to get him back up," Bobby reminded him. "Mebbe one of us should ride for help."

"There might not be enough time for that," Jesse replied.

"Then we've gotta think of somethin', and quick," Bobby answered.

"His horse! Bobby, get Clay's saddle and rope."

"That's it!"

Bobby hurried to where Taggart's saddle lay on the ground. He carried it back to where Mike stood, looking down at his rider and nickering questioningly.

"Get that saddle on him!" Jesse ordered.

Bobby tossed the saddle onto the gelding's back and tightened the cinches. He took Taggart's lariat from the saddle and dallied one end around the horn, then tied a loop in the other.

"One of us has gotta go down there and tie this rope around Clay," he noted.

"I reckon that should be you, since you're bigger'n I am. It'll take all the muscle you've got to lift that Ranger and slip the lasso under him," Jesse answered. "That is, unless you're still too scared."

"I ain't scared," Bobby retorted. "You just keep a tight grip on that rope. Make sure Mike doesn't move."

"You can count on me, pardner. But don't slip, whatever you do. And good luck."

"Thanks, Jess."

Bobby gripped the rope and disappeared over the lip of the embankment. Jesse stood at Mike's head, keeping a tight grip on the pinto's halter while he stroked the horse's neck and spoke soothingly to him.

After what seemed an eternity to Jesse, Bobby came back into view, more than halfway down the steep slope.

Bobby slid to the bottom, then scrambled to the downed Ranger.

"Bobby! Are you all right?" Jesse called.

"I'm fine!" Bobby shouted back.

"What about Clay?"

"His head's all bloody, but he's still breathin'. He looks in bad shape. We've gotta hurry. I'll get the rope around him, then you have Mike pull him up. Go slow and careful."

"Don't worry about me and Mike. Just get that rope tied!"

It was a struggle for the eighty-five pound Bobby to lift the two hundred plus pound Taggart's upper body and work the rope around the unconscious Ranger. He was exhausted when the lariat was finally under Taggart's armpits and tied around his chest.

"I'm ready, Jess. Get us outta here!"

"Hold on!"

Jesse urged Mike away from the cliff. Experienced in working cattle, the big gelding realized what was expected of him. He kept the rope taut as he backed slowly from the edge.

"Easy, Mike. Steady, boy. You don't want to hurt Clay more'n he already is," Jesse cautioned. "That's it.

Nice and easy. You're doin' fine, Mike. Keep goin', just like that."

Moments later, Mike dragged Taggart and Bobby back over the embankment's rim.

"Stop, Mike! You did great, boy!"

Jesse unwrapped the lariat from Mike's saddlehorn. The pinto trotted up to Taggart and nuzzled his rider's face. Taggart's only response was a barely audible moan.

"We did it, Jess!" Bobby shouted. "We got Clay outta there!"

"We sure did," Jesse responded. "But we're still in trouble. He's not gonna come to, and there's no way we can get him onto a horse by ourselves. We need a buckboard."

"That means we'll have to go for help after all."

"One of us will. The other will have to stay with Clay."

"Which one?"

"You'd better, Bobby. Monte's a lot faster than Freckles."

"All right, Jess. I'll head for your place. It's closest. You gonna be all right until I get back?"

"I'll be okay. Tell my pa to hurry back here. And have him send my brother for the doc."

"I'll be back quick as I can," Bobby promised.

He gathered Monte's reins, leapt onto the chestnut's back, and pushed him into a dead run.

5

Clay Taggart awoke in unfamiliar surroundings, and with a pounding headache. He was flat on his back in a comfortable bed, covered by a clean sheet. He opened his eyes to see a whitewashed ceiling. He groaned and touched a hand to his head. Most of his hair had been shaved away, and a bandage covered a good part of his scalp.

Hearing the Ranger moan, the woman at his bedside stirred.

"Ranger Taggart? Are you awake?" she softly asked.

Taggart turned his head to see a woman in her late thirties.

"I reckon so, ma'am. Might I ask who you are? And where am I?"

"My name is Bea Collins. You're at the Triangle C Ranch."

"Collins?"

"That's right. Jesse Collins' mother. How are you feeling?"

"I've got a wicked headache, but other than that not bad. Plus I'm a mite puzzled. How'd I get here? Last thing I remember was gettin' shot."

"Bobby Madison and Jesse. They were going fishing when they stumbled across you. Evidently you'd fallen over an embankment after that bullet struck. The boys found you there. I'll let them tell you the entire story, but somehow they got you back to the trail, then came for help. My husband brought you here. You were too weak to survive the trip to town. That's another seven miles. Doctor Palmer came out here to treat you. He confirmed our suspicions. You probably would have died before reaching Uvalde. The doctor said you have a rather severe concussion from the bullet wound. Fortunately, your skull wasn't fractured. Another quarter inch lower, however…"

"You don't need to finish that, ma'am," Taggart smiled, weakly. "Where is Jesse? I'd sure like to thank him. Bobby too."

"The boys are in school. They'll be along later. So will Lucy Squires. They'll be pleased to see you've regained consciousness."

"Lucy Squires? The schoolteacher?"

"That's right. Doctor Palmer said you needed to be watched twenty-four hours a day, until you awakened. Several women from town have been taking turns helping me do just that. Tonight is Lucy's turn."

"Well, what d'ya know?" Taggart whispered.

"What was that, Ranger Taggart?"

"Nothing. And please, call me Clay, ma'am."

"All right. As long as you call me Bea."

"It's a deal."

"Fine. Now, can I get you anything?"

"I am a bit hungry," Taggart admitted. "Just how long have I been unconscious?"

"Two days," Bea answered.

"Two days. That means I've got no chance of catchin' up with Travis Burnham."

"Travis Burnham?"

"The outlaw I was trailing, and the hombre who undoubtedly shot me," Taggart explained. "He's probably in Mexico by now. Don't matter. Once I'm outta this bed I'll be on his trail again."

"That won't be for several more days, at least," Bea answered. "I can't do anything about Travis Burnham, but I can surely do something about your empty stomach. You're not ready for a big meal yet, but how does beef broth and coffee sound?"

"That sounds just wonderful."

"Fine. I'll heat some for you. By the time you've finished eating, the boys should be here. I'll send for the doctor, too. He wanted to examine you once you awakened. Now you rest while I get your meal."

"Thanks, Bea. I appreciate everything your family's done for me."

"We only did what any decent folks would do," Bea answered. "So don't trouble yourself about that. Just recover as quickly as possible."

"Doctor's orders?"

"My orders, and no one disobeys them," Bea retorted, as she headed for the kitchen.

∧∧∧∧∧∧∧∧∧∧∧∧

Taggart had finished his meal and been dozing for an hour when Jesse and Bobby burst into his room.

"Clay! You're awake!" Jesse shouted.

"I am now," Taggart grinned.

"I told you he was sleepin', Jess," Bobby scolded.

"You were? I'm sorry, Ranger," Jesse apologized.

"No need to apologize, Jess. I've slept long enough anyway."

Bea hustled into the room.

"Clay, I didn't realize these boys were here. They snuck past me. I hope they didn't wake you."

"No harm done," Taggart assured her. "In fact, I'm glad for the company."

"Well, if you're sure. I have to start supper. However, if these boys are a bother you call me. Jesse, Bobby, don't you wear out Ranger Taggart. He still needs rest."

"We won't, Ma," Jesse promised.

"All right. Then I'll leave you men to talk."

Once Bea had left, Taggart propped himself higher on his pillows.

"Jess, Bobby, I've gotta thank you for bein' so brave. I understand if you hadn't hauled me outta that gulch I'd be coyote bait by now. I appreciate what you did."

"Shucks, Ranger. It wasn't much," Jesse demurred.

"That's right," Bobby agreed. "Your horse did most of the work. That, and you have Jesse's horse to thank for us findin' you. Freckles's the one who made us take that trail. Guess you were right. Pintos sure ain't dumb."

"Except for Freckles tossin' me over his head," Jesse corrected.

"Freckles? Mebbe you'd best explain," Taggart said.

"Sure. We were goin' fishin'," Bobby began.

"When we came to the old trail to Peter's Bluff, Freckles wouldn't take another step," Jesse broke in.

"Whoa, Hold on, boys. One at a time," Taggart ordered. "There's no hurry. I'm not goin' anywhere, so take it slow and easy."

And the boys did. For the next hour, they regaled the Ranger with their version of his rescue from the bottom of Peter's Bluff, embellishing the story but little. They were breathless by the time they finished their tale.

"And that's everything, Clay," Jesse concluded.

"Well, that's quite a story," Taggart answered. "Once I'm up and around I'll make sure your horses get an entire sack of peppermints. And I'll find something special for you boys, too."

"That's not necessary, Clay," Bobby protested.

"I know it's not, but you deserve a reward," Taggart insisted.

Jesse's mother poked her head in the door.

"Speaking of rewards, I just finished mixing a cake. Would you boys want to lick the icing bowl?"

"Would we?" Jesse exclaimed, then hesitated and looked at Taggart.

"Go ahead," Clay chuckled.

"Thanks!"

The boys raced from the room.

"Clay, I was afraid they were tiring you out, so I used that cake as an excuse," Bea explained. "But if you're up to it, the rest of the family is home. I'd like you to meet them."

"Sure," Taggart agreed.

"I'll bring them right in."

Bea departed, returning shortly with a rugged-looking man about her age, and two children who bore strong resemblance to Jesse.

"Clay, this is my husband Benjamin, Jesse's older brother Frank, and my daughter, Mary. Ben brought you here, and Frank fetched the doctor for you. Mary's been helping me care for you."

"Well, I'm beholden to all of you," Taggart stated.

Introductions completed, the Collins's and Taggart spent a few minutes in conversation, until they were interrupted by a tapping at the bedroom door.

"I hate to interrupt, but may I come in? I need to examine my patient."

"Certainly, Doctor," Bea answered. "Clay, this is Doctor Thaddeus Palmer."

"Glad to meet you, Doc," Taggart said.

"And I'm very pleased to see you awake," Palmer replied. "I couldn't be certain just how severe your concussion was. Now folks, if you can leave us."

"Of course. Supper is about ready. And don't forget you're joining us," Bea reminded him. "We'll see you shortly."

"Ranger, you gave everyone quite a scare," Palmer chided. He held up his right hand and extended two fingers.

"How many fingers do you see?"

"Two."

"That's fine. Do you have much dizziness? Any nausea? Blurred vision?"

"Nope. I'm just a bit lightheaded, Doc. And I'm starved."

"That's good. I'll permit you a light meal once I'm finished."

Palmer cleaned and readied Taggart's scalp, then took his temperature. He checked the Ranger's pulse, then put a stethoscope to Taggart's chest to check his heartbeat.

"You're doing fine, Ranger Taggart," he concluded. "You should make a full recovery."

"So I'll be outta this bed in a couple of days?"

"Not quite. You'll have that lightheaded sensation for a while, and that concussion will affect your balance. Riding a horse will be impossible, for at least a week. However, I am pleased with your progress. I'll return in three days to reexamine you. If you are still doing well, then you'll be able to get up for short periods. But no more."

"Doc, I can't do that. I've gotta get after the hombre who shot me," Taggart objected.

"Leave that to Sheriff Moran. And let me make this plain. If you get out of that bed too soon, you'll finish the job Burnham started," Palmer warned. "Now, I have other patients to visit. Follow my instructions, and I'll see you in three days. Don't, and you'll be dead. Is that clear?"

"As crystal."

"Good. I'll see myself out."

"Doc?"

"Yes, Ranger?"

"Thanks."

"You're quite welcome."

After Palmer departed, Taggart lay brooding. Despite the physician's stern warning, the desire to get after Travis Burnham burned like a fire deep in the Ranger's gut. He wasn't aware of Bea Collins entering the room with his supper until she called his name, twice.

"Clay. I was afraid you'd passed out again," she said.

"Nah. Just thinkin'. Lucy!" Taggart exclaimed, when he spotted the schoolteacher standing alongside Bea.

"I told you I'd see you again, Clay," Lucy smiled. "However, I seem to recall you promised not to have your hide punctured, to use your words."

"Luckily the bullet hit my thick skull, so there wasn't much damage," Taggart answered.

"That does explain a lot," Lucy retorted.

"I'm going to leave you two. Lucy, make sure he eats everything," Bea ordered.

"You won't have to worry about that. I'm famished," Taggart answered.

"I'll take good care of him," Lucy promised.

After Taggart finished his meal, he and Lucy talked for some time, until sleep once again claimed him. With Doctor Palmer still wanting the Ranger observed constantly, Lucy remained with Taggart, finally dozing off in her chair.

Bea Collins, checking on the Ranger before retiring for the night, tucked a blanket around the sleeping schoolmarm, then put an extra quilt over Taggart. She smiled once she had finished.

Looks like one good thing might come out of this, she thought. *I'd better tell the preacher to get ready for a wedding.*

6

Taggart spent several frustrating days recuperating. Sheriff Moran informed the Ranger he and his deputies had failed to locate Travis Burnham.

"We lost his trail not far from where he drygulched you," Moran had said. "I have no idea where he headed. I've got men watching the Burnham place, but it's unlikely he'll show there. My guess is he's in Mexico.

"You're probably right. But I still can't figure why he doubled back north," Taggart had answered.

Finally allowed out of bed, Clay was brushing his horse. He looked up at the sound of approaching hoofbeats.

"Someone's comin', Mike."

A moment later, the sheriff rode into the Triangle C yard and dismounted.

"Howdy, Clay."

"Howdy yourself, Bill. What brings you by? You look as if you're carryin' the weight of the world on your shoulders."

"Might as well be. Travis Burnham's turned up."

"He has? Where?"

"Pretty much everywhere around here. I just started gettin' reports from the past several days. He hit the bank in Blewett, then a saloon in Dabney. Rode north to Reagan Wells and robbed their general store. Headed east from there to Utopia, where he robbed another bank and killed the teller. Yesterday he hit the bank in Sabinal."

"He's makin' a circle," Taggart observed.

"Seems so," Moran agreed.

"And he's headed back here to Uvalde. I'd bet my hat on it!" Taggart exclaimed. "C'mon, Mike."

He grabbed the pinto's leadrope and started for the barn.

"You figure on goin' after Burnham?" Moran questioned, following along.

"Darn right," Taggart answered. He threw the blanket and saddle on Mike's back.

"You want some help?"

"No, except keep watch on the Burnham spread. I appreciate the offer, but I'll have a better chance of findin' Burnham on my own. He won't be lookin' for me. He thinks he killed me, remember?"

"I reckon you're right, but where do you start lookin' for him?"

"Right back where he bushwhacked me. I've a hunch his hideout is near there."

"Where? My men and I went over every inch of that spot," Moran protested.

"Dunno. But if he's in there, I'll find him," Taggart promised. "Bill, do me a favor. Tell the Collins' I rode after Burnham. Let them know I'll be back."

"Sure. But are you ready to be in the saddle? Doc Palmer…"

"Doesn't matter what the doc says. Burnham's got to be stopped."

Taggart slipped the bit into Mike's mouth, then mounted.

"Okay. I'll tell them," Moran agreed. "You be careful, Clay. Vaya con Dios."

"Gracias, Bill. Adios."

Taggart sent Mike out of the yard at a trot. He let the horse warm up for a mile, then put him into a gallop. An hour later, the Ranger was combing the area where he'd been ambushed.

"Burnham's holed up somewhere in here, Mike. I know it," he told his horse. "But this time we're ready for him."

Taggart dismounted, studying the area from which the shot had come. A chill went up his spine when he looked down into the gully where he'd nearly died. He turned away, and gazed to the top of the bluff.

"Somewhere up there," he muttered. "That's gotta be it. Mike, I'll have to leave you here and go on foot."

He tied the gelding to a live oak.

Taggart edged along the base of the bluff, seeking any opening large enough to hold a man and horse. He was about to give up when he spied some brush that was dry and withered.

"That doesn't look right," he muttered. "It's been rainin', so there's no good reason for those bushes to be dead."

Taggart yanked on one of the shrubs. It came easily out of the ground, revealing a dim trail climbing through a narrow defile.

"This is it!" Taggart exclaimed. He hurried back to Mike, untied him, and swung into the saddle.

"C'mon, Mike. We've got him now!"

Taggart walked his horse into the opening. Fresh hoofprints were evident in the dust.

"Pretty clever. Burnham hid this trail by cutting brush and stickin' it in front of the entrance. Would've worked, too, if he'd replaced it sooner, before it dried up. Well, he's not gonna slip away again."

Twenty minutes later, the defile opened into a small glade, with a cabin at its center.

"No horse in the corral," Taggart said. "Bet Burnham's not home. But I'd better make sure."

Taggart checked the shack and found it empty. He emerged from the cabin… and a bullet whistled past his cheek. The Ranger dove to his belly. When another slug ripped the air over his head, he jerked out his Colt and returned fire. Travis Burnham sent one more bullet in Taggart's direction, then whirled his bay around and raced for the opposite end of the glade.

Taggart ran for his horse and leapt into the saddle. He touched spurs to Mike's flanks, putting him into a dead run.

"We've got him now, pard. Go, boy!"

There were few horses in Texas which could match the big pinto's speed and endurance. Mike was well rested and eager to run. He streaked after the fleeing renegade.

The trail emerged onto rolling, open ground, interspersed with low hills and occasional shallow ravines. Although Burnham had a good start, Mike was steadily gaining on the outlaw's tiring bay.

"He's headin' for town. What the devil is he thinkin'?" Taggart muttered. He urged Mike to greater speed.

Burnham turned in his saddle to send several shots at his pursuer. Taggart returned fire, but with accurate aim from the back of a running horse impossible, neither man came near his target.

They pounded into Uvalde. Burnham pulled his bay to a stop in front of the school and jumped from the saddle. He sent one last shot at the Ranger to slow him, then burst into the building.

Taggart left his saddle while Mike was still at a run. He reloaded his sixgun as he raced up the school's steps. A bullet smacked into the wall over his head when he stepped through the door.

"Drop the gun, Ranger! Right now! Or I'll kill her!"

Travis Burnham was at the front of the room, Lucy Squires in his grasp. He held his pistol to the side of her head.

"I mean it, Ranger."

"Let her go, Burnham," Taggart ordered. "She's got nothin' to do with this. Neither do these kids. You don't want to kill a woman."

The children were huddled behind their desks, several of the younger ones crying.

"No. You let your gun drop," Burnham insisted. "I'll give you ten seconds."

"You don't wanna do this," Taggart replied. "Let her go and we'll take this outside, man to man."

"Ranger, this time you're dead for certain. Only choice you have is whether I kill this schoolmarm before I plug you. What's it gonna be?"

"Reckon you win, Burnham."

Taggart lowered his gun. Too late, he spied movement from the corner of his eye.

"Jesse, Bobby. No!"

The boys had slipped from their seats while Burnham was occupied with the Ranger. Now, they rushed to the front of the room and dove at their teacher. The collision separated her from Burnham's grasp.

For a split-second, Burnham's attention was diverted from Taggart. Nonetheless, he was already thumbing back the hammer of his sixgun when the Ranger lifted his Peacemaker and fired. Burnham pulled his trigger at the same moment. Taggart's bullet took the outlaw in his belly, while Burnham's hastily fired shot slammed into the Ranger's side.

The mortally wounded outlaw attempted to level his gun and put another slug into Taggart. Taggart shot him again, through the chest. The bullet smashed Burnham back. He twisted, fell across the teacher's desk, shuddered, then lay still. Taggart wrested Burnham's gun from his hand and tossed it aside. He slid his own gun back in its holster.

"Lucy, are you all right?" he asked.

"Yes. Yes, I am, Clay," she half-sobbed. "What about you?"

"I'll be okay. Get the kids out of here." Under his breath he added, "And get the doc. Now!"

Taggart's hands were clamped to his side, covering the crimson stain seeping through his shirt.

"All right."

Lucy hurried the children from the classroom. Once they were outside, Taggart collapsed.

7

Once again, Taggart awoke in an unfamiliar room. This time there was the pressure of bandages wrapped around his middle. The mingled scents of medicines and soaps permeated the air.

"Ranger Taggart. You're awake," the woman at his bedside noted. "I'll get the doctor." She left, soon reappearing with Doctor Palmer in tow.

"Ranger Taggart. We meet again," Palmer smiled. "Although just once I would like to visit when I'm not treating you for a bullet wound. Permit me to introduce my wife and assistant, Amanda."

"I'm pleased to meet you, Mrs. Palmer," Taggart nodded. "Doc, how'm I doin'?"

"You'll recover fully," Palmer explained. "However, you will be laid up for quite some time. That bullet was deep in your side. It took some doing to find it."

"Burnham?"

"Already buried. Sheriff Moran has notified Ranger Headquarters."

"Miss Squires and the kids?"

"All fine, thanks to you."

"I'd like to see 'em."

"In a few days, once your fever is lower," Palmer promised. "What you need now is rest. I've got some laudanum to help you do just that."

"Reckon it's no use arguing," Taggart said.

"That's right," Palmer confirmed. He gave the Ranger a large dose of the laudanum. Within minutes, Taggart was sound asleep.

∧∧∧∧∧∧∧∧∧∧∧∧

Several days later, as promised, Palmer allowed Taggart a few visitors. The first was Sheriff Moran. Later, Lucy Squires, accompanied by Jesse Collins and Bobby Madison, came by.

"Ranger Clay. We're sure glad to see you!" Bobby exclaimed.

"Yeah," Jesse added, "But I thought you said that gunfights were nothin' but fiction. Your shootout with Travis Burnham sure looked like one to me."

"It sure was," Taggart admitted. "Shows even a Ranger can be wrong. And speakin' of wrong, it was plumb foolish what you two pulled. Courageous, but foolish. You both could've been killed."

"So could've you," Bobby pointed out. "Good thing you were faster'n Burnham."

"Yeah, but takin' chances is my job," Taggart answered. "And even though you should've stayed out of it, I'm glad you didn't. You saved my life. Miss Squires' too. You're now unofficial Texas Rangers. Soon's you're old enough you can join up for real."

"You mean that?" Jesse exclaimed.

"I sure do," Taggart grinned. "Now, if you don't mind, I'd like a few minutes to speak with Miss Squires. You can come back once we're done."

"Sure, Clay," Bobby answered. "C'mon, Jess, let's go."

"Clay I want to thank you," Lucy began, once the boys had left.

"You were pretty brave yourself," Taggart answered.

"I had to be, for the children."

Doctor Palmer stuck his head in the door.

"Only a few more minutes, please."

"All right," Lucy conceded.

"Guess we don't have time to talk," Taggart grumbled.

"We'll have plenty of time, while you recuperate," Lucy answered. "And hopefully for a long time after that."

"Lucy, I'm a Texas Ranger, and always will be," Clay explained. "I'll be leavin' for Austin soon as I'm able. After that, who knows where I'll be goin'? Besides, you don't know me very well."

"I know what you are," Lucy replied. "And we'll have lots of time to get to know each other. I want to learn everything about you."

"It's a hard life, bein' a Ranger's gal," Taggart warned.

"I realize that. But if you love someone you take him as he is."

"But…"

"No buts, Clay Taggart," Lucy said. "When you leave for Austin, I'm going with you… as your wife."

"I haven't asked you yet."

"You will," Lucy assured him.

She kissed him on the cheek, then turned for the door. She stopped, and looked back at the bemused Ranger.

"Yes, you will."

Once a Ranger

1

It was a blistering hot afternoon the day I rode into Junction, the kind of Texas summer day so scorching it would send ol' Beelzebub himself searching for shade and a cold beer. I knew I sure needed one.

However, my sorrel needed a drink first. I walked him up to the trough in the town plaza, dismounted, and let him drink his fill. Once he was finished, I tied him to the rail in front of the Crossroads Saloon.

As much as I wanted that beer, I had some business to attend to first. I gave the saloon a wistful glance, then headed across the road to the First Bank of Junction.

The bank's interior was dark and cool after the bright sunshine. I paused to allow my eyes to adapt, then stepped to the counter. The teller looked disdainfully at me from behind the iron grill. He clearly wasn't impressed by the dusty figure I made. I didn't much care, but I couldn't blame him. It's hard for a man to stay presentable during days of riding through the Texas heat. Add in the two week's worth of dark whiskers stubbling my jaw and I reckon I must've looked downright disreputable.

"May I help you, sir?" the teller queried, looking down his nose.

"Perhaps. I've just ridden into town. I'm supposed to meet an acquaintance, who was to make a substantial deposit in our names upon his arrival. My name is Daniel Brown. My friend's is Jeremiah Carter."

"I don't believe anyone by that name has been in, sir," the teller replied, his interest obviously piqued by my mention of that large deposit. "But let me check with Mister Hollister. He's the bank president.

The teller disappeared behind a door marked "Private". He reappeared a moment later with a middle-aged, balding man at his side.

"Mister Brown, I am Slater Hollister, president of the First Bank of Junction," the heavyset banker announced.

"I'm pleased to meet you, Mister Hollister," I replied.

Hollister's grip as we shook hands was moist, his soft hand sweaty. His substantial paunch testified to years of soft living.

"And might I say the same. Regrettably, your friend must not have arrived, as no one has made a goodly deposit for the past several weeks. When exactly were you expecting him?"

"He's due anytime. I'd hoped he had already arrived. However, I'm not concerned. I'm sure he'll turn up in a day or so. In the meantime I'll partake of the hospitality of your town. I've been traveling for several days, and look forward to some rest."

"That's a fine idea," Hollister agreed. "You'll find Junction more than suitable for satisfying your needs. And when Mister Carter arrives, my bank will be ready and capable of handling all your financial transactions."

"I'm sure it will be, but I'm reassured to hear that," I replied. "Now if you don't mind, I'd like to wash some of this trail dust from my throat."

"Of course, of course," Hollister answered. "I hope you enjoy your stay."

"I'm certain I will," I assured him. "Until Jeremiah arrives. Good day, sir."

"Good day to you."

Now it was time for that beer. I retraced my steps to the saloon. Where the chairs in front of the place had been empty when I tied my horse, a wizened old man now sat. He nodded to me when I climbed the stairs to the Crossroads' entryway.

"Howdy, mister," he drawled. "Right hot day, ain't it?"

"It's warm enough," I agreed, taking off my Stetson and wiping sweat from the band.

"Sure makes a body thirsty. Would you be disposed to buy an old man a drink?" he pleaded.

"Why not? I reckon I can spare the price of a beer," I grinned. "C'mon."

I pushed through the batwings with the codger at my side.

At this time of day, there were few customers in the Crossroads. I found a space at the nearly empty bar. My newfound friend stood alongside me.

"Howdy, mister. New in town?" the barkeep asked. "What's your pleasure?"

"Yep to your first question, don't know how long I'll be in town, but I'm waitin' for a friend to ride in from San Angelo," I answered, anticipating his next questions. "And two beers. One for me, and one for…"

"Caleb." The old man supplied his name.

"Caleb, how many times have I told you to stop hanging around outside my place and pesterin' the paying customers?" the saloonman snapped. "Now git!"

"Aw Purdy, I really need a beer," Caleb whined.

"It's all right," I assured the bartender. "Give him a beer."

"Your choice, mister," Purdy shrugged. He drew two glasses of the amber brew.

"Thank you, mister," Caleb told me as he lifted his mug.

"My name's Dan. And you're welcome," I replied.

The oldster downed half his glass, then headed for the free lunch.

"Don't you be cleanin' off that lunch counter on just one beer you didn't even pay for," Purdy shouted after him.

"Just a coupla' sandwiches," Caleb called back.

"Sorry, Dan," the barkeep apologized. "I hate to see a new arrival in Junction taken advantage of by that broken-down old coot. I'm Hank Purdy, by the way, the owner of this establishment."

"Dan Brown. And that old man ain't really botherin' anyone. Seems harmless enough. Who is he, anyway?"

"Caleb Sutton," Purdy explained. "Been here in Junction as long as anyone can remember. Claims he rode with the original Texas Rangers back in Sam Houston's day, when Texas was still part of Mexico."

"Him a Ranger? Hardly seems possible," I replied. "Even in his prime he couldn't have stood more'n five foot three or four. Wouldn't have weighed a hundred and twenty pounds fully dressed with his boots on and soakin' wet, neither. Now he looks as if he strapped on a Colt the weight of it'd tip him right over."

Age had withered Caleb Sutton so he now stood little more than five feet tall, and couldn't weigh more than one hundred pounds. His fingers were twisted by arthritis, the knuckles badly swollen.

"I know. No one believes his tall tales," Purdy snorted. "But as you say, he's harmless enough, except for his cadgin' free drinks. And he does earn his keep by sweepin' out the feed store, and the jail. Speakin' of which, here comes our deputy marshal. Steve, get over here," he called to a youth stepping through the batwings. "Got a beer ready for you."

"Sure thing, Hank," the deputy answered.

The deputy stalked up to the bar and took the spot at my left. He looked me over thoroughly.

"Howdy, stranger," he greeted me. "I'm Steve Malvern, deputy marshal in this town. Who might you be?"

"Name's Dan Brown. I'm waitin' on a friend to show up from San Angelo, to answer your next question. Dunno how long I'll be in town. Anythin' else you want to know?"

The deputy couldn't have been more than nineteen. He was downright skinny, with pale gray eyes and light brown hair. The big Smith and Wesson on his right hip appeared too heavy for its owner. It threatened to pull the gunbelt over the kid's thin hips and down to his ankles. A peach fuzz mustache, barely visible on his upper lip, was his apparent attempt to enhance an appearance of maturity. It didn't work.

"I reckon that'll do for now," Malvern answered, not quite able to meet my steady gaze.

Purdy placed a beer in front of the young lawman.

"Any word from Sheriff Dobbs?" he queried.

"Not yet. I don't imagine he'll reach San Saba for a few more days. Ridin' with those prisoners is bound to mean slow goin'."

"I just hope he makes it there in one piece. Those Dahlman brothers are poison mean. Pure rattlesnake venom. I'll rest easier once Dobbs is back. The whole town will."

"I can handle any trouble until the sheriff returns," Malvern retorted.

"I'm sure you can," Purdy answered, attempting to mollify the deputy's feelings.

"Darn right I can," Malvern shot back. He drained the last of his beer.

"Reckon I'd better finish my rounds. I'll stop in before you close up for the night, Hank."

"I'll see you then," the saloonman answered.

After the deputy left, I took advantage of the free lunch counter, lingered over another beer, then decided to call it a night.

"Hank, thanks for the hospitality. Those were mighty good beers," I told him.

"Appreciate that," he replied. "You got a place to stay?"

"I reckon I'll bunk in the hayloft at the livery stable. Since my friend hasn't arrived, I'm gonna ride out early tomorrow and take the trail to San Angelo. With luck I'll meet him before goin' too far."

"That sounds like a good idea," Purdy agreed. "I'll keep the beer cold in the meantime."

"Seems reasonable," I answered. "Hasta luego."

"'Night, Dan."

I left the saloon, picked up my sorrel's reins, and led him to the nearby livery barn. For an extra four bits, the hostler readily agreed to let me bed down in the hayloft. Once my horse was cared for I climbed the ladder to the loft, pulled off my hat, boots, and gunbelt, and settled down for a hard-earned night's rest.

2

As I'd told the bartender, I was in the saddle at first light the next morning. And as I'd also told him, I headed northwestward on the road to San Angelo.

However, unlike the impression I'd left, I only took that road little more than three miles, then turned left onto a little-used side trail. I followed that trail another mile, then turned right, up a dry stream bed. The rock-strewn watercourse showed few signs of my horse's passing. Another quarter mile up led to a nest of scattered boulders. I pulled my horse to a stop, cupped my hands around my mouth, and gave the low, melancholy call of a mourning dove. A moment later another dove answered my call. I repeated the signal, heeled my sorrel into motion, and sent him around the rocks.

Four men were seated around a smokeless campfire there. They had just finished breakfast and were now enjoying cigarettes. They looked up at me, but said nothing until I had dismounted. One of them detached himself from the rest of the group, filled a tin cup with coffee, and brought it to me while I unsaddled my horse.

"Howdy, Dan. What'd you find in Junction?" he asked, handing me the cup.

"About what I expected, Jerry," I answered. "Soon's I get Dandy rubbed down we'll go over everything. And get the boys ready to ride."

"'Sta bueno," Jerry Carpenter, my long-time partner and the segundo of my outfit, replied. "I'll tell the others."

While I rubbed down my gelding, I could hear the other men mulling over the bit of information I'd given Jerry. I knew they were anxious to get back into action, and I didn't intend to keep them waiting any longer.

I turned my horse loose with the others in a rope corral, then headed for the fire.

"Jerry tells us we're ridin' out," Vance Brigham spoke up, "Reckon that means easy pickin's for us."

After Jerry, Vance had ridden with me the longest. Tough as whang leather, he was the one man I wouldn't want to tangle with. Vance combined the loyalty of a bulldog with the tenaciousness of a terrier.

"That right, Dan?" Beau Thibodeaux echoed. Thibodeaux was a Cajun from the Louisiana bayou country, mean as a snake and twice as ugly.

"This outfit never takes anything for granted. You all know that," I retorted. "But if everyone does his job, we should have no trouble."

260

"We always follow orders, don't we?" Ed Thornton grumbled. He was the youngest, little older than that deputy in Junction. His tow hair, pale blue eyes, and smooth-skinned face made him look more like a sixteen year old farm boy than a hard-riding outlaw and cold-blooded killer. Thornton was sure of himself, sometimes too cocky, but his skill with both gun and knife justified that arrogance.

"Yes, you do," I conceded, "Which is why we've always been successful. I expect we will be again. And after this bank job in Junction, we'll head for Mexico. We'll have enough money to live well in Chihuahua for a long time.

"Tequila and senoritas. That's what I've been waitin' to hear," Thibodeaux grinned.

"Never mind that. Let's get down to business," Carpenter ordered. "Dan, what'll we be up against?"

"Gather round and I'll tell you."

I squatted on my haunches, the others settling into a circle while I used a stick to draw a rough map in the sand.

"This here's the First Bank of Junction," I explained. "Sheriff's office is on the opposite corner. Saloon's across the street, hotel and general store next to that. There's alleyways alongside each of them if we need to use those to escape."

"What about the livery stable, in case one of our horses gets plugged and we need a replacement real quick?" Brigham questioned.

"It's at the end of town. Too far away to do any good," I explained. "If we lose one of the horses we'll have to grab another one from a hitchrail, or double up until we make our getaway."

"How about the bank itself?" Carpenter asked.

"Should be easy enough. There's three teller's cages and the vault. The vault was wide open. Appears to be kept that way during business hours. Four of us can get in there, clean the place out, then get out real quick."

"That sounds fine, Dan," Thornton said. "What about the law?"

I had to grin. Leave it to Ed to ask about the law. He'd killed several lawmen in his short outlaw career, and was always looking for the opportunity to gun down yet another.

"Nothin' to worry about there. In fact, it'll be even easier than usual," I explained. "The sheriff's out of town, escortin' a couple of prisoners to San Saba. The only law in town's a young snot-nosed deputy. He'll be no problem at all. If he does butt in, you'll take care of him, Ed."

"That's fine and dandy," Thornton smirked. The expression on his face told me that deputy was already good as dead.

"I didn't finish," I continued. "There's also a Texas Ranger."

"A Ranger?" Brigham exclaimed. "Hold on a minute, Dan. I don't mind tacklin' a job that's a mite tough, but tanglin' with a Texas Ranger's a whole other story. We don't need that grief."

"I can handle any Ranger," Thornton declared, with an oath. "I've been waitin' for the chance to drill one of those hombres right through his lousy guts."

"Just relax," I cautioned. "This particular gent who claims to be a Texas Ranger is an old coot who's at least eighty years old. And I doubt he was ever a Ranger. No one in town believes he was. It doesn't matter. He's a harmless old drunk who spends his days talkin' folks into buyin' him beers. We've got nothing to worry about from him."

"Dan had you goin' for a minute there, didn't he, Vance?" Thibodeaux chuckled.

"Holloway, one of these days…"

"You're gonna rip my guts out. I know, Vance," I laughed. That threat had been a joke between us for years.

"Anything else we need to know?" Carpenter asked.

"That's about it. We'll start ridin' out of here in a bit. Ed, you and Beau will leave first. When you get to town, head for the saloon and have a couple of beers. Vance, you'll leave thirty minutes after them. You can also stop at the saloon for a beer."

"But I don't know Ed or Beau," he concluded.

"That's right. Take a table by the front window, where you can watch the street. Jerry and I will reach town a half-hour later. When you spot us, leave the saloon and drift across the street. Ed, you and Beau do the same, five minutes later. Jerry and I'll go into the bank first. You two follow right behind us. Vance, your job is to hold the horses and warn us if it looks like trouble's brewin'."

Brigham nodded.

"And plug anyone who gets in the way. Right, Dan?"

I nodded.

"Any other questions?"

"What about the deputy?" Thornton asked.

"Don't worry, Ed. I'll save him for you," Brigham promised.

"That's settled," I said. "Anything else?"

There were no replies.

"Seems not," Carpenter grunted.

"All right. We'll rest for another couple of hours, then we'll head out and meet up in Junction. That'll put us in town just before the bank's closing time. We'll hit it ten minutes before they lock the doors. Check your guns and ammunition."

While the others went over their weapons, I dug a piece of mirror, bar of soap, and a razor from my saddlebags. I propped the mirror on a rock, lathered my face, and commenced scraping the whiskers from my neck and jaw. I didn't really expect my newly-shaven countenance to fool many folks, but it might keep a few from recognizing Dan Holloway and Dan Brown as one and the same.

Once I'd finished shaving, I settled back against a boulder, stretched out my legs, and tilted my Stetson over my eyes. I'd get some more shut-eye before we rode for Junction.

3

The streets of Junction were virtually deserted when Carpenter and I came into town. Most of the populace was indoors, taking shelter from the oppressive mid-afternoon heat. We sat casually in our saddles, letting our horses set their own pace. I noted with satisfaction that Ed's, Vance's, and Beau's mounts were tied in front of the bank, idly switching their tails at pestering flies.

Brigham had wandered out of the Crossroads and was seated in a tilted-back chair under the saloon's wooden awning, his feet up on the rail. He nodded almost imperceptibly when we rode by. I pretended not to notice his signal.

Carpenter and I rode a half-block past the bank, dismounted, and tied our horses. We pulled out the makings, rolled quirlies and lit them, then stood against the wall of a millinery shop to smoke. Vance crossed the street, also rolled a smoke, and stood alongside our horses. Once we had entered the bank he'd untie our mounts and bring them to the front.

Five minutes later, right on schedule, Thornton and Thibodeaux exited the saloon and sauntered across the dusty street. Carpenter and I waited until they reached the board sidewalk, then pulled our bandannas over our faces and stepped into the bank. Thibodeaux and Thornton were right behind us. Once we were inside, we drew our guns and fanned out. There was only a single customer, a woman at one of the teller's cages. We quickly had her and the two tellers covered.

"Don't you scream, honey," Thornton warned the woman, who nodded her compliance.

"This is a holdup!" I announced. "No one will get hurt unless one of you tries something stupid. Now everyone get your hands in the air."

I stuck my Colt right against the nose of the same snooty teller I'd dealt with the previous day.

"You," I ordered. "Tell your friend to empty all the cash drawers. And get your boss out here, now!"

"Barnaby, better do what they say," the clerk told the other teller. "I'll get Mister Hollister."

He headed for the bank president's office, fully aware of the gun Thornton kept trained on his back. He knocked on the door and called for his boss.

"Mister Hollister. We have an urgent matter which needs your attention."

"I'm quite busy," came a muffled reply from behind the closed door. "Can't you handle whatever it is, Hal?"

"I'm afraid not," the teller answered. "We need you out here."

"Very well."

"Good. Now back away from that door," I ordered the teller.

Slater Hollister emerged from his office... to Beau Thibodeaux's sixgun being rammed into his substantial belly.

"What... what is this?" the banker gasped.

"It's a holdup," Thibodeaux grinned. "Start cleaning out your vault, Mister Banker."

"I will not! This is an outrage!" Hollister snapped.

Thibodeaux's pistol slashed up and down, to connect solidly with the banker's head. The blow drove Hollister to his knees, the gun barrel opening a gash on his scalp. Thibodeaux hit him again and Hollister rolled onto his back, out cold.

"He's not gonna be much help," Thibodeaux noted. "Reckon I'd better empty that vault myself."

He leapt the counter, grabbed two canvas sacks, and proceeded to rifle the vault.

The two clerks efficiently cleaned out the cash drawers. Once Thibodeaux had finished his work in the vault, we had four bulging sacks filled with cash.

"Thank you for your cooperation," I told the clerks, adding to the woman, "Ma'am we apologize for causing you any fright. Now, don't anyone try to follow us or call for help for fifteen minutes. Anybody sticks his head out that door and it'll get blown off."

We started to edge out of the bank.

Hal, that snooty teller, had more guts than smarts. Despite the guns covering him, he dove behind the counter, snaked a pistol from under it, and came up shooting. His first shots missed, and Carpenter made sure he didn't get another chance. Jerry shot him through the stomach. The teller folded, groaning in pain.

"Let's get outta here! Those shots are gonna bring half the town down on us!" I shouted.

We turned and ran out the door.

Deputy Steve Malvern had heard the shots and was crossing the street at a run. Vance Brigham already had his gun leveled at the deputy and was thumbing back the hammer, but it was Ed Thornton who gunned the young lawman down. The deputy had his gun only half out of leather when Thornton nailed him in the chest. The kid was slammed to his back in the dirt. He never knew what hit him.

That deputy marshal was the last lawman Ed Thornton ever killed. A shot fired from down the street smashed into the side of his head and buried itself in his brain. He dropped in his tracks.

"What the..." Brigham started to curse. He never finished, for a bullet tore into his stomach. He dropped the horses' reins, doubled up, collapsed, and rolled under their hooves, screaming. The panicked animals galloped away.

I turned to see Caleb Sutton walking toward us, coolly as could be, a Colt Peacemaker in his right hand. I'd never know where he'd gotten that gun, but he held it steadily in his arthritic hand, his aim never wavering. Every time that big .45 bucked in that old man's hand another of my partners went down.

Sutton fired, and Beau Thibodeaux spun to the dirt. Sutton's slug had pierced the Cajun's side and punctured a lung.

Sutton lifted his thumb off the hammer again. Dust puffed from Jerry Carpenter's shirt and crimson spread across his chest. My longtime compadre pitched to his face with a bullet through his heart.

Sutton had shot four times, each time finding his target. My four companions lay dead or dying.

I aimed at Sutton, thumbed back the hammer of my Colt, pulled the trigger, and shot at just about the same moment he fired at me. Sutton never flinched, but I staggered back at the shocking impact of a bullet ripping into my belly.

Sutton kept walking toward me. I tried to lift my Colt to shoot at him again, but the agony of that bullet buried deep in my guts had drained all my strength. Before I could get the gun level, Sutton shot me through the belly again. I jackknifed, dropped to my knees, then crumpled face-down.

With the toe of his boot, Sutton rolled me onto my back, then wrested the Colt from my hand. He glared down at me, but never said a word.

That old man had only six bullets, but he'd made every one count. Not once had he missed his target. Six shots, six mortal hits.

Vance Brigham had rolled onto his side, hands clamped to his stomach. He looked at me through pain-glazed eyes.

"Thought... you said... we'd have no trouble... Dan."

He shuddered, gasped, and lay still.

Now that the shooting was over, a crowd was quickly gathering. Several men grabbed my shoulders and ankles to lift me from the ground. A few moments later they carried me into the doctor's office.

"Got a patient for you, Doc Carstairs," one of them said.

"Figured as much. I heard the shootin'," came a gruff answer. "Bring him inside and put him on the table. Any more comin'?"

"Nope. This hombre and his partners tried to rob the bank. Rest of 'em are dead," the voice replied. "So's Steve Malvern, the deputy, and Hal Conrad from the bank. Slater Hollister's got a nasty gash and bump on his head, but he insists he's all right."

"Who shot this man?" the doctor questioned.

"Caleb Sutton. He shot all those renegades. Five of 'em."

"Caleb Sutton. Well I'll be," Carstairs exclaimed. "He downed five men, you say?"

"Yep. Five. Never missed a shot. Who would've figured?" the voice answered. "Reckon ol' Cal was a Texas Ranger like he claimed after all. Well, we've gotta get back to the bank, Doc. Need to get those bodies to the undertaker."

"You'll have another one for him shortly," Carstairs answered. "I can't help this one."

Once the others had left, Carstairs opened my shirt to confirm what he already knew. He wiped the blood from my belly and tsked softly when he saw the bullet holes.

"There's not much I can do for you, mister," he said. "Not with two bullets in your intestines. About all I can offer is some whiskey or laudanum."

"No thanks," I gasped.

My guts were already on fire. Once that whiskey hit the agony would increase tenfold, and laudanum would do little to ease the pain.

"Whatever you'd prefer," Carstairs shrugged. "I'll give you some time to yourself. You might want to make peace with your Maker."

Carstairs left me alone. I lifted my head slightly so I could see the holes in my belly. There wasn't much blood oozing from them. I knew that meant nothing. Inside, I was bleeding heavily, the coppery taste of blood filling my mouth only adding to my torment.

I had no idea how long I'd been lying there, the pain in my gut steadily worsening and sweat pouring off my brow, when the door opened and another man was carried into the room. He was placed on the table alongside mine.

It was Caleb Sutton.

Carstairs bent over the old man and went to work on him.

"Doc?" I managed to rasp.

"Yeah, mister?"

"Is he…?"

"He's dying, if that's what you want to know," Carstairs snapped.

"Guess… I didn't miss him… after all," I grunted.

"Yes, you did," the doctor growled. "He wasn't shot. Apparently the excitement was too much for his heart. It's giving out. However, he's dying knowing he finally received the respect he should have gotten years ago."

Carstairs covered the dying old Ranger with a blanket. That done, he turned to me, took my pulse, and shook his head.

"You don't have much longer. Perhaps an hour at the most," he said. "Anything you want to say? Anyone I should notify?"

"No one, Doc," I whispered. "Just leave me be."

"Suit yourself," he replied. "I'll return shortly."

Once the doctor left, I glanced at Sutton. The old man sighed deeply, and a slight smile played across his face. As he breathed his last, a white light seemed to envelope his body. I knew he was at peace.

A sharp pain, far worse than any previous, ripped through my belly. I doubled up on my side, trying in vain to scream through the blood welling from my mouth. I realized there'd be no white light for me. The only thing I saw as I drew my final breath was an inky curtain of black as it descended, darker and more terrifying than the stormiest night.

Ambush at Railroad Canyon

1

Lucy Squires Taggart glared distastefully at her Texas Ranger husband while he dressed.

"Clay, please tell me you're not going to wear that shirt," she pleaded.

"Why not? What's wrong with this shirt?" Clay questioned.

"It's all faded and worn. The elbows are ready to wear through, and it's been patched too many times. And those old bloodstains. They'll never wash out completely," Lucy explained.

"What does it matter?" Clay protested as he buttoned the shirt closed and tied a bandanna around his neck. "I'm gonna be on the trail for weeks. In two days it'll be all dusty and sweat-stained anyway."

"I don't care. You're not starting out wearing that shirt," Lucy retorted. She rose from the bed and walked over to the bureau, from which she opened a drawer to remove a clean, neatly folded shirt.

"Here. Wear this one," she ordered.

"But I like the one I have on," Clay objected. "It's already broken in and comfortable. Besides, the renegades I'll be after sure won't care whether I'm wearin' fancy duds."

Lucy slid her hand inside the shirt Clay had donned and undid the buttons. She slipped the old shirt from his shoulders, then ran her hand gently over his chest and belly. She lifted her lips to his for a long, lingering kiss.

"For me. Please?" she whispered.

"All right. Anythin' for you, darlin'," Clay grinned. He took the fresh shirt and shrugged into it.

"Better?"

"Much better," Lucy stated. "I'll make breakfast while you feed Michael and wash up."

"You mean Mike," Clay corrected.

"I mean Michael," Lucy insisted. "And don't try sneaking that ragged old shirt into your saddlebags."

"All right." Clay gave in.

Clay buckled his gunbelt around his lean hips. Lucy wrapped a robe over the thin nightgown she wore. The gown's flimsy material and low cut revealed the fullness of her bosom, which even the heavier robe could not fully conceal. Clay's gaze followed her appreciatively as she walked from the room.

"I'm still takin' my favorite shirt," he muttered, tucking the garment behind his gunbelt. He went out the front door and headed for the small barn. Mike, his black and white overo, whinnied a greeting from his corral.

"Howdy, pardner. You ready to ride, or are you just hungry?" Clay called to his horse. Mike nickered a response, then when his rider ducked under the fence buried his muzzle in Clay's belly, causing the Ranger to grunt.

"Reckon you want a peppermint," Clay chuckled, when Mike nuzzled his hip pocket. "I've got one for you right here."

He slipped the gelding a candy, then filled his manger with oats and hay, adding fresh water to his bucket.

"Reckon you're all set for now," Clay told his horse, "Soon's I put on the feedbag myself we'll be headin' out."

By the time Clay finished caring for Mike and cleaning up, Lucy had breakfast on the table.

"You're gonna make me fat, honey," Clay warned, looking over the ham, bacon, eggs, hotcakes, and biscuits piled high on the table, along with a pot of steaming black coffee.

"I doubt that," Lucy answered. "I know how little good food you get on the trail, so I'm filling you up now. Whatever's left over I'll wrap so you can take it along."

Husband and wife settled down to their meal, eating mostly in silence.

"Clay, isn't there anything else you can tell me about your assignment?" Lucy asked, while they were lingering over last cups of coffee.

"Not a thing. All I know is I'm heading for the Panhandle. The railroad's having trouble up there. That's all Captain Morris told me. I'll have him get word to you if he's willing."

"That's all I can ask." Lucy sighed. "You should be leaving."

"Let me help you with the dishes," Clay offered.

"I'll take care of them. You shouldn't keep the captain waiting," Lucy answered. "And I have to get busy myself, or I'll be late for school. I can't keep the children waiting, or heaven knows what mischief they'll get into."

"I reckon you're right," Clay agreed. "Time I got movin'."

Lucy packed the leftover breakfast while Clay retrieved his saddlebags, then headed for the corral. He quickly saddled and bridled Mike.

Lucy soon joined them. She stroked Mike's nose, speaking softly to the big gelding.

"Michael, you make sure and bring Clay back safely to me," she told the pinto. "I've planted a big crop of carrots just for you."

Mike nickered, and nuzzled Lucy's cheek.

"You're gonna spoil him," Clay complained.

"Oh, like you don't, with all those peppermints," Lucy shot back.

"Guess I can't deny that," Clay conceded.

Clay took Lucy into his arms, holding her tightly. Their lips met, and they remained locked in their embrace for several minutes. Finally, Clay pulled away and swung into the saddle.

"Be careful, Clay," Lucy asked.

"I promise you that," Clay assured her. He leaned from the saddle to give Lucy one more kiss, then heeled Mike into a trot.

"I know you've got that old shirt in your saddlebags, Clay Taggart," Lucy called after him.

Clay turned in his saddle, to smile and wave in reply.

"Michael she calls you," Clay muttered, patting his overo's neck. "And you fall for that, horse. Never would've guessed a pretty face would turn your head."

Mike snorted explosively.

"I reckon you're right," Clay chortled. "I fell for that pretty face too."

While he rode along, the Ranger reflected on the changes to his life in the two months since he'd met the pretty schoolmarm down in Uvalde. As she'd told him would happen, they had indeed gotten married. Lucy had come to Austin with him and found another teaching position. And now Clay, who had always been content with a bunk in the Ranger Headquarters barracks, had scraped together enough money for a down payment on that small house and barn in Manchaca, a tiny hamlet on the outskirts of Austin. Lucy's feminine touch was evident throughout the house, with lace curtains at the windows, gingham covers on the bed, and flowers growing at the front door. Even Clay's guns and Stetson had been relegated to a corner of the kitchen.

Clay gave a rueful chuckle.

"Sun's already up an hour, Mike. We'd best pick up the pace."

He heeled Mike into a long-reaching gallop.

2

"Looks like we're gonna have ridin' pards this trip, Mike," Clay observed as he reined up in front of Ranger Headquarters, dismounted, and looped Mike's reins over the hitchrail. He recognized the two mounts already nosing the rail, Dade French's steeldust, Spook, and Dusty, Jim Huggins' long-legged chestnut.

Clay entered the building and strode down the hallway to Captain Joseph Morris's office. Huggins and French were already seated. The captain looked up from behind his desk when Clay walked in.

"See boys, told you when a man gets married you just can't count on him," Morris joked.

"I reckon that means me too, Cap'n," Jim Huggins laughed. The veteran sergeant was married, with a daughter and son.

"Don't forget, you've also got a wife, Cap'n," Clay retorted.

"Please don't remind me," Morris sighed. "Dade here's the only one of us with sense enough not to get hitched."

"Boy howdy, that's for certain," Dade agreed. He took a puff on his quirly. "No female's gonna tie me down."

"I wouldn't bet a hat on it," Clay chuckled.

"That's enough discussion of the marital state," Morris ordered. "Clay, pour yourself a cup of coffee and pull up a chair."

"All right."

Clay took a mug from the shelf, lifted the battered coffeepot from the stove in the corner, and poured the mug brimful. He settled into a cane bottom chair.

Morris opened the manila folder on his desk. He put on a pair of pince-nez spectacles to scan its contents, then leaned back in his chair. He lit his pipe and took a long pull, sending a blue smoke ring toward the ceiling.

"You boys are headin' for the lower Panhandle. There's a heap of trouble brewin' up there."

"What kind of trouble?" Dade asked.

"Indian trouble, and outlaw trouble. Is there any other kind?" Morris replied.

"Women trouble," Dade laughed.

"You're not gonna have time to worry about that kind of trouble," Morris assured him.

"I'm kinda surprised to hear talk of Indian trouble. The Comanch' haven't been a problem for quite some time," Jim said.

"Well, from the reports I've gotten, they're raidin' again," Morris explained. "However, that's not your main assignment. The Army's still supposed to be handling the Comanches. You'll just try'n round up any you might stumble across."

"That leaves the outlaws," Clay answered.

"It sure does. You'll have your hands filled with them," Morris snapped. He turned and pointed to the wall map behind him.

"You know folks are startin' to settle up that way, and counties are bein' organized. One of those is Scurry County. Its seat is a town called Snyder. However, there's no law to speak of in that whole region, so the settlers are pretty much at the mercy of any renegades preyin' on 'em."

"So you want us to round up those renegades and quiet things down," Jim said.

"That, and more."

Morris traced a line on the map with his finger.

"There's a railroad building along this route. Plans are to extend the line into New Mexico, then north to Denver, although I think the backers are bein' real optimistic believing they'll ever build all the way to California. I figure their road will end up bein' absorbed by the Texas and Pacific before too long. In the meantime, their trains are bein' robbed on a regular basis. Their construction crews are also bein' harassed, by both Comanches and renegade whites. Besides the settlers who've lost their lives, several railroaders have been killed. The railroad's asked for our help. I want you to stop the robberies and those attacks."

"Plus any other Indians or desperadoes we might find," Clay grinned. "Seems simple enough."

"These things are never as easy as they appear. You know that, Clay," Morris chided.

"I reckon that's so, Cap'n," Clay conceded.

"That's it? Dade asked.

"That's enough, ain't it?" Morris retorted.

"I figure it is. Let's get ridin'," Jim said. He and the others stood up.

"Vaya con Dios, men," Morris said. "Watch your backs."

"And our guts," Dade replied, with a thin smile. "I'm not overly fond of takin' a bullet, from either front or back."

"I mean it. Be careful," Morris insisted.

"Count on it," Clay replied.

Morris stood at his desk to watch the three men untie their horses, mount, and lope down Congress Avenue. Once they were out of sight, he turned back toward his desk. He ran a hand through his graying hair, started for the stove, then changed his mind.

"I don't need coffee. I need a drink," he muttered. He opened the bottom drawer of his desk to pull out a bottle and glass.

Morris filled the tumbler, downed its contents, and refilled it. His frosty blue-gray eyes took on a troubled expression. He gazed at the tumbler's amber contents for a moment, then tossed them down.

"Wish I could be ridin' with them," he muttered. "I've got a feelin' they'll have their hands full. Sure hope they can handle whatever's thrown their way."

3

The three men riding out of Austin gave no outward sign of being Texas Rangers. Their garb was that of the common drifting cowpoke, faded shirts and jeans, bandannas, leather vests, scuffed boots, and sweat-stained Stetsons. Rangers wore no uniforms, and few wore badges, although Huggins, Taggart, and French carried silver stars on silver circles they'd hand-carved from Mexican ten peso coins in their shirt pockets, out of sight until needed.

Taggart was tall and lanky, with dark brown hair and eyes. French was slightly shorter than average, with a wiry build and swarthy complexion. With his jet black hair and eyes, he was often mistaken for a Mexican or half-breed Indian. He found that useful for undercover work, playing those roles to perfection. Huggins was the veteran of the trio. He was also tall and lean, his brown hair running to gray at the temples.

They set a steady pace on their northwestward run. With two hundred and fifty miles to their destination, it would take nearly a week of hard riding before they reached the lower Panhandle.

One day's ride out of Roscoe they settled into the best campsite they'd found since leaving Austin, a grassy hollow alongside a small creek. Scattered boulders sheltered the hollow and blocked the steady wind. The tired men cared for their horses, ate a quick supper, then rolled in their blankets.

"Man, I can hardly wait to reach town so I can sleep in a hotel room and get some good chuck," Dade commented.

"Along with a bath and shave," Clay added.

"Our horses can use a good grainin' and rest too," Huggins noted. "Now let's get some shut-eye."

They were soon sleeping.

Sometime later, Clay was awakened by a sixth sense warning of danger. The usual stirrings of the night creatures were silent. He quietly slid his Colt from the holster alongside him, then glanced at his partners. Dade and Jim were also awake, staring into the darkness.

Clay could make out several vague figures slipping through the dark in their direction. Noiselessly they approached, wraithlike. Two were heading for the Rangers' picketed horses.

"Comanches!" Clay hissed. He leveled his Colt at one nearing the horses and fired. The Comanche screamed, then collapsed with Clay's bullet in his side.

Instantly the other warriors opened fire at the Rangers, some with rifles, the others showering arrows down on the camp. The Rangers returned fire, and three more of their attackers went down.

Dade grunted when an arrow tore along his ribs. His return shot knocked another Indian off his feet.

One of the braves climbed a boulder and leapt at Jim, a long-bladed knife in his hand. Jim whirled and fired, his bullet catching the Comanche in the belly while still in mid-air. The Comanche shrieked and crumpled to the dirt, writhing. Jim put a finishing shot into his chest.

As quickly as they had appeared, the Comanches retreated, fading into the night.

"You both all right?" Clay called.

"I'm fine," Jim answered.

"Seem to be," Dade responded. "An arrow scraped my side, but it ain't much. Reckon they'll be back?"

"I doubt it, but we'd better keep a close watch just in case," Clay stated. "Meantime, let's check these dead ones."

Guns still at the ready, they examined the bodies. Jim whistled in surprise when he rolled the Comanche he'd shot onto his back.

"This one ain't a full-blooded Comanch'," he exclaimed. "Look at his eyes. They're blue."

"Hair's light for an Indian, too," Dade added. "Looks like we might have some white men runnin' with these renegades."

"Else he's a half-breed, or a white who was captured as a boy and's been livin' with the Comanches," Clay noted. "Kinda like Quanah Parker, one of their great chiefs. His father was an Indian, but his mother was a captured white woman."

"You're right," Jim agreed. "At least we don't have to worry about these botherin' anyone else."

"What're we gonna do with 'em?" Dade questioned.

Clay looked at the gray of the false dawn streaking the eastern horizon.

"It's not that long to sunup," he observed. "We'll just leave 'em here. Their compadres'll come back for them, since Indians don't like leavin' their dead behind."

"Makes sense," Jim agreed. "However, in case those others have revenge on their minds, I suggest we ride out right now, before they come back with reinforcements."

"That's not a bad idea," Clay admitted.

Moments later, their horses were saddled and the Rangers were back on the trail.

4

It was early the next evening when they reached Roscoe. For a Wednesday night, the town was surprisingly busy. The road was filled with men and women, the boardwalks packed shoulder to shoulder. Men jostled each other as they forced their way through the crowd.

One drunken railroader stumbled into Mike. Clay's normally placid pinto pinned back his ears and bit the man's shoulder, ripping away a chunk of flesh.

"Hey, you! Your horse..." The railroader started to challenge Mike's rider, but wilted under Clay's steady gaze. Muttering under his breath, he turned, and melted back into the crowd.

"This town's sure a rip-roarin' place," Dade observed. "Wonder why?"

"Dunno, but we'll find out. There's the marshal's office."

Jim pointed to a makeshift office and jail, a block away.

They rode up to the building, dismounted, and looped their horses' reins over the rail. They stepped inside to find a young, harried-looking deputy.

"Don't tell me you three have a complaint," he muttered when they stepped through the door.

"Nope. We're Texas Rangers," Jim replied. "Sergeant Jim Huggins, Rangers Clay Taggart and Dade French."

"Rangers! I'm sure glad to see you," the deputy exclaimed. "I'm Pete Townsend. I've got my hands full, as you probably guessed, from that mob outside."

"Seems a mite rowdy out there all right," Clay noted. "What's the big ruckus about?"

"The railroad's finally got the trackbed finished from here to Snyder, so they've given all their workers the day off tomorrow to celebrate, and a bonus besides. Then they start layin' rails the day after."

"Looks like they've started celebratin' a bit early," Dade chuckled.

"You don't know the half of it," Townsend replied. "That's why I'm glad for your help. You sure got here at the right time."

"Well, I hate to disappoint you, deputy," Jim answered, "but we're only stoppin' here for the night, then headin' toward Snyder in the morning. We'll do what we can while we're in town, but we're after the renegades doin' the killin' and stealin' in these parts, not drunken railroaders."

"That's not the news I wanted to hear," Townsend complained. "Mebbe you can at least help me keep a lid on this town tonight."

"We'll be glad to," Jim answered. "Soon as we get our broncs settled in and some grub in our bellies."

"All right," Townsend agreed. "Livery stable's two blocks down on the left. Tell ol' Zeke there I said the town'll pay for puttin' up your horses. Far as chuck, head for the Kansas Café. It's across from the livery. Best steaks within a hundred miles. The hotel's right across the street. I'll make sure they hold a room. You gonna want some drinks?"

"We could be talked into a few," Dade grinned.

"Then once you're done with supper, head for the Gilded Lily, another block past the stable. I'll meet you there in say, two hours."

"That'll be enough time for us to finish," Clay answered. "See you then, deputy."

∧∧∧∧∧∧∧∧∧∧∧∧

The Rangers had finished their suppers and were in the Gilded Lily Saloon, nursing beers, when Townsend entered the barroom, accompanied by another man. They headed straight for the Rangers' table.

"Rangers, got a gentleman here who's been waitin' for you to show up," Townsend announced. "Jasper Wheeler, chief construction superintendent of the Roscoe, Snyder, and Pacific railroad. He just got back on the supply train. Mr. Wheeler, Rangers Huggins, Taggart, and French."

"That's Jim, Clay, and Dade," Huggins replied. "We're glad to meet you. Please, sit down and join us."

"The same. And make it Jasper," the railroader responded. "Pete knows that. I don't know why he's being so formal."

He took the chair alongside Taggart.

"First time introduction," the deputy shrugged. "Jasper's got a proposition which might solve both our problems."

"What do you mean?" Clay asked.

"I'll get to that in a minute," Wheeler answered before the deputy could respond. "First, I need a drink. How about refills for you Rangers? And Pete?"

"I could stand a beer," Townsend nodded.

"Another one'd go down good," Jim agreed.

"One more for me, too," Clay added.

"Another shot of rye here," Dade concluded.

"Fine." Wheeler signaled to the bartender, and placed the order. Once their drinks had been brought, he lit a cigar, leaned back in his chair, and explained Townsend's statement.

"Pete tells me you men are heading for Snyder in the morning," he began.

"That's right," Jim confirmed.

"There's no need for that. Pete's already told you about the celebration we've planned for tomorrow."

"He has," Jim replied.

"There will be very few men in Snyder until the day after tomorrow. Since most of our supplies, and the crew's quarters, are still here in Roscoe, we've brought all the men back here, except for a few watchmen in Snyder. The day after tomorrow several work trains will be headed back there. You Rangers can ride with me to Snyder in my private car. I'll have a boxcar prepared for your horses. That way you can stay here and help Pete keep things under control."

"You expectin' that much trouble?" Clay asked.

"Not really, but the men have been working hard and have quite a bit of steam to blow off, so there are bound to be a few quarrels. I'd appreciate your help in keeping those from getting out of hand. By staying and taking the train, you'll be able to help out here and save a day's riding. The train will get you to Snyder in only a couple of hours, compared to a full day on horseback. You'll reach your destination early Friday morning rather than tomorrow night, which won't make much difference as far as your assignment is concerned. What do you think?"

"It sounds reasonable," Dade answered. "However, the decision is the sergeant's. How about it, Jim?"

"Seems like a good idea," Huggins answered. "We'll go along with it. Pete, you still need our help tonight?"

"I don't think so," the deputy answered. "Things are settlin' down. The real shindig doesn't start until tomorrow, and you boys have been ridin' hard the past several days. I can handle any trouble tonight. Y'all just take it easy until tomorrow."

"Fine. We'll be at your office at seven," Jim stated.

"That's settled," Wheeler concluded. "I have some final details to attend to, so I'll take my leave. Any more refreshments you would like are on the Roscoe, Snyder, and Pacific. I'll instruct Moses at the bar to that effect."

"Not quite so fast," Clay interrupted. "We need to discuss the attacks on your men."

"We'll talk about that on the train," Wheeler replied. "Until tomorrow, gentlemen. Good night."

"I've got to make my rounds, so I'll be leavin' too," Townsend added. "See you in the mornin'."

After the railroader and deputy left, Clay, Jim, and Dade lingered over a few more drinks.

"I think I'm gonna sit in on a poker game," Dade decided. "Either of you care to join me?"

"I might play a hand or two," Jim agreed. "How about you, Clay?"

"I'll skip it this time. I'm bushed," Clay answered. "Think I'll head back to our room and turn in."

"Okay. We'll see you in the morning," Jim said.

"We'll try not to wake you when we come in," Dade added. "G'night, Clay."

"'Night, both of you."

Clay headed across the street to the hotel, got the key to their room, and headed upstairs. Leaving the door unlocked for his partners, he undressed, then crawled under the blankets. He was asleep the moment his head hit the pillow.

∧∧∧∧∧∧∧∧∧∧∧∧

All three men were up with the sun the next morning. Clay was at the washstand shaving, while Jim and Dade were still stretched out under the covers.

"How late'd you get in last night?" Clay asked. "I never heard a thing after I fell into bed."

"Not too late," Jim answered. "The card game broke up soon after you left. But we do have another friendly wager to settle."

"How's that?"

"Dade, you want to explain it?"

"Sure," French agreed. "Clay, those railroaders started braggin' last night about how tough they are, and how any one of 'em could lick any of us Rangers in a standup fight. You know we couldn't let that pass."

"So, which one of you fought?"

"Neither. That's where you come into the picture."

"What?" Clay turned and glared at his partners.

"You're the best scrapper of the three of us," Dade explained. "We challenged their best fighter to a boxing match, you and him. It's set for eleven this morning at the livery stable. One of the corrals will be used for a ring."

"You're both loco if you think I'm gettin' myself beat to a pulp just so you can win a bet," Clay snapped. "Either that, or you had more red-eye than I realized. Forget it. If you want to brawl with one of those hombres, do it yourselves."

"Clay, you have to fight. Think of the reputation of the Rangers," Dade insisted. "If you don't go in that ring, we'll be laughingstocks."

"I'm thinkin' of my hide," Clay retorted.

"You're not turnin' yellow, are you Clay?" Jim broke in. "Besides, the hombre who's takin' you on ain't all that tough. You'll win, easy."

"Last time I leave you two alone while I get some shut-eye," Clay grumbled. "Should've known better. You're not givin' me any choice, are you?"

"Reckon we're not," Jim admitted.

"Besides, it's easy money. Those railroaders have cash to burn with those bonuses in their pockets. We'll clean up," Dade said.

With a sigh, Clay gave in.

"All right. But you'd better not be lyin' about my chances."

"Not at all, pard," Dade assured him.

"We'll even buy your breakfast," Jim added. "Just don't eat too much, in case you catch a punch in the gut. That wouldn't be a pretty sight."

"Wonderful. The condemned man gets a last meal," Clay muttered.

"Jim's just joshin'. You've got nothing to worry about," Dade replied.

"That's what scares me," Clay answered.

∧∧∧∧∧∧∧∧∧∧∧∧

The Rangers and Deputy Townsend made several patrols of Roscoe. So far things had been fairly uneventful, the deputy only having had to break up one fight.

"The day's still young. Once these railroad men have some more whiskey in their bellies things'll heat up," Townsend predicted. "Right now, a lot of them are waitin' for the boxing match."

"Speakin' of which, it's quarter to eleven. Reckon we'd better head for the stable," Jim said.

They started down the street.

"Sure glad I'm refereein' this fight, instead of takin' on Pat Doyle," Townsend noted.

"What do you mean, Pete?" Clay demanded.

"Just that…" Pete stopped short when Jim and Dade glared at him. "Just that I…"

"Never mind. I get your drift. Dade, Jim, I thought you said I'd have no problem."

"You won't," Dade attempted to assure Clay. "Doyle's a pushover. He won't last five minutes against you."

"Your pardner's right," Pete agreed.

"Somehow, I'm not buyin' that," Clay retorted.

"You're not backin' out, are you?" Jim asked.

"Reckon it's too late," Clay answered.

They reached the alleyway, and turned down it to the stable.

"Looks like quite a crowd," Jim remarked.

The makeshift ring was surrounded by spectators, three deep.

"Here comes the Rangers!" one of them shouted. The crowd parted to allow Clay and his companions access to the corral.

Patrick Doyle was already in the ring. The big Irishman had jet black hair and bright blue eyes. He was taller than Taggart by a good three inches, and outweighed the Ranger by at least twenty pounds. Doyle had already peeled off his shirt. His arms, shoulders, and chest bulged with muscles developed by years of laying track for the railroads. His body had not an ounce of fat.

"That's who I'm fightin'?" Clay exclaimed.

"That's him," Dade confirmed.

"The only way I'll beat that hombre is with both barrels of a ten gauge shotgun," Clay answered.

"He's not all that big," Jim replied.

"For a live oak," Clay retorted. He unbuckled his gunbelt and stripped off his shirt, bandanna, and Stetson, then handed them to Huggins.

"You're gonna have a hard time explainin' to Lucy why she's a new widow," he warned the sergeant, as he ducked under the fence and into the corral.

The spectators, seeing the two men together for the first time, began betting heavily on the railroader.

Pete Townsend called both men to the center of the ring.

"Men, there won't be any rounds. You'll fight until one of you is knocked out or quits," he explained. "The rules are simple. No gouging, kicking, biting, or hitting below the belt... unless I'm lookin' the other way. Good luck."

He backed from between the combatants.

Clay and Doyle circled warily for a few moments, each sizing up his opponent. Doyle threw the first punch, a left jab to Clay's chin. Clay ducked under the blow and shot a right hook to Doyle's stomach. The railroader barely flinched at the impact.

Clay landed a left to Doyle's jaw, then Doyle sank his fist deep into the Ranger's belly. All the air was driven from Clay's lungs, his guts feeling as if they'd been turned inside out. He jackknifed into a powerful right to his chin. The blow straightened him up, and Doyle slammed another huge fist into Clay's belly. Clay folded to the dirt, then rolled onto his back.

His head roaring, gasping for breath, Clay was vaguely aware of Townsend beginning the ten count. He lay there, helpless against the pain, struggling to draw air into his lungs. When Townsend reached seven, Clay managed to roll onto his stomach, pushed himself to his hands and knees, and forced himself to his feet just before Townsend counted ten.

Doyle came at Clay again, aiming another left at the Ranger's head. Clay avoided the punch and landed one of his own, a right that opened a cut over the railroader's left eye. Before Doyle could recover, Clay landed another blow to his right eye, which quickly swelled shut.

Doyle smashed a left into Clay's chest, staggering him. Clay countered with a hook to Doyle's ribs. Infuriated, Doyle swung wildly at Clay's head, missing when Clay ducked under his huge fist.

Both men stood toe to toe, hammering each other unmercifully. Doyle was half-blinded by his closed right eye and the blood flowing into his left. Clay was bleeding heavily from a slice one of Doyle's punches had opened along his right cheekbone.

Doyle landed another hard punch to Clay's midsection, a left hook which sank wrist-deep into the Ranger's belly. The impact folded Clay over Doyle's fist and lifted him a foot into the air. Somehow he managed to stagger backwards and avoid the railroader's following blow.

Doyle closed in to finish Clay off. Clay ducked under a punch which would have taken his head half-off, to land several short, vicious jabs to Doyle's gut. The blows had their effect on the tiring railroader. He grunted with pain and began to jackknife.

Clay took one step back and, with the last of his strength, launched a wicked uppercut at Doyle's chin. The punch took Doyle in the soft tissue behind the jawbone, where throat and chin meet. Doyle gagged, fought for air that wasn't there, and toppled backwards, eyes glazing. He crashed to the ground and lay unmoving.

Clay staggered to the fence and leaned against it, arms draped over the top rail. He stood, chest heaving, while Townsend counted over Doyle. Once he reached ten, Townsend hurried to Clay, to lift the Ranger's left arm in victory.

"The winner by a knockout! Texas Ranger Clay Taggart!"

The spectators reacted with cheers for the victor and moans for their lost money. Dade and Jim rushed into the ring to join their partner.

"Told you that you'd beat him, Clay," Dade crowed.

"Yeah. That was some fight," Jim agreed. "We sure cleaned up, thanks to you, pardner."

"What are you gonna do now, Clay?" Dade questioned.

"Soon as Doyle comes to, I'm gonna buy him a drink," Clay answered. "He's earned it."

5

"You don't look all that much the worse for wear, Clay, considering that was one of the toughest boxing matches I've ever seen," Jasper Wheeler noted when the Rangers boarded his private car the next morning, and settled into plush green velvet chairs. "You cost me quite a bit of money, by the way. I bet a bundle on Doyle."

"Thanks." Clay attempted a grin that was more of a lopsided grimace. "It helped that your men didn't stir things up too much last night."

Despite Pete Townsend's dire predictions, the railroaders' celebration, while rowdy, had only been marred by a few minor altercations.

"I warned them to stay in line," Wheeler explained.

"It worked," Dade laughed.

The locomotive's whistle blew, and the train lurched into motion.

"We'll be having breakfast shortly. After that you may ask me all the questions you wish," Wheeler noted.

The Rangers enjoyed a sumptuous breakfast while the train chugged along. After they were finished, and enjoying a last cup of thick black coffee, Dade and Wheeler puffing on cigars, the superintendent finally allowed them to question him.

"Do you have any idea who's behind the attacks on the railroad?" Jim asked.

"Not a clue," Wheeler admitted. "Everyone seems to be in favor of the line, along with the progress and prosperity it will bring to this entire region. We hope to eventually extend our tracks all the way to Denver."

"Well, someone sure wants to stop you," Clay replied.

"Perhaps not. Don't forget, settlers and others have also been robbed or murdered," Wheeler pointed out. "We too may just be victims of those same gangs."

"I don't think so. Not from the information Captain Morris provided," Jim disagreed.

"Jim's right. There's been too many attacks on your crews," Dade noted. "What have you done about that?"

"What we can, which isn't adequate," Wheeler conceded. "My men are railroaders, not fighters. I have Patrick Doyle, the man Clay fought yesterday, in charge of defending the crews, but he's not a rifleman. None of us are, which is why I'm counting on you Rangers."

"We'll do everything we can to protect your men and get to the bottom of this," Clay responded.

"Sure would be great if we had an idea where to start, however," Jim added.

"I'm confident you'll solve this dilemma," Wheeler replied. "In the meantime, why don't you just relax and enjoy your ride. We'll be in Snyder in ninety minutes or so. We're still running the trains more slowly than we will once all the detail work is finished."

"Sounds like a good idea to me," Clay said. He stretched out his legs and tilted his Stetson over his battered face.

Clay and his partners dozed for a bit. About an hour later, Clay awakened and glanced out his window. A stagecoach was racing at breakneck speed on the road paralleling the tracks. The driver was whipping his team mercilessly, urging them to even greater speed.

"Jim, Dade. Look out there."

Clay pointed to the coach.

"What in blue blazes is that fool doing?" Dade asked.

"Looks like the idiot's tryin' to outrun this train," Clay answered.

"There's a crossing about a mile ahead," Wheeler observed. "It appears that driver is trying to beat us there."

"He should be shot for abusin' those horses like that," Jim said. "When he rolls into Snyder I'm gonna have a long discussion with him… and he sure won't enjoy it."

"If he reaches that crossing at the same time as this train there won't be anything of him left to talk with," Clay responded.

They watched with growing trepidation while the stagecoach hurtled alongside the train, the jehu ignoring the engineer's frantic blasts of the whistle.

"He's gonna kill himself and everyone on that stage," Clay muttered.

"Darn fool!" Dade added.

The locomotive rumbled over the crossing just ahead of the stage. The coach's driver pulled back hard on the reins, causing the leaders to rear. They stopped just before crashing into the tender.

"I'm not gonna talk to him. I'm gonna pound some sense into him," Jim snapped. "And make sure he loses his job."

"I'll finish what you start," Clay added.

"What you just observed won't be a problem much longer," Wheeler said. "Once we start regular service, the stage line will be out of business. We have offered all their workers employment with the railroad; however, I don't believe that particular individual is suitable."

"I'd agree with you," Clay answered. "Endangering folks like that. Jasper, how much longer until we reach Snyder?"

"About thirty minutes," Wheeler replied. "I've already sent word ahead to reserve a room for you and stalls for your horses. You'll be settled in no time."

"We appreciate that," Jim answered, "But we need to make a stop about five miles before town."

"Oh? Why?" Wheeler asked.

"We're gonna drop off Dade and his horse. He's gonna head out and do some pokin' around on his own," Jim answered.

"That's right. I'm now Kiowa Dave, half-breed renegade," Dade grinned.

"Dade's real good at playin' a half-breed or Mexican," Jim explained. "That way, he can often find out information a Ranger never could."

"I understand," Wheeler answered.

A half-hour before reaching Snyder, the train ground to a stop. Dade descended from the coach and retrieved Spook from the boxcar, then disappeared into the brush.

The remainder of the journey was uneventful. Once the train pulled into Snyder, Clay and Jim unloaded their horses and left them at the stable. They settled in chairs in front of the newly-built hotel to await the stage's arrival.

Jim and Clay never did get the opportunity to confront the stage driver about his reckless conduct. When the coach's team stopped just short of crashing into the train, the shotgun guard, infuriated at the driver's risking the lives of everyone on board, had grabbed the reins from the driver's hands and sent him flying from the seat with an oath and a well-placed kick to his rump, along with a stern warning never to show his face in town. The guard then completed the run to Snyder.

Not knowing when or where the renegades might strike next, the Rangers decided on a random pattern of accompanying the track crews, alternating with patrolling the area.

"What about your partner?" Wheeler asked, as Clay and Jim prepared to depart Snyder.

"Don't worry about Dade," Clay assured him. "He'll find us when he needs to."

"All right. Good luck. And be careful," Wheeler urged.

"We will. See you in a few days," Jim answered.

6

Two days after leaving town, they came across the hoofprints of several horses, both shod and unshod.

"What d'ya think, Clay?" Jim asked.

Clay dismounted and studied the tracks.

"I'd say we've either got a bunch of renegades, Indian and white, or else some Comanches who've been raidin' and stealin' horses," he answered. "Either way it means trouble."

"Looks to me like they're not all that far ahead of us," Jim observed. "Let's see if we can catch up to 'em."

Clay climbed back into his saddle. They pushed their horses into a hard gallop.

Two miles later, they topped a rise to see their quarry surrounding a small ranch. They were keeping up a steady volley of gunshots. Several men lay dead in the yard, while from the house others were returning the raiders' gunfire.

"Let's even up the odds a bit," Jim said.

"All right," Clay agreed.

They pulled the Winchesters from their scabbards and urged their horses down the hill at a dead run. Halfway down the slope, they pulled in the horses and opened fire, raking the raiders with a hail of lead. Three of them were knocked from their saddles, with Ranger slugs in their backs. Others turned to meet the unexpected threat, only to fall with bullets in their chests.

Another rider burst from the scrub, adding his own accurate shooting to that of the Rangers. He put a bullet through the belly of a renegade who had drawn a bead on Clay's stomach, just as he pulled the trigger. His aim spoiled by the slug's impact, the outlaw's shot went wide as he slumped over his horse's neck, then tumbled to the dirt.

Completely rattled by the unexpected attack from behind, the remaining outlaws whirled their horses and ran. Two of the survivors returned the Rangers' fire, only to be cut down. The rest disappeared into the thick brush.

"Leave 'em go," Jim ordered. "They could pick us off one by one real easy in those thickets. Let's check on the folks inside."

Their unexpected ally reined up alongside them.

"Bet you're surprised to see me," Dade French grinned.

"You might say that," Jim drawled. "Where the devil did you come from?"

"And where in blue blazes did you get that outfit you're wearin'?" Clay demanded. "You're dang lucky one of us didn't plug you."

Their Ranger partner was clad in buckskin leggings and moccasins, his upper torso only half-covered by a open leather vest. A battered U.S. Army campaign hat was perched on his head, while he carried a bow and quiver slung over one shoulder.

"We'd better explain ourselves to these ranchers first," Jim ordered. "They'll still be a mite jumpy."

With the shooting stopped and the raiders fled, several men had emerged from the house. They had their guns trained on the threesome.

"Appreciate the help, but would you hombres mind statin' your business," one of them called.

"We're Texas Rangers," Clay answered. "Came across the tracks of those renegades and followed 'em. Seems like we caught up to 'em in the nick of time."

"I reckon you did," the rancher replied. " You fellas saved out bacon, that's for certain. You're on the Triangle H. I'm Bob Harte. These are my boys, Beau and Brent. My wife Ellie and daughter Sally are inside."

"Sergeant Jim Huggins, Rangers Clay Taggart and Dade French," Jim responded.

"Glad you came along. But Mister, you sure don't look like any Ranger I've ever seen," Harte challenged Dade.

"I'll explain as soon as we take care of things here," Dade answered.

"Once the wounded are inside and treated, we'll help you bury the dead," Jim added.

Clay dismounted. He walked up to one of the dead raiders and rolled the body onto its back.

"Looks like we've got another mixed bunch. This jasper's white," he noted.

"I figured as much," Jim replied. "Let's get to work."

"All right. Lemme introduce you to the rest of my men," Harte replied. "You can put your broncs into that second corral."

Mike, Dusty, and Spook were unsaddled and turned into the enclosure.

The introductions were completed, the wounded taken into the house and cared for. The dead cowboys from the Triangle H were buried in carefully dug graves, the dead outlaws dumped into a common pit, but prayers spoken over all. Once that was done, the Rangers and the crew from the Triangle H washed up. Dade changed back into his normal trail garb. Everyone headed inside for supper.

Mrs. Harte and her daughter had set a table overflowing with beefsteaks, potatoes, vegetables, bread, butter, and plenty of hot coffee. They refused to allow any discussion until everyone had eaten their fill.

After the meal, they settled in the parlor with cups of coffee, most of the men smoking.

"All right, Dade. You've stalled long enough. Explain those Indian duds," Jim demanded.

"Sure," Dade agreed. "I was sleepin' a couple nights back when a big Comanche warrior jumped me. He nearly got my scalp, but I managed to stick my knife between his ribs. I was gettin' ready to roll his body into a ravine when I decided I should dress in his clothes, since they make me look even more like a half-breed. Figured I might have a better chance of stumblin' across some of the hombres we're after ridin' around like a part Indian, part white man. I stripped out of my clothes, stuck 'em in my saddlebags, and put on that Indian's outfit."

"How'd you find us?" Clay asked.

"Pure dumb luck," Dade explained. "I happened upon the tracks of those renegades' horses, same ones you were following. It was just fortunate timing we all turned up in the same place at the same time."

"We'd better explain things to the Hartes," Clay said.

"We are a mite puzzled," Bob admitted.

"We've been assigned to track down the hombres attacking the railroad's crews building the line to Snyder," Clay explained. "Also, to take care of any other renegades we chance to find."

"I decided to have Dade work incognito, since he can pass as a half-breed or Mexican real easy," Jim took up the narrative. "He's done that many times. We split up, and Dade's been poking around on his own. As he said, it was coincidence we all arrived here at just about the same time."

"A very fortunate coincidence," Sally Harte added. She was gazing unabashedly at the darkly handsome French.

"You really look much better in your regular clothes, sir," she said.

"Why, thank you, ma'am, but my name's Dade, not sir."

Sally blushed.

"Bob, would any of you have an idea who might be tryin' to stop the railroad, or why?" Jim asked the rancher.

"Not a clue," Harte admitted.

"Everyone's real pleased at the idea of the line goin' through," Brent added.

"My brother's right," Beau concurred. "It'll make shippin' our cattle a lot easier, only havin' to drive 'em to a railhead in Snyder, plus getting supplies should be faster and easier."

"We'll also be able to travel without having to depend on the stage line," Ellie added.

"Everyone around here feels that way?" Clay asked.

"Everyone we know," Bob confirmed.

"Well, someone's sure tryin' to shut down the railroad," Dade answered. "All we have to do is figure out who."

"You can't do much about that tonight," Bob replied, "So why don't you Rangers bunk here until mornin'?"

"Sounds reasonable," Jim agreed. "We'll just spread our blankets out in the bunkhouse, if that's agreeable."

"It sure is," Bob said. "You'll get a good night's sleep, and a good breakfast before you ride out."

Clay yawned and stretched.

"Speakin' of sleep, I'm ready for some."

"I reckon we all are. Let's call it a night," Jim answered.

The next couple of weeks were uneventful, at least as far as the Rangers were concerned. With no incidents, the railroad's tracks pushed steadily northwestward. Dade continued his solitary undercover surveillance, occasionally bringing in a renegade he'd found and arrested. Clay and Jim also made several arrests during their patrols.

Clay and Jim were eating supper with most of the track crew when Jasper Wheeler entered the mess tent. The construction superintendent filled a plate with buffalo steak, potatoes, and beans. He added a cup of coffee, placed that on a tray along with his meal, and sat alongside the Rangers.

"I appreciate the fine job you Rangers have been doin'," he remarked. "Things sure have quieted down."

"You haven't finished the line yet," Clay pointed out.

"That's true, but we are nearing the finish," Wheeler answered. "By the way, where's your partner? I haven't seen him around."

"Dade? Don't worry about him. He's out there somewhere, keepin' his eyes peeled," Jim replied. "He'll show up when we need him."

"Good. With your help holding off any more attacks, we've been layin' track real fast. We're even a bit ahead of schedule," Wheeler said. "I just hope the weather holds out, because in a few days we've got a big chore ahead of us."

"What do you mean?" Clay asked.

"We'll be pushin' through a long canyon. We've already completed a lot of leveling of the terrain in there, and we're finally done. We'll start placin' the tracks inside that canyon shortly."

"A canyon? How wide? How high are the sides?" Jim asked.

"It's not very wide at all," Wheeler answered. "There's enough room for two sets of tracks, although right now we'll only be laying one. There's anywhere from ten to fifty feet to spare on either side. I'd say the walls range from eighty to two hundred feet above the railbed."

"Which makes it a perfect spot for an ambush," Huggins observed.

"Or to blow up the walls and block the rails entirely," Clay added.

"Dang! I never thought of that!" Wheeler exclaimed. "You're both absolutely right."

"I figure we'd best ride out first thing tomorrow, and check that canyon out," Clay said.

"We'll have to contact Dade, too," Jim added. "Jasper, how far ahead is this place?"

"About seven miles."

"Good. We'll head there at first light."

"What should we do?" Wheeler asked.

"Just keep on workin'," Clay told him, "And keep a sharp watch."

"You can count on that," Wheeler assured him.

∧∧∧∧∧∧∧∧∧∧∧∧

By the time the sun was just clearing the eastern horizon the next morning, Clay and Jim were already in the saddle. They took their time, letting the horses set their own pace while their riders studied the surrounding landscape. A bit more than two hours later, they entered the rocky defile. Even though they weren't expecting any trouble, at least not yet, their skin crawled and the napes of their necks prickled, the hair standing on end when they rode into the canyon's shadowed mouth. The beetling cliffs seemed to close in on them. Even their normally unflappable horses were uneasy, prancing and snorting their displeasure. When their riders reined them in, Mike and Dusty kept up their fidgeting.

"This sure is the perfect spot for an ambush, Jim," Clay noted. "A few men up on those cliffs could pick off just about the entire crew."

"Worse. A few sticks of well-placed dynamite could bring the entire shebang crashing down," Jim answered.

"Let's find a way to the top and take a look around up there," Clay suggested.

"That's a good idea," Jim agreed. They put their horses into a walk, while they searched for a trail which would lead them out of the canyon.

Three-quarters of a mile later, they found the spot they were seeking.

"What d'ya think, Jim?"

"It looks like it could be a trail, but not much of one. Let's give it a try."

Jim urged a reluctant Dusty onto the narrow path. Clay and Mike followed closely behind.

The trail hugged the base of the cliff for some distance, then began a steep climb. In some spots the horses had to struggle to keep their footing on loose shale. In several places, the trail doubled back on itself, switchbacking along the rock face. By the time the Rangers were halfway up the cliff, the trail was barely wide enough for their horses to plant all four feet.

"You reckon we made a mistake?" Clay asked, while they gave their horses a short breather.

"Dunno, but I know one thing for certain, there's no turnin' back," Jim replied. "Only way to go is up."

And up they did go, for another hour, before the trail finally emerged onto a level shelf. A short distance later, they stopped on a flat tableland.

"I don't mind tellin' you, I never figured we'd get outta that spot in one piece," Clay said.

"Me neither," Jim agreed. "I thought sure we'd be lyin' in a million little pieces at the bottom of that slope. Let's rest a spell before we poke around up here."

Jim and Clay rode over to a small clump of redberry junipers. Jim headed Dusty toward one of the trees to tie him, then unsaddle. As he swung off the horse, an arrow whistled past and buried itself in a juniper's trunk, just above his head. Jim grabbed his Winchester from its scabbard and dove to his belly. Close behind him, Clay did the same, diving behind a cluster of low rocks. Both men scanned the terrain, searching for the Indian who'd shot that arrow.

Raucous laughter came from behind a fallen cottonwood log.

"Boy howdy, if I were a real Comanche or Kiowa you two hombres would have my arrows in your guts, and

I'd be scalpin' you right about now. You're gettin' mighty careless."

Dade French appeared from behind the log, bow in hand. He was still clad in the moccasins, leggings, vest, and cavalry hat he'd taken off the Comanche he'd killed.

"French, you no good…," Clay began. "Where'd you come from?"

"Over yonder." Dade waved toward the horizon. "Been doin' some scoutin'. How about you two?"

"Checkin' out this canyon for ambush sites. The railroad's gonna be pushin' through here in a few days," Jim answered. "We figure whoever's tryin' to stop the line will hit it somewhere around this spot."

Dade pulled his arrow from the juniper trunk.

"You're figurin' right," he answered. "I've been trailin' a bunch of men for the last few days. They been following the track-layin' crews. Day before yesterday, they met up with some others. They're holed up five or six miles east of here. They sure look like they're up to no good. And you'll never guess who's with 'em."

"Who?" Clay asked.

"The stagecoach driver who nearly ran his rig into the train," Dade answered. "That's not all. Dale Montague, the owner of the stage line, is also with them. It looks like Montague's the one behind all this trouble."

"Which makes sense," Jim replied. "Once the railroad goes through the stage line'll be out of business. Wheeler told me he offered Montague a manager's job, but that Montague turned him down flat. I guess he doesn't realize there's no way he'll ever stop progress. Sooner or later a railroad's bound to be built through here. If not this one, then another."

"We'd better stop him," Dade said.

"That's not as easy as it sounds," Clay replied. "We've got no proof against Montague, or anyone else, for that matter."

"So what's our next step?"

"We're gonna have to let 'em pull off their drygulchin', Dade," Jim answered, "and be ready for 'em when they do."

"Then we've got to make plans, right quick," Dade said.

Clay glanced up at the sun.

"It's just about noon," he said. "Why don't we have some chuck? We can work on what needs doin' while we chow down."

"That sounds good," Jim answered.

8

"I still don't like the way we've gotta handle this, not one bit," Jasper Wheeler protested. Three mornings later, he, Clay, and Jim were in the superintendent's private car, which was coupled to the end of a string of flat cars holding rails and ties. The locomotive pulling the work train was edging slowly into the canyon, while the track crew laid rail as quickly as possible.

"We're not exactly thrilled with bein' sittin' ducks either, Jasper, but we've got no choice," Clay answered.

"Clay's right," Jim concurred. "As we told you, those hombres have been watchin' us all along. They're pretty clever to be able to do that without me or Clay spottin' 'em. If they're that smart, they'd know for certain something was up if they didn't see us with the crews, or if a whole bunch of your men suddenly turned up missin'. We've got to lure 'em into a trap. With Dade and Pat Doyle comin' up from behind them when they make their move, that should be enough of a surprise to rattle 'em good. We'll make out all right."

"I hope you're assessment is accurate, Sergeant," Wheeler retorted. "Because if it's not, I'll be filing a complaint with Austin."

"If it's not, we'll most likely be dead," Jim replied, with a rueful chuckle. "In that case, your complaint to Headquarters would be the least of my worries."

"We'd better get ready, Jim," Clay said.

"I reckon you're right," Jim agreed. "Jasper, by the end of the day you'll either have your tracks through this canyon, or they'll be buried under tons of rock."

"That's real encouraging," Wheeler answered, his voice dripping with sarcasm.

Clay and Jim headed outside. They retrieved their horses from the care of a trackman, mounted, and began patrolling the right of way. For two hours, nothing happened... until a crackle of rifle fire marked the beginning of the ambush. Three trackman and a gandy dancer fell dead under the first volley of lead.

"Let 'em have it!" Clay shouted. He and Jim unshipped their rifles, and rode with reckless abandon straight for the cliff face. At the same time, a score of railroaders rose from where they'd lain hidden behind the rails on the flatcars, and returned the drygulchers' fire. From Wheeler's car, the sharp crack of a Winchester carbine indicated the superintendent had joined the fray.

Under the cover of the railroaders' fire, which was far more volume than accuracy, the two Rangers drew closer to the cliff base. They dove from their horses into the jumbled rocks at the bottom of the talus. From there, they could still see and fire back at the bushwhackers above, from the relative safety of the jagged boulders.

"Looks like the trackmen managed to pick off a few of 'em," Clay shouted, seeing several bodies sprawled on ledges overhead.

"Yeah, but that was pure luck," Jim shouted back. "I'll take it, though."

He levered his rifle and fired at a figure above. His bullet tore through a gunman's belly. The man screamed in terror as he grabbed his middle and jackknifed over the cliff. He landed five feet from Clay.

"Jim, I sure don't want to get squashed by one of those hombres you drop," Clay chuckled. He ducked when a bullet drove chips from the rocks just in front of him.

"If you don't keep your head down you won't have to worry about that. A slug'll take care of you," Jim retorted. He fired again, and another raider died with Ranger lead in his chest.

"We'd better hope Dade and Pat Doyle get their job done, or neither one of us is liable to get out of this fix," Clay shot back. He shot, and another raider tumbled over the rim of the canyon, with Clay's bullet in his stomach.

For what seemed an eternity, but in reality was less than thirty minutes, the battle raged. With both the Rangers and railroaders, and the outlaws, in good cover, it was difficult for either side to gain an advantage. After the first casualties, men were more cautious about coming from behind their shelter and exposing themselves to sudden lead death. While Clay, Jim, and the railroad men kept the raiders busy, Dade and Pat Doyle had their own hands full. They had come in behind the drygulchers, catching them by surprise. Several of their targets were dead or wounded, with the rest dug in atop the cliff.

"Whatever we do, Pat, we can't let anyone else get back to that plunger box!" Dade ordered. The outlaw band led by Dale Montague had rigged the cliff with dynamite. They had then lain in wait until the train entered the canyon, intending to explode the ledge and send tons of rocks cascading onto the tracks and men below. Only Dade's and Doyle's timely appearance had kept their plan from succeeding. Their first shots had knocked two men away from the plunger.

"Don't worry about that," Doyle called back. He aimed at a man drawing a bead on one of the fighters below and fired. His bullet struck the outlaw in the neck, breaking it and killing him instantly.

"Got him!" Doyle shouted triumphantly. He shot again, this time putting a slug into the back of a crouching renegade. The man arched in agony, half-rose, then toppled onto his side.

"Nice shootin' for a railroad man, Pat!" Dade praised. "Lemme see if I can do as good."

Dade fired three times, and three men went down. A fourth outlaw turned to face the disguised Ranger. Dade jacked the lever of his rifle, which jammed. The outlaw shot, his bullet clipping Dade's right leg. Dade went down to one knee, threw his useless rifle aside, pulled the bow off his shoulder and an arrow from the quiver he still carried. He notched the arrow to the bow, aimed, and shot. The arrow drove deep into the outlaw's belly. He screamed, jackknifed, and staggered blindly over the canyon's rim.

"You win, Dade," Doyle conceded.

Slowly the tide turned, the outnumbered Rangers and railroaders more than making up for their lack of manpower with superior shooting. Suddenly, one of the men atop the rim dashed for the plunger box. Dade sent several rounds at the zigzagging figure. One of them clipped the top of the man's shoulder. He stumbled from the impact, fell and rolled, then came back to his feet. Before Dade could shoot again, the man was at the plunger's controls.

"That's Dale Montague!" Doyle hissed.

Dade rose to his knees from behind his cover.

"Montague! This is the Texas Rangers. Don't touch that handle. I've got my rifle aimed plumb at your belly!"

"You pull that trigger, Ranger, and I'll blow all your friends to Kingdom Come!" Montague screamed.

"I'm tellin' you, don't do it!" Dade repeated his warning.

Montague ignored Dade, and grabbed the plunger's handle. When he did, Dade shot him through the belly. Montague doubled up and slumped over the box, pushing down the handle to complete the circuit. Dade and Doyle ducked behind their rock shelter as a goodly chunk of earth and ledge went up in a tremendous explosion, shards of rock raining everywhere.

The thunderous explosion was followed by a silence almost as deafening. Dade and Doyle rose from their cover, shaking rock dust from their clothing. Where Montague had stood there was now a giant crater. Besides the stage line owner, several of his men had been blasted to oblivion. Others lay dead or wounded, while a few stunned survivors were struggling to their feet.

"Well, you warned Montague not to touch that plunger, Dade," Doyle said, dryly.

"He should've listened," Dade replied. "Let's round up these hombres, then check on Jim and Clay."

Once they had rounded up and secured the few surviving outlaws, Dade and Doyle scrambled down the cliff to the canyon floor. They found Jim, Clay, and the rest of the railroad crew awaiting them. Two more of the railroaders had been killed, and several others wounded.

Clay sported a bandage across his forehead, where he'd been grazed by an outlaw's slug.

"You boys all right?" Jim called, when he spotted Dade and Doyle.

"Yeah, Sarge. We're fine. I've got a nick in my leg, but that's nothin'," Dade responded. "How about you?"

"Clay stuck his head in front of a bullet," Jim answered. "Luckily the slug hit him in his thick skull, so there was no damage."

"Thanks a lot, Jim," Clay muttered.

"I still don't understand what happened," Jasper Wheeler puzzled, looking at the smoke and dust still curling from the cliff top.

"It's pretty simple, really," Clay explained. "Dade did a little night work. He moved the dynamite when no one was lookin'. Lucky for us Montague and his men didn't expect anyone would find their little surprise. They were so confident they weren't being watched they didn't bother to guard the explosives after they planted them. Instead, they backed off and waited until the tracks got close. Pretty stupid on their parts, and pretty fortunate for us."

"I'd say more than 'pretty' fortunate," Wheeler answered. "But why didn't you let me know?"

"We had to make sure of absolute secrecy," Jim replied. "Even though we knew you could be trusted, you never know who might overhear something. Then someone gets drunk in a saloon in town, lets something slip, and the next thing you know our plan gets shot to pieces… not to mention our hides."

"You mean to tell me no one bothered Dade?"

"That's one reason I kept wearin' this outfit," Dade answered. He was still clad in the same moccasins, leggings, open vest, and tattered cavalry hat. "I figured no one's gonna bother a crazy half-breed who's wanderin' around. I even visited with a couple of Montague's men, and talked 'em out of a bottle of whiskey. They never suspected a thing."

"Well, now it is high time you got shut of those filthy duds," Jim ordered.

"Soon as we take care of the details," Dade grinned.

"We're certainly grateful for the Rangers' help. You've saved us a lot of time, trouble, and money… not to mention lives," Wheeler said. "What are your plans once you're finished here?"

"We'll stick with you another week or so, just to make sure there's no further trouble," Jim answered. "Then we'll head for home."

"Fine. Well, I guess once the dead are buried and the injured cared for, we won't do any further work today," Wheeler decided. "Whenever you're ready, you men are welcome to bunk in my car. There's plenty of room."

"We'll take you up on that, just as soon as we wrap things up," Jim accepted.

The wounded were tended to, the prisoners locked in a cattle car, with two railroaders assigned to guard them. While the railroad men rounded up the outlaws' horses and buried the dead, the exhausted Rangers slept. They would sleep the clock around.

Partners

1

"Looks like those hombres headed right into the canyon, T. That shoe with the piece chipped out of it shows plain enough," Texas Ranger Jack Blanchard told his buckskin paint gelding. Blanchard had dismounted and was examining the hoofprints left by the horses of the men he'd been following the past three weeks.

Blanchard glanced at the lowering sun as he swung back into the saddle.

"We'd better get movin', or else those renegades are liable to slip away under the cover of dark," he muttered. Blanchard pushed the paint into a trot.

The canyon into which Blanchard had tracked the men held a clear stream running down its center, a stream which emptied into the Red River, not far to the north. The Ranger knew he had to find his quarry before they reached the Red and swam their horses to safety in the Indian Territories, out of reach of Texas law.

Blanchard's deep blue eyes scanned the canyon from side to side, his gaze missing nothing as he attempted to spot the six men he was after, before they were able to put an ambush bullet in his back.

When a flock of crows, squawking in protest, suddenly rose from a thicket halfway up the canyon wall Blanchard instantly rolled from his saddle. He grabbed his Winchester as he dove from his horse and slid on his belly into a patch of scrub and mesquite. Rifle slugs tore through the brush over his head.

Blanchard rose to one knee, aimed, and fired just below a puff of powdersmoke. He heard a scream of pain and saw a man half-rise from his hiding place, then tumble to the canyon floor.

Blanchard aimed and fired again, then was slammed back against the rock wall behind him by a bullet plowing high into his chest. While the Ranger hung there, paralyzed with pain, a second slug tore into his belly. Blanchard clawed at his bullet-torn gut and began to jackknife. Yet another bullet took him in the chest, knocking him into the rocks a second time. Blanchard slid halfway to the dirt, then toppled onto his side.

2

Jack Blanchard's eyes slowly opened, his vision blurry as he stared up at a rough, unfamiliar surface. As he became more aware of his surroundings, he sniffed at the familiar scent of wood smoke, which was mixed with several other odors he could not identify. He sensed, rather than felt, a heavy pressure across his chest and belly, accompanied by a dull ache, far different from the sharp, incapacitating pain he had endured when those bullets tore into him. When his vision cleared somewhat, he realized he was gazing at the cracked rock roof of a cavern.

Blanchard moaned and stirred slightly. Instantly a man's face appeared above the gravely wounded Ranger, the sharp-featured visage of a young Comanche warrior.

"You are awake," the Comanche noted in presentable English. "That is good."

"Who... who are you?" Blanchard stammered. "Where am I?"

"I am Blue Hawk," the brave replied, "You are in a cave, not far from the place I discovered you, badly wounded."

The Comanche pulled back the blanket covering Blanchard to reveal the Ranger's upper torso. An evil-looking mixture of herbs and roots covered Blanchard's chest, and another was plastered over his belly.

"I must change these poultices," Blue Hawk explained. "This will hurt."

Blanchard grimaced and yelped when Blue Hawk removed the dressings from his body, the dried poultices pulling away bits of flesh and dried blood.

"Your wounds are healing well," the Comanche stated with satisfaction.

"Dunno… dunno how. I've been gut-shot," Blanchard objected. "You're wastin' your time, Indian. A man can't survive takin' a bullet in his belly, I've always been told. And I've never met one who has."

"That is true, in most cases," Blue Hawk agreed. "However, a belly wound can be survived, especially if treated with Comanche medicines. White men aren't as wise as they think when it comes to doctoring."

"But…"

"Stay quiet. You need more rest," Blue Hawk urged. He removed a fresh batch of the herbs and roots from a pot simmering on the fire. He pressed the steaming concoction into the bullet holes in Blanchard's chest and belly.

That done, Blue Hawk filled a pottery mug with a foul-smelling brew.

"Now you'll drink this," he ordered.

"That smells awful," Blanchard protested, when the Comanche held the mug to his lips.

"It tastes even worse," Blue Hawk assured him. "But it will help you sleep some more, and also help you regain your strength."

"All right," Blanchard conceded. He took a long swallow of the brew. Almost immediately his eyelids grew heavy and his head fell back.

"That's right, Ranger," Blue Hawk whispered. "Sleep is what you need."

∧∧∧∧∧∧∧∧∧∧∧∧

When Blanchard next awakened, the pain was almost completely gone. While he still felt tired, he also felt much stronger. The poultices had been removed from his chest and belly, his wounds now merely covered by some light bandages.

Blue Hawk immediately sensed the Ranger had awakened.

"How do you feel?" he asked, as he placed a hand on Blanchard's forehead. "Your fever is gone."

"I feel much better," Blanchard admitted. "I am kinda hungry, though."

"I told you those medicines would help you recover, Ranger," Blue Hawk answered. "I'll have some stew dished out for you in a minute."

"How'd you know I'm a Texas Ranger?" Blanchard demanded.

"I found your badge in your shirt pocket, when I removed the shirt to treat your wounds," Blue Hawk explained. "But while you know my name, I do not know yours," he added.

Still covered by a blanket from the waist down, Blanchard shifted to a half-seated position, leaning his back against the cavern wall, his legs stretched out in front of him.

"It's Jack. Jack Blanchard."

"Well, eat this, Jack Blanchard," the Comanche ordered. He handed the Ranger a tin plate full of steaming venison stew, along with a mugful of an herbal brew.

While Blanchard eagerly devoured his first meal since being shot, he gazed curiously at the Indian.

"How long have I been here?" he asked.

"Sixteen days."

"And you stuck with me all that time?"

"I did," Blue Hawk confirmed.

"That just doesn't figure," Blanchard protested. He swallowed another mouthful of stew, then continued.

"Why didn't you just let me die, or finish what those renegades started and kill me? You could've finished me off with no trouble."

Blanchard was well aware of the animosity which existed between the Texas Rangers and most Indian tribes. He himself had killed his share of Comanches and Kiowas during his Ranger career, and had seen many of his Ranger comrades succumb to Indian arrows or bullets.

"There is only one reason," Blue Hawk explained. "I left the Territory reservation to find the white men who attacked my village and killed my wife, son, and two daughters. I followed their trail into Texas."

"What's that got to do with not killin' me?" Blanchard persisted when Blue Hawk paused.

"I was getting close to those men. I could feel it," the Comanche continued, "Then just before the sun set sixteen days ago, I heard gunfire in this very canyon. Before I reached the spot from where it came, the firing had faded away, and there were no men left in the canyon, except two. One was already dead. The other, who was badly wounded, carried a Ranger star in his shirt pocket. The dead man I knew was one of the men who attacked my village. Since it was clear you had killed him before you were shot, I realized the Great Spirit wanted me to care for you, until you recovered or were taken by Him. And that if you survived, you and I were fated to hunt down those men together."

"I've got to say I'm grateful. Surprise, but grateful," Blanchard admitted. "Can you tell me what this hombre I downed looked like?"

"Dark of hair and eyes, both so brown as to appear black," Blue Hawk described. "Tall and heavy, with a scar under his left eye. Your bullet struck him just under the heart."

"Blue Hawk, did you happen to recover my horse and saddle," Blanchard asked.

"I did," Blue Hawk confirmed. "Your horse is staked outside, along with my pony. Your saddle is cached in the back of this cave."

"There's a leather-bound book in my saddlebags. Would you please get it for me?" Blanchard requested. "I believe I know who that man was, but I want to be certain."

"I will do that," Blue Hawk agreed. He disappeared toward the rear of the cavern, beyond the fire's light. He returned shortly, with the book in his hand.

"Here you are, Ranger."

Blue Hawk handed Blanchard the book, which had leather covers loosely held together by a length of string.

Blanchard quickly thumbed through the book, his copy of the Ranger's Fugitive List, otherwise known as the Ranger's Bible. It contained the descriptions of every known wanted man in the state of Texas. Blanchard stopped about a third of the way through the book when he found the listing he sought.

"Sure enough, that was Mack Duquesta," he said. "He was one of the Horton outfit. That means there are five of 'em left."

"I do not know their names," Blue Hawk softly answered, "But I do know the spirits of my wife and children cry out for justice, and they will not rest until it is obtained. And my own soul cries out for revenge on the men who murdered my family."

"I can tell you their names," Blanchard stated. "Holt and Bob Horton, the cousins who lead that bunch. Then there's Dave Smith, Ryne Durant, and Sledge Bascomb. There's not a decent bone in any of 'em."

"We will be on their trail soon enough. And they will not escape me again," Blue Hawk fiercely declared.

"How soon can we get ridin'?" Blanchard asked.

In response, Blue Hawk took the now-empty plate from Blanchard and set it aside. He hunkered alongside the Ranger and removed the bandages from Blanchard's chest and belly.

"Your wounds are healing very quickly," the Comanche noted. Indeed, the bullet holes were now merely puckered scars, still livid but beginning to fade. "You do need some more time to recover your strength. I would say within two days."

"That's too long," Blanchard objected. "Those renegades already have a better'n two week jump on us."

"That is true. However, I have been studying their habits and following their trail for nearly two months now," Blue Hawk replied. "I will know where to find them."

"Reckon I don't have much choice," Blanchard conceded. "I guess a couple more days won't make much difference."

"That's right," Blue Hawk concurred. "Now, you should get more rest."

"I don't need rest as much as I need coffee," Blanchard retorted, adding as he ran a hand over his whisker-stubbled jaw, "And a bath and shave."

"I can get your razor and soap from your saddlebags. There is a pond right outside this cavern where you can bathe," Blue Hawk offered.

"I sure appreciate that," Blanchard answered. He tossed aside his blankets and came to his feet. The Ranger swayed only slightly as he stood up, then steadied himself.

Once Blue Hawk handed him the razor and bar of yellow soap, Blanchard headed outside. T, his paint gelding, nickered a greeting when he saw his rider standing in the entrance of the cave.

"Sure is good to see you again too, ol' pard," Blanchard called to the horse.

"Ranger, I mean Jack."

Blue Hawk spoke from where he stood alongside Blanchard.

"Yeah, Blue Hawk?"

"That is a fine pony you ride. I must admit, had our trails crossed under different circumstances, I would have killed you for your horse. You would have died with my arrow in your belly, for killing a white man to steal a horse as fine as yours would bring great honor to any Comanche warrior."

Blue Hawk chuckled as he glanced at Blanchard's unruly thatch of thick blonde hair.

"And taking a yellow scalp such as yours would bring even more honor, as well as being powerful medicine."

"I might have had something to say about that," Blanchard disagreed with a laugh of his own. "Mebbe I would've put a bullet in your guts instead. But I'm sure glad things didn't happen that way. We'll ride as partners until we catch up to the Hortons. Once that job is done we can go our separate ways."

"That is the Great Spirit's will," Blue Hawk agreed.

"Seems so," Blanchard concurred. "Meanwhile, I'd better take that bath."

"I will have coffee ready by the time you are done," Blue Hawk announced.

"You know how to brew coffee?" Blanchard asked in surprise.

"I learned many of your white man's ways while living on the reservation, including how to speak your language," the Comanche stated. "I found your Arbuckle's in your saddlebag, so it will be waiting for you. I will also have a cup. By the way, don't bother looking for the peppermint stick. I'm taking that for myself."

3

True to Blue Hawk's word, at sunup two days later the unlikely pair, a Texas Ranger and a Comanche warrior, rode away from the hidden cavern.

For nearly two weeks they followed the trail of the Horton gang, swimming their horses across the Red River numerous times as they pursued the desperadoes from Texas into Indian Territory and back. It was late afternoon on the twelfth day after leaving the cave when they pulled their horses to a halt atop a low ridge.

"We're gettin' closer to those hombres. I can feel it in my gut," Blanchard declared. He pushed back his Stetson to scratch his forehead.

"We're gonna catch up with 'em by tomorrow at the latest."

"We are even closer than you think, Jack," answered Blue Hawk. "Do you see the mouth of that arroyo in the distance, say about nine miles off?"

"I do indeed," Blanchard replied. "You sayin' that's one of Horton's hiding places?"

"It sure is," Blue Hawk confirmed. "And my 'gut', as you put it, tells me they are in there now."

The Comanche slid from the back of his tough pinto war pony. He dug in his saddle pouch and removed several items, then pulled off his deerskin shirt and leggings, stripping to only his breech clout.

Blanchard also swung from his saddle.

"What're you doin', Blue Hawk?"

"Preparing for battle."

The Comanche brave broke into a singsong chant as he began to smear crimson and black war paint on his face and chest.

When Blanchard rummaged in his own saddlebags, then peeled off his shirt, Blue Hawk broke off his chant and stared at the Ranger in puzzlement. Blanchard had taken off his good spare shirt and was shrugging into the shirt he had been wearing when he was shot, the shirt that was now bullet-torn and bloodstained.

"Now it is my turn to ask. What exactly are you doing, Jack?"

"Simple," Blanchard explained as he pinned his badge to the shirt. "When we ride up on the Hortons and their men, I want those renegades to think they're seein' a ghost... my ghost, the ghost of the man they thought they'd killed back in that canyon."

ʌʌʌʌʌʌʌʌʌʌʌʌ

Three hours later, Blanchard and Blue Hawk were bellied down under the cover of thick scrub, from where they studied the Horton gang's well-concealed hideout.

"Looks like there's still only five of 'em," Blanchard observed. "There's six horses in the corral, one for each of those hombres, plus Duquesta's cayuse."

"It appears they are all in the cabin," Blue Hawk added. "There seems to be no back way out."

The only building in the arroyo was a ramshackle structure built right against the draw's steep wall. They arroyo itself was a box, ending in sheer bluffs not many yards beyond the shack.

"You're right about that," Blanchard agreed. "However, there's also no cover for at least a hundred yards around that cabin, which means we'd be easy targets if we tried to rush that shack. We'd be cut down before gettin' half-way across the clearing."

"That is not much of a problem," Blue Hawk disagreed. He set aside the Winchester he carried, the rifle which he'd taken from alongside Mack Duquesta's body when he'd found the dead outlaw and the wounded Ranger. He pulled the bow from over his shoulder and an arrow from his quiver, then twisted some oily creosote branches around the arrowhead.

"You want I should make like a primitive savage and strike some flint on rock to make a spark, or do you have a match, Jack?" Blue Hawk asked with a grin.

"I've got a match right here," Blanchard replied. He dug in his shirt pocket and came up with a lucifer. He struck the match on his belt and handed it to the Comanche.

Just as Blue Hawk lit the arrow and notched it to his bow, one of the outlaws stepped from the cabin's doorway, and stood rolling a quirly.

"Blast it!" Blanchard exclaimed. "That's Sledge Bascomb. Blue Hawk, he'll spot us before you can hit that cabin,"

"Don't worry," Blue Hawk calmly answered. "I'll light that cigarette for him."

He pulled back the bow's string to release the arrow.

Bascomb gave a shriek of shock and pain when the flaming arrow ripped into his stomach, driving him back against the cabin's front wall. He slumped to the ground, his shirt still smoking where the blazing missile had pierced through the garment to bury itself in the outlaw's vitals.

"Guess I missed. That's a real shame," Blue Hawk said.

Instantly, yells and curses of surprise came from inside the cabin. The door was flung open.

"Keep them inside the shack while I get another arrow ready," Blue Hawk ordered Blanchard.

The Ranger swept the cabin with rifle fire, one of his bullets tearing into Dave Smith's gut as the outlaw stood framed in the doorway. Smith clutched his belly and jackknifed across the sill, writhing and moaning in pain. Unseen hands dragged the gut-shot renegade inside the cabin and slammed the door closed.

Blanchard tossed aside his now-empty rifle and grabbed Blue Hawk's Winchester to keep the outlaws pinned down, while Blue Hawk swiftly made and shot three more fire arrows into the cabin's front wall, yet another onto the roof. The tinder-dry logs quickly caught, and aided by a stiff breeze blowing up-canyon the flames spread rapidly. The entire front wall of the shack was soon a mass of flames.

"That should smoke 'em outta there real quick," Blanchard noted with satisfaction. He handed Blue Hawk's rifle back to the Comanche and picked up his own Winchester. They quickly reloaded the weapons.

"You men inside!" Blanchard shouted. "This is the Texas Rangers. Toss out your guns and come out with your hands up, or else you'll roast in there. Come out shootin' and we'll cut you down before you can run ten feet!"

The only response was a fusillade of bullets from the shack's two windows. Lead sliced through the brush sheltering the lawman and Indian.

"There's no point in wastin' our cartridges until that fire drives 'em outta there," Blanchard said.

He dropped to his belly and sighted his rifle on the cabin door. Alongside him, Blue Hawk did the same.

As the flames climbed the cabin's walls and began licking at the roof, the heat and smoke soon became too much for the outlaws to bear. Their curses faded to strangled coughs and their gunshots trailed off.

"They will be coming out at any moment," Blue Hawk stated.

Four minutes later the cabin door was flung open and three men emerged, stumbling in their attempt to flee the burning building, still firing their rifles in a desperate attempt to down the Ranger and Comanche.

Blue Hawk took careful aimed and shot. His bullet plowed through the center of Bob Horton's chest, slamming the outlaw against the flaming cabin. Horton screamed in terror as his clothing caught fire. The dying renegade pitched to his face, managed to drag himself a few feet, then gasped, shuddered, and finally lay unmoving.

Blanchard levered and fired his rifle three times, all three of the slugs ripping into Ryne Durant's belly.

Stopped in his tracks when the bullets tore through his middle, Durant folded, then dropped to one knee before toppling onto his side, hands clamped to his gut.

Holt Horton, still shooting, charged at the Ranger and Comanche. Blanchard and Blue Hawk fired as one, Blanchard's bullet hitting Horton in the face, Blue's Hawk's in the chest, where it stopped in a lung. Horton was smashed flat on his back, dead.

"I guess that takes care of all of 'em," Blanchard muttered. He came to his feet. "Smith sure ain't still alive inside that shack."

Virtually the entire cabin was engulfed in flames.

Cautiously, Blanchard and Blue Hawk approached the cabin. Neither man speaking, they removed the dead men's gunbelts and holsters, then dragged the bodies to the cabin and tossed them inside. The blazing structure was now the Horton gang's funeral pyre.

Silently, Blanchard and Blue Hawk watched the cabin burn until it was merely a pile of smoldering timbers, a few sparks and wisps of smoke curling into the dusk.

"My family has been avenged," Blue Hawk whispered.

4

Blanchard and Blue Hawk spent that night in a shallow draw, about two miles from where the Horton gang had met its fate. They had driven the outlaws' horses before them, and picketed them to graze on a good-sized patch of grama grass. Now, early the next morning, the pair was readying breakfast before preparing to ride on.

"I'd best write up my report for Austin before we head on out," Blue Hawk," Blanchard explained. "I'd also better write you a receipt sayin' those horses are rightfully yours."

He dug two sheets of paper and the stub of a pencil out of his saddlebags.

The Ranger and Comanche had agreed Blue Hawk would receive possession of the outlaws' horses as some compensation for the loss of his family, and as a token of appreciation for his assistance in nursing Blanchard back to health and helping him track down the renegades. The outlaws' weapons would be taken back to Austin by the Ranger.

Blanchard thought for a moment, then added, "In fact, I'd best ride along with you until you're back across the Red and into the Territories. Anyone who sees a lone Comanch' herdin' six shod horses on this side of the river is liable to shoot first, without botherin' to check the ownership of those broncs until it's too late."

"You are right," Blue Hawk agreed. "So we will ride together for one more day, then tomorrow I will cross back to the reservation."

While Blanchard wrote a brief report and the receipt, Blue Hawk made a scant breakfast of jerky and cornmeal. Once they had eaten and cleaned up, Blanchard handed the receipt to Blue Hawk.

"Don't let anything happen to this, at least until you get back home," he warned.

"I will make sure of that," Blue Hawk assured him. He tucked the document into a pocket of his shirt.

A short while later the pair pointed their horses northwestward, back toward the Red River some twenty-five miles away.

∧∧∧∧∧∧∧∧∧∧∧∧

The Ranger and Comanche rode steadily all day, the six horses they were herding slowing their pace. Sundown found them still a few miles short of the river. They reined in alongside a clear creek, which watered a grassy glade.

"This is as likely a place as any to spend the night," Blanchard observed. "There's plenty of grass and water for the horses."

"You are right, Jack, since we can't make the Red tonight," Blue Hawk agreed. "We can get a good night's rest, and finish our journey in the morning."

Blanchard swung out of his saddle, then yawned and stretched. He slipped the bridle from his horse's head, then loosened the cinches and pulled the saddle from the gelding's back.

"Reckon that feels good, eh T, Boy?" he asked the paint as he scratched the paint's ears.

"I reckon it's high time I got rid of this shirt, too," the Ranger chuckled. He was still wearing his bullet-torn, bloodstained shirt.

"I agree." Blue Hawk smiled as he climbed from his pony's back. "Frankly Jack, you smell."

Blanchard pulled his badge from his shirt, peeled off the ruined garment, and tossed it in the creek, watching until it floated out of sight. He turned away from the stream, then whirled, his hand dropping for his Colt, too late. An arrow hissed across the clearing and thudded into the middle of the Ranger's belly, burying itself deep in his gut. Blanchard grasped futilely at the arrow's shaft. He staggered back against his horse's side, doubled over, then spun to the ground, landing heavily on his back.

When the Ranger fell, a war-whooping Comanche burst from a clump of redberry juniper, with a knife in his hand. He raised the weapon high to plunge its blade into Blanchard's heart. Blue Hawk raced to Blanchard's side and grabbed his fellow warrior's wrist, wrenching the knife from his grasp to stop the fatal thrust.

"Dark Bear, no!" In his native tongue, Blue Hawk screamed in grief and rage.

"Blue Hawk, why did you stop me?" Dark Bear asked, puzzled. "I have freed you from your captor and killed our enemy. Now I will take his scalp."

"This man is not my enemy, but my friend," Blue Hawk replied. "Did you not see he wasn't holding me as a prisoner? Instead, we were riding together. He helped me find the men who murdered my family. Without his help, their deaths would not have been avenged."

"But he is a white man, and a Texas Ranger," Dark Bear objected. He had seen Blanchard pull the badge from his shirt before tossing it in the creek.

"He is also a brother, and I will protect him as best I can," Blue Hawk retorted. He knelt alongside Blanchard.

"Jack, I am sorry," Blue Hawk murmured. "Dark Bear is my cousin. He did not realize what he was doing."

"It's all right, Blue Hawk," Blanchard half-whispered. "Although I don't think any of your Comanche medicine will help me this time."

The Ranger's hands were still wrapped around the arrow's shaft. Surprisingly little blood was running from the wound to trickle over the flesh of Blanchard's belly. However, internally he was bleeding profusely, blood filling his abdominal cavity.

"I am afraid you are right, my friend," Blue Hawk sorrowfully answered. "I will stay with you until your soul flies to the Great Spirit. And may there be a curse on Dark Bear until he makes amends for what he has done."

"Does Dark Bear understand English?" Blanchard asked.

"Very little," Blue Hawk answered.

"Then please tell him this for me. I understand why he put this arrow in me. Had our roles been reversed, and I saw a Comanche and white man together, I might have done the same as he did, and put a bullet into the warrior to save the white man's life. Dark Bear only did what he believed was right. I hold no malice toward him, and I don't want your curse on him."

In Comanche, Blue Hawk repeated Blanchard's words to his cousin. When he finished, Dark Bear responded, at first calmly, then his voice rising when he glared at

Blanchard and gestured angrily. Dark Bear's eyes glittered as he fixed his gaze on the dying Ranger.

Blue Hawk answered Dark Bear in equally harsh tones, then turned away from his fellow Comanche.

"Jack, Dark Bear offers his thanks for your forgiveness, and as is your wish I will not curse his spirit. However, I will not do as he requests and allow him to take your scalp!" Blue Hawk spat. "He also feels he has earned your horse and weapons."

Blanchard let out a deep sigh. Blood was now running from his mouth. He choked on it as he replied.

"Let Dark Bear take my scalp," Blanchard said. "After all, he earned it. He shot me fair and square, believing he was saving you. I just wish he'd got me in the chest rather'n my gut. I'd've died quicker and it wouldn't hurt so much. Your cousin has the right to my scalp, but he'll have to wait until I'm dead to collect it. That won't be long now."

"What of your horse and weapons?" Blue Hawk questioned.

"My horse is yours. You said yourself that under different circumstances you would have killed me to steal him. I know you will treat T well," Blanchard answered. "My rifle and Colt are also yours. Let Dark Bear keep my Bowie knife as a trophy of war."

"That is more than fair, Jack," Blue Hawk agreed.

Blue Hawk repeated Blanchard's statement for Dark Bear, who nodded his understanding to the Ranger.

"Blue Hawk, I must ask one more favor," Blanchard requested.

"What is that?"

"Please make sure someone gets word to Ranger Headquarters what happened to me. Don't tell 'em how I died, though, or they'll come after Dark Bear. Just say that I was killed fightin' the Hortons and their bunch."

"I'll do that," Blue Hawk agreed. "What about your family?"

"I've got no kin," Blanchard answered. "My mother and father are both dead, and I've got no sisters or brothers. The Rangers were the closest thing I had to a family."

"I understand," Blue Hawk nodded. "I am also grateful you do not want revenge on Dark Bear."

Blanchard shuddered as a wave of agony wracked his body. Sweat was beading on his forehead and running down his chest and stomach, mixing with the blood around the arrow's shaft.

"I won't be hangin' on much longer, Blue Hawk," he told the Comanche. "We made a great team though, didn't we?"

"We did indeed, Jack," Blue Hawk answered. "May the eagle swiftly fly your spirit to the Great Spirit."

"Thanks, pardner," Blanchard whispered.

"I will not be able to give you a proper funeral, as is the white man's custom," Blue Hawk continued. "Nor will I be able to provide you a Comanche burial ceremony. However, I will make sure the scavengers will not ravage your flesh and scatter your bones."

"I'd be grateful for that," Blanchard answered, his voice weak and fading. "Reckon... it's time to see what's on the... other side of... the Great... Divide."

Blanchard was wrenched with pain. The Ranger rolled onto his side in a death spasm, gave out a long groan, then his body went slack.

"You were as brave and honorable as any Comanche warrior, Texas Ranger Jack Blanchard," Blue Hawk sorrowfully whispered.

True to Blanchard's word, Dark Bear was allowed to take his scalp, but out of respect for the Ranger he'd killed, and at Blue Hawk's insistence, Dark Bear sliced the scalp carefully and cleanly from Blanchard's skull. Once that was done, Dark Bear took Blanchard's Bowie and departed, leaving the grieving Blue Hawk alone with his dead companion.

T, Blanchard's pinto, had remained nearby, waiting and watching. Now, he walked up to his deceased rider, nuzzled him, and nickered sadly.

"I know you'll miss Jack," Blue Hawk soothed the horse. "I promise you I'll care for you just as he did. Right now, though, it will be better if you don't see what I have to do."

He led the horse away and picketed him with the others.

Blue Hawk gathered dried branches and stacked them to prepare for his Ranger compadre's final journey. Once he had sufficient fuel, he gently lifted Blanchard's body from the ground and laid it reverently on the pyre. He picked up Blanchard's silver star on silver circle badge from where it had fallen and placed it on the Ranger's breast.

The preparations completed, Blue Hawk lit a length of dried mesquite and touched it to several places at the base of the pyre. As the flames rose, he broke into a Comanche death chant, the mournful dirge seeming to mix with the sparks rising into the night sky. When the flames reached Blanchard's body, a single tear rolled down Blue Hawk's cheek.

Gunfight at Taylor Ridge

Introduction

Conventional wisdom states the traditional Western story is dying or already dead, particularly among young people. It's claimed the younger generations have little or no interest in our American Western heritage, either the facts of history or the legends which have made the cowboys, gunslingers, lawmen, Native American Indians, cavalrymen, and settlers of the American West enduring icons for generations throughout the entire world.

In the presentations I give at schools, libraries, and other venues throughout the United States, I have found this not to be true. Young people are still extremely interested in the stories and history of the West. I am concluding this anthology with the following true story, which illustrates perfectly this interest.

1

After what seemed weeks of dreary, rainy weather, Sunday dawned warm and sunny, so I took advantage of the fine weather to get my horse out for some exercise, and to get in some patrol hours. Yankee and I are members of the state horse patrol, volunteers who help keep an eye on the state parks and forests. As always, I substituted a cowboy hat for the riding helmet which is part of my uniform.

Once I saddled up, I headed for my usual assigned areas of Buell Forest and Taylor Ridge. I had been riding for about an hour when Yankee pricked up his ears and sniffed the air, a sure sign that something or someone is nearby. When we rounded the next bend in the trail, we came upon a gentleman who was out exploring the woods, along with his five year old grandson, Dylan. Dylan was excited to see my horse and, to his eyes, a cowboy. He was also all wound up because he'd outgrown his old cowboy hat, and only the day before had gotten a new black one similar to the one I was wearing. Dylan's granddad and legal guardian, Vinny, told me Dylan couldn't decide whether he wanted to be a biker or a cowboy when he grew up. Vinny also related how he and Dylan watched all the cowboy movies on the Encore Westerns Channel, and Dylan knew who Roy Rogers, the Lone Ranger, and Gene Autry were. He added that Dylan even owned a Roy Rogers and Trigger pocket knife. Very surprising for a kid in 2008.

While we were talking, Dylan was petting my horse, who loves both attention and kids. Dylan worked his way from Yankee's right shoulder to his nose to his left shoulder, all the while looking curiously at me. Finally, Dylan brought up the question he'd obviously been dying to ask.

"Mister, how come you aren't wearing your cowboy pistol?"

I explained that I wasn't allowed to carry a gun while on duty, then kiddingly asked him if he could draw and shoot like a cowboy. He and his grandfather both said yes, so of course I couldn't let that challenge pass. I braced myself for a showdown.

"Draw, mister!" I shouted.

Dylan and I jerked our "Colts" (the index finger and thumb sixshooters kids have used as pretend pistols for generations), and naturally I let Dylan beat me to the draw. When he aimed and fired, I yelped, clutched my stomach as if Dylan had just put a bullet through it, and collapsed over my horse's neck. Dylan was thrilled.

We had several more gunfights while I was still in the saddle. Dylan shot me in most of them, but I did manage to gun him down a couple of times. During one, I thought I'd finished him off, but Dylan never went down. Instead, he came back with the retort heard innumerable times in games of cowboys and Indians.

"Your bullet just nicked me!"

He then proceeded to plug me yet again. I dropped over Yankee's withers with Dylan's bullet in my chest.

While I was lying slumped over my horse's neck, Dylan came up with his next question.

"How come you don't fall off your horse when you get shot like the real cowboys (okay, the movie cowboys) do?"

I explained that I wasn't about to take a chance on breaking any bones by falling out of the saddle and hitting the ground. However, I did tell him I'd get off my horse so he could gun me down once more. That way he and his granddad would get to see Yankee's "wounded cowboy" trick.

Yankee performs several tricks, including giving kisses, hugs, neck massages, handshakes, and he will steal a bandanna from my shirt pocket. If I tell him I'm a horse thief and am attempting to steal him, he'll bury his nose in my middle and shove me aside. However, his absolute favorite trick is one I call the "wounded cowboy", an old Western movie stunt. I act as if I've been shot and fall face-down to the ground. Yank will then shove at my side with his muzzle until he flips me onto my back, then will nuzzle and lick my face until I "come to".

Of course, Dylan wasn't about to give me the chance to get all the way out of the saddle. He nailed me as soon as my right foot hit the ground and my left was still in the stirrup. I gave Yankee his voice cue, "I've been shot, Yank!", as I staggered, then dropped to the dirt in front of him. Yankee immediately put his nose to my ribs and shoved at my side until he rolled me onto my back, then nuzzled my face until I came back to life, much to Dylan and his granddad's delight.

We had to repeat the performance several times. Yankee, being the good-natured horse and ham that he is, stood stock-still, putting up with me as I flopped all over and under him while Dylan shot me again and again. Even when I ran out of the horse treats which are Yankee's reward for performing, he still nuzzled me back to life every time I was shot down by that tow-headed five year old gunslinger I'd by now nicknamed "Dylan the Kid".

We must have had twenty or more gunfights, and like me Dylan died pretty good in some of them too, staggering and spinning dramatically before dropping to the ground "dead" when I shot him. He also sure knew his cowboy language. Dylan knew what an ambush was (I learned that the hard way when he sprang up from where he'd hidden behind a fallen log and shot me in the back), and also a lot of the old Western movie slang. I found that out during one of our showdowns. Dylan looked me straight in the eye while we got ready to draw.

"I'm gonna gut-shoot you, Mister!" he growled.

We both drew. Dylan beat me to the draw, and promptly shot me four times in the belly. I jackknifed and bit the dust. Sure enough, Dylan the Kid had gut-shot me. He knew exactly what that expression meant.

I got even, though. In the very next showdown, I drilled Dylan right through his bellybutton. Dylan screamed in feigned agony as only a five year old boy can while he grabbed his belly, doubled over, and pitched to the dirt.

Before he even bounced back up, Dylan shot me again. I crumpled to the ground, and now we were both lying in the wet leaves and mud, blazing away at each other with our imaginary sixguns, laughing uncontrollably as we shot each other time and time again.

Finally, I had to move on. Before I rode off; however, there was time for a bit more fun.

Dylan had been pleading for a ride on Yankee. I had reluctantly told him that since I was on duty, patrol regulations and liability issues forbade me from allowing anyone but myself to ride my horse. However, after having shot it out with Dylan, I couldn't bring myself to simply ride away. I broke the rules, and put Dylan into the saddle to give him a short ride on Yankee. While we headed down the trail, Dylan kept yelling joyously at the top of his lungs.

"I'm riding a real cowboy horse!" he shouted repeatedly.

When we returned to where Dylan's grandfather was waiting, naturally we had to have a few more gunfights. Dylan was just too reluctant to quit our play, and frankly I wasn't quite ready to give up either, although by this point I was certain my body was going to be feeling the effects of all those falls by the time I got home.

When I was at last ready to get on Yankee's back and head for home, I told Dylan to shoot me while I was climbing into the saddle, and I would show him another of Yankee's tricks. When I mounted, Dylan shot me as soon as he could aim at my stomach over my horse's back, while my left foot was in the stirrup and I was swinging the right over my horse's rump. I fell belly-down across Yankee, to show Dylan and Vinny how my horse would carry a "dead cowboy" slung over the saddle, just like in the movies.

Dylan again pleaded to have a couple of more shootouts before I left, and of course I couldn't refuse him. In one, I shot Dylan. After taking my bullet in his chest, Dylan staggered into a tree before spinning around and falling face up right in front of my horse. Yankee immediately dropped his nose to nuzzle Dylan back to life. The look on Dylan's face while Yankee nuzzled him was priceless. I was totally surprised at Yank's actions, since he had never been willing to perform this trick with anyone but me.

But how did Dylan return Yankee's favor? He looked up at me as he aimed at my chest.

"You didn't get me, Mister! I was just playin' possum!"

Dylan the Kid plugged me dead center and shot me out of the saddle. He shot me again as I tumbled off Yankee, then once more when I hit the dirt.

Yep, the boy knew his cowboy movie stuff, all right. Played dead until he knew I didn't have my gun at the ready, then promptly let me have it.

I promised Dylan and Vinny one more trick from Yankee before I rode off. I explained to Dylan that if he shot and killed me, Yankee would take his dead rider home.

Dylan got behind me and shot me in the back. I grunted as I arched in death agony, then crumpled over Yankee's neck. Trained not to move until I am fully seated and upright in the saddle, Yankee stood perfectly still until I whispered to him.

"Take me home, pardner."

Yankee slowly walked off, carrying his "dead" rider slumped in the saddle.

As I rode away, Dylan the Kid's final words to me weren't "Good-bye" or "It was nice meeting you". No, Dylan had a much more appropriate farewell.

"It was fun shootin' you, Mister," Dylan shouted after me.

I whirled my horse and shot that five year old gunslinger right through his guts. Two can play possum.

I honestly don't know who had more fun that afternoon, me, Dylan, or his granddad Vinny. All I know is for an hour or so I felt like a ten year old again, playing cowboys with my best friend. Every one of the worries and inhibitions of an adult disappeared that day, at least for a while, as Dylan and I shot it out. And surprisingly, I never felt one ache from all those gunbattles and the falls I took.

There are plenty more kids like Dylan out there, kids who are the potential next generation of Western readers. I've met many of them during my presentations at public libraries, schools, and bookstores. Most of these kids have little knowledge of the American West and its history, but give them a few good stories and they are ready for more.

As we know, there is no longer a ready audience for the Western novel, so it's up to us as authors and educators to reach out, find those future readers, and encourage their interest. We need to keep pushing the Western genre every chance we get, and in any way we can. So if playing gunslinger with a five year old is what it takes to make a kid a lifelong fan of Westerns, then that's what I'll do. Besides, playing cowboy, even after all these years, is still a heckuva lot of fun, especially since I now have the horse I'd always wanted as a kid.

There's an epilogue to this story. I had promised Vinny and Dylan we would keep in touch. However, a couple of months later, their house was empty. Vinny's mother had been suffering with terminal cancer. Vinny had told me he and Dylan might have to move once she passed on. I figured since I had no idea where they had gone, I wouldn't see them again. But several months later, they showed up at one of my programs about the frontier West at our local public library. Luckily they had moved to the same town where I live, in fact only a few blocks from my place, and had read an announcement about the presentation in our local weekly newspaper. Dylan and several others youngsters who were there helped out with the reenactments, and I'm certain some of them, at least, went home with a better appreciation of the West and Westerns.

###